FLYAWAY VACATION SWEEPSTAKES!

This month's destination:
Exciting ORLANDO, FLORIDA!

Are you the lucky person who will win a free trip to Orlando? Imagine how much fun it would be to visit Walt Disney World**, Universal Studios**, Cape Canaveral and the other sights and attractions in this area! The Next page contains tow Official Entry Coupons, as does each of the other books you received this shipment. Complete and return *all* the entry coupons—the more times you enter, the better your chances of winning!

Then keep your fingers crossed, because you'll find out by October 15, 1995 if you're the winner! If you are, here's what you'll get:

- Round-trip airfare for two to Orlando!
- 4 days/3 nights at a first-class resort hotel!
- $500.00 pocket money for meals and sightseeing!

Remember: The more times you enter, the better your chances of winning!*

*NO PURCHASE OR OBLIGATION TO CONTINUE BEING A SUBSCRIBER NECESSARY TO ENTER. SEE BACK PAGE FOR ALTERNATIVE MEANS OF ENTRY AND RULES.

**THE PROPRIETORS OF THE TRAD[...] THIS PROMOTION.

D0211434

FLYAWAY VACATION
SWEEPSTAKES
OFFICIAL ENTRY COUPON

This entry must be received by: SEPTEMBER 30, 1995
This month's winner will be notified by: OCTOBER 15, 1995
Trip must be taken between: NOVEMBER 30, 1995-NOVEMBER 30, 1996

YES, I want to win the vacation for two to Orlando, Florida. I understand the prize includes round-trip airfare, first-class hotel and $500.00 spending money. Please let me know if I'm the winner!

Name_____

Address _____ Apt. _____

City   State/Prov.   Zip/Postal Code

Account #_____

Return entry with invoice in reply envelope.

© 1995 HARLEQUIN ENTERPRISES LTD.   COR KAL

FLYAWAY VACATION
SWEEPSTAKES
OFFICIAL ENTRY COUPON

This entry must be received by: SEPTEMBER 30, 1995
This month's winner will be notified by: OCTOBER 15, 1995
Trip must be taken between: NOVEMBER 30, 1995-NOVEMBER 30, 1996

YES, I want to win the vacation for two to Orlando, Florida. I understand the prize includes round-trip airfare, first-class hotel and $500.00 spending money. Please let me know if I'm the winner!

Name_____

Address _____ Apt. _____

City   State/Prov.   Zip/Postal Code

Account #_____

Return entry with invoice in reply envelope.

© 1995 HARLEQUIN ENTERPRISES LTD.   COR KAL

"It is there, so close I can almost feel it," Marion whispered.

"What?" Dunstan's low, urgent response told her that he was awake and alert for danger.

"My past."

He grunted, rather irritably, and she wondered if he was heartily sick of chasing after her. Who could blame him? He had a home and duties, while she had only blank nothingness. "I am afraid, Dunstan," she said. "I do not want to remember."

"Then, do not," he said gruffly, and suddenly Marion felt his arm around her, pulling her into the curve of his body. "Sleep," he ordered in a rough whisper.

She had forgotten how warm he was, but the reminder made her snuggle up against his side. His heat surrounded her immediately, driving away the chill in the air, the horrors of the night and the dread of a history that loomed over her like a black cloud....

Dear Reader,

This month, gifted author Deborah Simmons returns to Medieval times with her new book, *Taming the Wolf.* This amusing story follows the travails of a knight who is determined to fulfill his duty and return an heiress to her legal guardian, only to discover that the young lady does not wish to go! Needless to say, she convinces him that she is in the gravest danger, and he is soon transformed from jailer to rescuer. Don't miss this wonderful tale.

Ever since the release of her first book, *Snow Angel,* Susan Amarillas has been delighting readers with her western stories of love and laughter. This month's *Scanlin's Law* is the tale of a jaded U.S. Marshal and the woman who has waited eight years for him to return. We hope you enjoy it.

For those of you who like adventure with your romance, look for *Desert Rogue,* by the writing team of Erin Yorke. It's the story of an English socialite and the rough-hewn American soldier of fortune who rescues her. And from contemporary author Liz Ireland comes her debut historical, *Cecilia and the Stranger.* This month's WOMEN OF THE WEST selection is the charming tale of a schoolteacher who is not all he seems, and the rancher's daughter who is bent on finding out just who he really is.

Whatever your taste in historical reading, we hope you'll keep a lookout for all four titles, available wherever Harlequin Historicals are sold.

Sincerely,

Tracy Farrell

Senior Editor

Please address questions and book requests to:
Harlequin Reader Service
U.S.: 3010 Walden Ave., P.O. Box 1325, Buffalo, NY 14269
Canadian: P.O. Box 609, Fort Erie, Ont. L2A 5X3

DEBORAH SIMMONS

TAMING THE WOLF

Harlequin Books

TORONTO • NEW YORK • LONDON
AMSTERDAM • PARIS • SYDNEY • HAMBURG
STOCKHOLM • ATHENS • TOKYO • MILAN
MADRID • WARSAW • BUDAPEST • AUCKLAND

ISBN 0-373-28884-0

TAMING THE WOLF

Printed in U.S.A.

Books by Deborah Simmons

Harlequin Historicals

Fortune Hunter #132
Silent Heart #185
The Squire's Daughter #208
The Devil's Lady #241
The Vicar's Daughter #258
Taming the Wolf #284

DEBORAH SIMMONS

Always drawn to writing, Deborah began her professional career as a newspaper reporter. She turned to fiction writing after the birth of her first child when a longtime love of historical romances prompted her to pen her first book, published in 1989. She lives with her husband, two children and two cats on seven acres in rural Ohio, where she divides her time between her family, reading, researching and writing.

For my own brother, Robert W. Smith

Prologue

England 1270

The sound of approaching riders made Marion freeze, her hands still upon the reins and colder than the autumn winds that whipped against her cloak. Although they were nearly two days gone from Baddersly Castle, she still feared pursuit from her uncle and his soldiers. When both he and his steward were away, she had made her escape, ostensibly to go on a pilgrimage, but even a journey taken in the Lord's name would ill please Harold Peasely. He would track her down, and when he found her.... Marion shuddered at the thought.

If only she could reach the convent, she would have sanctuary, for even her uncle could not touch her there. She could live a selfless, holy existence, locked inside the walls safe from harm, with a group of women who would be a family to her—because she would never have one of her own.

Marion swallowed thickly at the cost of her asylum. Once she had entertained dreams of a husband and children, but her uncle had no intention of giving over his wardship of her lands and wealth to another man. He had kept her hidden away, subject to his wild tempers and so often alone. . . .

With a piercing glance, Marion focused her attention on the oncoming travelers, relaxing slightly when she saw that they did not wear her uncle's colors. Closer inspection revealed that they were a dangerous-looking, ill-kept group, however, and Marion worried anew.

Although the Church proclaimed that pilgrims were not to be harmed, assassins and outlaws roamed the roads, and the group of young serfs and freedmen Marion had hired to accompany her were poor protection. Little more than boys, the Miller brothers might wield clubs, but they would be no match for armed brigands.

As if to confirm her worst fears, the men ahead suddenly spurred toward them, thundering forward on great horses and raising cruel weapons. Marion gasped as they smote the leader of her train, John Miller, with one mighty blow. Her palfrey balked, and beside her, her servant, Enid, screamed wildly, drawing the attention of one of the attackers, a bearded giant who was soon looming over them. Before Marion could draw a breath, the fellow dragged the shrieking Enid from her seat.

Marion's heart contracted in horror, and for a moment she simply stared, immobile, as the man pawed at her servant. Then, forcing her limbs to action, she drew her small dagger with calm deliberation. She moved as if in a dream, the world about her seemingly slowed, the clank of weapons and the screams of her companions fading to a low buzz, while she urged her mount toward the fiend who held Enid.

Marion knew she must aim her blade at his heart, and she poised to strike, but years of submission to those bigger and stronger stilled her hand and she remained motionless as the nightmare unfolded around her.

Finally, it was too late. The brute saw her. Laughing at the sight of her puny knife, he lifted an arm to knock her aside like a pesky fly. Marion fell to the ground below, landing hard on her back, the wind knocked from her and her head spinning and spinning....

Chapter One

Campion. Marion drew in a breath at the sight of the massive stone walls, rising high in the air and marching majestically into the distance. Its myriad towers looked so fine, so great and strong, that a tingle of apprehension ran along her spine. What awaited her here?

Anxiously, Marion glanced toward the dark-haired knights who led the train, and she felt her tension ease. Over the past weeks of travel, she had grown to trust the men who had found her in the roadway. But then, she had little choice in the matter, for they were all she knew.

She remembered nothing else.

It was because of her head injury. Geoffrey, the learned one, said that sometimes a blow to the brain could steal one's memory, and she had to believe him, for she knew naught of herself or her past. All that had happened before the de Burgh brothers appeared in her life was a vast, empty—and rather chilling—void.

Although she lived and breathed and walked and talked, it was eerie, this lack of history. Hearing the song of a bird, she could easily identify it as a sparrow. She could even recall a recipe for roasting the creatures, but how and when she had learned the ingredients escaped her. Her past was a blank.

They called her Marion. It meant naught to her, but they had found the name inscribed in what they thought was her psalter. They said that she was a lady, and only a lady would have such possessions as they discovered—fine clothes, a mirror, books, coins and jewelry. Then they took her with them, for they did not know who she was, and were in a hurry to return home.

"Come, lady!" Geoffrey called. Obviously happy to have finally reached his destination, he urged her on, through the outer bailey and inner bailey toward massive doors, flung open in welcome. He helped her dismount quickly, and Marion smiled at his eagerness as he led her inside. Although a knight, Geoffrey was a gentle, scholarly man, and she liked him readily.

Then Marion looked around, and her eyes widened in wonder at the enormous hall, the like of which she could swear she had never seen before. Light poured in through the tall, arched windows set high in the walls, and chairs and settles were scattered among the benches as evidence of the de Burgh fortune.

It was very impressive—and very dirty. Marion tried not to wrinkle her nose at the smell of overripe food, stale rushes and dogs, which the chill air could not dispel. Even with her faulty wit, she could tell that Campion was in need of a chatelaine.

The thought made Marion pause, while tiny prickles trickled up the back of her neck, along with a sense of discovery. *She* could do it. She knew it with utter certainty, and with that certainty came a swell of longing and excitement. Not only could she do it, but she would do it well and find happiness in the task.

"Ho! Simon! Geoffrey!" Suddenly, there was such a din that Marion nearly covered her ears. The party was set upon by various large dogs, barking their heads off, followed closely by several large, dark-haired men, shouting even louder. She stepped back as the giants joined the equally big Geoffrey and Simon and jostled and hugged and swung at them in what she hoped was a friendly fashion.

They all seemed to talk at once in shouts and grunts while she watched, amazed by the affection apparent beneath all the gruff bellowing. And then, as if by some unspoken agreement, the noise ceased and all turned to face an approaching figure.

He was not as tall, or nearly as broad as his sons, but Marion immediately guessed that the man who drew near was their father, the earl of Campion. His hair was still as dark as theirs except where it was streaked with silver. His face was more gaunt, his mouth less generous, but the resemblance was there, marking him as an attractive man, despite his years.

Marion watched him closely, her eyes flicking away only to gauge the reaction of others to his presence. Though a patriarch and a nobleman, he did not appear to be a cruel lord and master, nor did he seem full of his own importance. He moved very gracefully, with a dignity that commanded respect, not through brute force but through wisdom, and Marion felt the tightness that had settled in her chest ease at the sight of him.

Although Campion was obviously above the kind of boisterous behavior of the others, he was nonetheless pleased to see his sons. It was evident in his smile and in his voice when he spoke their names. "Simon, Geoffrey," he said, his tone low and rough with the measure of his affection. And then, while Marion looked on in astonishment, the elegant earl opened his arms and loosely clasped the towering body of the mail-clad Simon.

Marion's longing returned in a rush, more piercing this time. Had she ever been part of such a family? She watched, fascinated, as the earl did the same with Geoffrey. Then, suddenly, Campion's attention was upon her.

His brows lifted a fraction in polite curiosity, and she nodded her greeting before bending her head, anxiety curling in her breast.

"Sir, we came upon a pack of thieves attacking the Lady Marion's train," Geoffrey explained. "Although we dispatched them, we were not in time to save her injury. She was thrown into the roadway and now knows not her own name. All of her people were either slain or fled in fright, so we have offered her our protection until she might regain her... health."

"My lady," Campion said, bowing slightly in a formal salute. "We shall be pleased to have you with us. It has been too long since a damsel has graced our hall. I am Campion, and these are my sons," he said, lifting a hand to take in the group.

"You have met Simon and Geoffrey. May I introduce Stephen," he said, and another de Burgh stepped forward, this one with a lock of the familiar dark hair hanging loosely over his forehead. He had a different air about him than Simon or Geoffrey, a careless attitude that did not seem to fit Campion's line.

"My lady," Stephen said. He flashed white teeth in a mocking grin, and she decided he was too handsome for his own good.

"Robin, my lady." A man of about twenty years spoke this time. His hair was a shade lighter than the rest, and his friendliness was genuine, as if he were paying court to her. Marion nodded her greeting with pleasure.

"Reynold." More gaunt than the others and walking with a stiff gait, as though one leg pained him, came Reynold. Although he appeared to be younger than Robin, he seemed angry and bitter beyond his years. He did not return her smile.

"And, finally, Nicholas." At the earl's words, no one stepped forward, and Campion repeated the name with just a hint of exasperation. Marion almost laughed aloud then as the youngest de Burgh bounded toward her. He was probably no more than fourteen, a softer, smaller version of his brothers.

"Yes, sir?"

"Please meet our guest," Campion directed with a nod toward Marion.

"Greetings!" Nicholas said, eyeing her up and down with the eager curiosity of the young. She could see that he was bubbling over with questions for her, but apparently his father also recognized the signs, for he quickly forestalled the interrogation with a reproving look.

Campion then glanced around the hall. "Wilda," he called. Although he did not raise his voice, a young servant girl was soon at his elbow.

"Yes, my lord?" She spoke respectfully, yet with a sincerity that caught Marion's attention. She realized that even the servants went about their work with pride here at Campion. It was a situation that struck Marion as oddly unusual, but she could not say why.

"This lady will be staying with us," Campion said. "Please show her to a room with a hearth, and send something up from the kitchens for her. 'Tis late, and she will wish to seek her rest after the long journey."

"Yes, my lord." Wilda nodded warmly, the casually given welcome touching Marion to the bone. Although she realized that she had been graciously dismissed, Marion could not leave yet. Ignoring the urge to scurry away, she turned to face the earl.

"My lord, I cannot thank you enough for your hospitality. I promise you that you shall not regret it," Marion said. Then she did hurry after Wilda, before he could change his mind about letting her stay.

She had seen little enough of the castle and its inhabitants, but Marion liked what she saw. Although big and gruff, the de Burgh brothers were handsome and appealing, their father was gentle and kind, and his people were happy. It seemed to Marion's dazed senses that the very walls reached out to her in welcome.

Already, Campion seemed like home.

"Come, I have ordered some food and drink for you two," the earl said to his returning sons.

"And me, too, sir!" Nicholas said.

Campion smiled at his youngest. "For all of us, then."

Although supper had been cleared away, he sent a servant for bread, cheese, apples and ale. Once these were brought and they were all seated at the high table, Campion nodded toward Simon to speak. He listened intently as his warrior son reported on his trip south to collect monies from a recalcitrant tenant.

"Then, on the way home, when we were hurrying against winter's winds, we came across a small band being attacked by murderous thieves. We killed the devils, but some of our men were injured in the skirmish," Simon said.

"The odd thing is, the ruffians were not your usual bandits. They fought very well, like trained soldiers," Geoffrey put in, "and on fine horseflesh, far better than you would expect such men to own."

Simon snorted his dispute. "They fought to the death, as the bastards will when cornered, 'tis all."

The earl glanced back at Geoffrey, but the boy said nothing further, deferring instead to his brother, as usual. It was not Geoffrey's way to argue, and yet Campion knew that his scholarly son was probably speaking the truth. Geoffrey might not be as bold as Simon, but he noticed things. He sat back, watched, assessed and made his plans accordingly. That was his strength, and that was why Campion often sent him to accompany his more single-minded brother.

"Some members of the attacked train fled into the woods," Simon said with a scowl of contempt. "They appeared to be youths hardly fit for working in the fields, let alone escorting a female of any consequence. The only remaining survivor was the woman. When we revived her, she could not tell us who she was, nor did she or the caravan have any colors or clues to identify them."

Geoffrey spoke up again. "'Tis plain she is a lady, sir, by the quality of her clothes and by her bearing and speech. I talked with her at length on the road, and she is well educated. She can read and write and has some knowledge of accounts, too."

"And yet she does not remember her own name?" Campion asked.

"No, sir," Geoffrey said. Campion held his gaze for a moment, a silent question passing between them, but Geoffrey did not flinch. Without putting the query into words, Campion knew his son believed the woman spoke the truth. Campion then glanced at Simon, to get his opinion, but the older brother obviously did not think the lady worthy of further conversation. He was already fiddling with his scabbard, impatient to be off.

"And who christened her? You?" Stephen asked, laughing at his own jest. Campion shot him a look and did not miss the replenished wine cup in his hands. Stephen was becoming difficult.

"We have called her Marion," Geoffrey said, ignoring Stephen's contemptuous chuckling, "for we found the name in one of her books."

"Oh! And are you smitten with her, brother?" Stephen taunted.

"Geoffrey's in love!" Nicholas shouted. A round of jeering followed that announcement, and Campion let it play itself out. He could tell with one glance at Geoffrey's disgusted expression that his son had no interest in the girl other than compassion.

"No?" Stephen said. "Then perhaps 'tis our Simon who has felt Cupid's prick?" There was some laughter at

Stephen's play on words. Lord, he was a clever boy. If only he would use it to advantage, instead of wasting it. "Our good brother likes his women short and well rounded, I see!"

Suddenly, the room quieted as Simon shot to his feet. "Wish you a fight?" he growled, looming over Stephen, who leaned back against the wall in a casual pose.

"Lord, no," Stephen replied. He affected a yawn. "It has been positively peaceful without you about—crowing like a cock at the veriest whim."

"That is enough," Campion said. "Simon, sit down. And Stephen, you will be kind enough to keep a civil tongue in your head concerning our guest." Stephen's penchant for finding fault with anything and everything was beginning to annoy his father. The girl might not be breathtaking, but she was pretty in an arresting way.

If Stephen could have seen past the current fashion for boyish figures and golden ladies, he might have noticed that the unruly brown curls framing her heart-shaped face would be a riot of thick locks when freed. He might have noted that her skin, although not as ghostly white as some, was pale and pure, and that those great dark eyes could hold their own against another's of brighter hue.

Campion kept his thoughts to himself, however, having no wish to watch his sons battling one another for the favor of their visitor. Let them ignore her comeliness, but he would not have them treat her rudely, and the look he gave them made that clear.

After a long, threatening moment, Simon sat down, sending a scowl at his black-sheep brother, who grinned shamelessly. One day, Stephen would get his deserts, Campion thought to himself with a flash of premonition, then he focused his attention on the matter at hand. "We shall continue to call her Marion," he said. "Now, tell me where you found her. Perhaps she was only going to a village or visiting amongst her neighbors."

"Nay, sir," Geoffrey said. "A cart held supplies for a long journey, perhaps a pilgrimage." He paused, as if uncertain how much to say, and then continued on determinedly. "I wanted to go back along the road and ask about her, but Simon . . . did not feel the issue warranted a delay."

Campion nodded, but said nothing. Geoffrey's words held no censure, but Campion knew that the two must have been at odds over the fate of the lady. Simon had no use for women and would have put the return of his company before the mystery of a lone female. And who was to say he was wrong? Perhaps, if they had probed the area, they could have returned her safely to her home. Perhaps not. And with the unpredictable weather and poor state of the roads to contend with, Campion hesitated to second-guess Simon.

He rubbed his chin thoughtfully. "It could not hurt to discover who lives in the area and to send out inquiries, but with winter nigh, I am not certain how much success we shall have. Ask the lady for something of her own, something identifiable—a piece of her jewelry, perhaps—and we shall send it along with a messenger to court."

Campion sighed softly, his decision made, and put his palms on the table. "Until we discover her identity, however, the lady shall stay with us and shall be treated as such," he ordered, his gaze sweeping the circle of his sons.

He noted, with chagrin, that the members of this womanless household did not look very well pleased by his verdict. Only Nicholas seemed intrigued by the idea of a visiting female, and Campion could see a wealth of problems in the youth's healthy curiosity. Simon and Reynold looked positively dour, Robin and Stephen rather amused, and Geoffrey somewhat pained. He obviously was feeling sorry for the poor girl.

Campion, on the other hand, had no fears for the lady. Though small, she looked strong enough to withstand much—even the fierce pack of de Burghs—without flinching. There was more to the mysterious Marion than met the eye, he would swear to it. He remembered her huge eyes, soft as a doe's, and he sat back, rubbing his chin thoughtfully.

Perhaps, he wondered, smiling himself... perhaps she might even tame the wolves to her hand.

What beautiful beasts, Marion thought, admiring her own handiwork. It had taken her all winter, but she had finally finished the tapestry last week, and now it brightened the great hall with its bold colors.

It was her own design, a rendering of eight wolves—the de Burgh device—rampant across a field of green, with Campion Castle rising behind them. Of course, the work had been greeted with much humor by the brothers, who taunted Nicholas for being depicted as the runt of the litter and complained loudly about being turned into creatures of various hues. The only de Burghs who did not voice their disapproval were the earl, who was as polite as always, and his eldest son, Dunstan, who did not live at Campion.

For the past week, the hall had been filled with mock howling that would have deafened another woman, but Marion was undisturbed. She took in stride Simon's grunts, Stephen's baiting, Robin's tricks, Reynold's sharp words, and Nicholas's curiosity, for they were like brothers to her now.

Seated by the fire with some sewing, Marion mused on her good fortune. A total stranger, without name or fortune or family, she had been taken in by the de Burghs and accepted. She now served as chatelaine in almost every capacity, and the joy of purpose in her life was heady. But Campion and his handsome, dark-haired sons had given

her more than a home and a position—they had given her
their grudging affection. That was what made her smile
and kept the smile upon her face so much that they teased
her unmercifully about it.

Startled from her pleasant thoughts by the sound of the
great doors banging open, Marion looked up, the needle
still in her hand, to see a giant of a man stride into the
hall. He was dressed as a knight and accompanied by
others similarly garbed, though none was quite as impos-
ing as the man who led them.

Mercy, but the fellow was huge, Marion thought. He
looked to be even bigger than the de Burghs, who towered over everyone at Campion. Who was he? He walked
into the hall as if he owned it, arrogance apparent in every
step.

Suddenly, Marion felt an odd sensation of recognition. There was something familiar about that gait, strong
but graceful, and yet it was like none she had ever seen
before. While she watched, trying to place the massive
warrior, he lifted his helm to shake out a head of dark hair
that gave away his identity in an instant.

Dunstan.

For a moment, Marion remained in her seat, studying
him with blatant interest. Although the family often spoke
of Campion's firstborn, he lived at his own holding and
Marion had never seen him before. She began to stare
openly as her curiosity gave way to admiration. Although a good distance from him, she could see his features plainly enough. But no one, *no one* could ever use
the word *plain* in association with Dunstan.

The eldest de Burgh was the handsomest man Marion
had ever seen. He was huge, taller and broader even than
Simon, and wore his heavy mail with ease. He looked like
a predator, dark menace emanating from his formidable
form, but Marion did not shy from the sight. In fact, she
was surprised to find her heart increasing its pace, for the

first time in her short memory, at a pair of wide male shoulders and muscular legs.

But that was not all that stirred her. The hair that fell to his shoulders was nearly the color of a raven's wing; his face was broad, his cheekbones high, his jaw firm, and his lips... they were neither too full nor too thin, but just right. She gaped.

Oh, Marion knew the de Burghs were a glorious group of specimens, with their thick hair and striking features, but the others had never affected her in this way. They were men, and they were dear to her, but Dunstan rose above his brothers like cream to the top of the crock.

Although he looked to be hard, even more of a soldier than Simon, his face held none of his younger brother's tautness, and his mouth, even pulled tight, looked warm and beckoning.... Mercy! Marion lifted a hand to her throat, for she had never before looked at a man and felt the ground give way beneath her feet.

As if drawn by her perusal, he suddenly looked toward her, and Marion realized just how much she had been neglecting her duties. She shot to her feet, forgetting the handwork in her lap, which promptly fell to the floor. "Arthur!" she called to a passing servant in a shaken voice. "Some wine and food for my lord Dunstan." Then she stooped to retrieve her materials, flustered as she had never been before and all too conscious of her own clumsiness.

She was even more dismayed when a mail-clad knee appeared in front of her. With something akin to amazement, she raised her head to find the object of her admiration before her, holding out the fallen thread. Silently, breathlessly, Marion looked at his hand for a long moment. He had removed his gauntlet, and she gawked at his flesh as if she had never seen such before. And, truly, she had never noticed how appealing such a simple appendage could be.

For one so big, his fingers were neither stubby nor meaty, but long and relatively slender. They were callused and rough, as befitted a warrior, but they held the object gracefully in a light grasp. Marion's attention shifted to the dark hairs sprinkled on the back of the hand, and she felt herself blushing, as if she were glimpsing some intimate part of his great body, and her heart thudded wildly. Her gaze fled to his face.

He was not really smiling because the corners of his lovely mouth were not curved upward, but it was not a frown, either. It seemed to tease her, that mouth of his, and the sight of his lips this near to her made Marion tingle all over, as if she had just been dropped, shivering, into a hot bath. She lifted her eyes to his.

"They are green!" she murmured, with pleased surprise.

"What?" His voice was a deep one, befitting his size, and had a husky sound to it that made Marion tingle all the more.

"Your eyes. They are different from your brothers'. I always wished for green eyes, instead of plain brown," she explained. And no ordinary green were Dunstan's, but the color of the deepest, darkest forest, shrouded in mystery . . . and promise.

He looked confused. Thrusting the thread at her, he straightened and gave her a peremptory look. "Who are you?"

"Marion," she answered simply, rising to her feet. When they both stood at full height, she had to lean back her head to look at him.

"Marion, who?" he asked a trifle churlishly.

"I have no other name," she answered softly. And then she smiled at him. It was easy to do, for he was a beautiful man—even when he was studying her suspiciously, as he was now.

"And you are a visitor to Campion?"

"A guest," Marion corrected, for a visit implied eventual departure, and she had no intention of leaving.

She watched him slant a glance at the servant, who returned to set out ale and food upon the high table for Dunstan's men. She nodded her thanks to Arthur, who then withdrew, and turned to find Dunstan's curious gaze upon her again. "When did you come to Campion?" he asked.

Marion smiled even wider. Did he think she had done away with his father and six brothers? Usurped someone's position here? Exceeded some unwritten authority on guest behavior? "Nigh on six months ago, my lord. 'Tis hard for me to believe that I have seen you not. Can it be you did not attend to your lord father for such a time?"

Marion saw a spark of annoyance in his eyes and noted that he was not a one to be teased. "My own lands keep me busy, lady," he said brusquely. "If you will excuse me." With a dismissive nod, he turned to join his men, and Marion stifled an urge to reach out and tug on his sleeve. She wanted to call him back, to hold him to her side, but she realized, unfortunately, that whatever earthshaking thing was between them, it was obviously onesided. Dunstan did not seem the slightest bit interested in her, beyond normal inquisitiveness.

And why should he? Marion asked herself. She was no court beauty, no sophisticated lady, or even a fresh, young thing in her first flowering. She was short, unremarkable and past marriageable age. For the first time since her arrival at Campion, Marion did not feel at home.

She went back to her sewing and tried to concentrate upon its intricate design rather than the exact hue of Dunstan de Burgh's eyes, but she kept sneaking surreptitious glances at him. Since he was seated far away at the high table and surrounded by his men, all she could see was a pair of broad shoulders and a mane of dark hair, but it was enough . . . or too much, depending upon one's outlook, Marion thought gloomily.

She had often longed to meet Campion's heir, but now that he was here, she found herself wishing for his speedy departure. She was too old to begin harboring the girlish fancies that his appearance seemed to inspire. Sometimes she wondered if there had ever been a man in her life, but afraid to truly look into her past, she could only rely on her senses. And they told her that there had never been anyone like Dunstan de Burgh.

A sudden burst of noise heralded the entrance of Dunstan's younger brothers, and Marion felt her errant smile return. They rushed to greet their sibling with a loud volley of rather dubious exchanges: grunts from Simon, insults from Stephen, compliments from Geoffrey, and jests from Robin. Campion followed his sons in at a more stately pace, but he had no reservations about pulling his towering heir into a rough embrace. "'Tis good to see you," Marion heard him say, and then they all talked at once.

Listening absently, Marion waited for a formal introduction, but it did not come. The men held a low conversation and then filed up the stairs, presumably to the solar, for a private conference.

What was it about? Marion did not like the urgency of their meeting, nor could she imagine the reason for such grim manners. Was there a threat to Campion? Although the castle seemed impregnable, war was always a possibility, and she did not want to imagine the de Burghs going off to battle.

Moving closer to the fire to ward off a chill, Marion realized that for the first time since entering the safety of Campion's walls, she felt uneasy, a prickly sense of dread disturbing the hairs upon her neck. Whether it denoted danger to herself or to her newfound family, Marion did not know, but she had to fight an urge to rush to the solar and throw herself into someone's arms...preferably Dunstan's.

Chapter Two

Looking up from the papers that had been delivered to him, Campion leaned back and sighed, his heart heavy with their contents. It had been a long and bitter winter with little activity, but the queries he had sent out months ago had borne fruit, and now... Now he wished they had not.

The earl regretted those simple actions, taken before the snows, but it was too late to call them back now. He was well aware that a man often set in motion events that traveled beyond his control, and such had been the case in the autumn when he had asked after a lost lady with no memory.

Reaching a decision, Campion laid his hands upon his knees and surveyed his sons. He felt pride at the sight of them gathered around him in the solar. It had been some time since they had met together. Was it last summer, or had it been spring the last time he had had the pleasure of seeing them all before him?

Campion was glad that the court courier had traveled first to Wessex, with messages for Dunstan. Otherwise, his firstborn might never have come. He felt a small measure of doubt as he wondered if there might be another reason for Dunstan's visit. Campion was unsure, for his eldest son had become distant and close-mouthed ever since taking over his own holdings.

He is a grown man, keeping his own counsel, Campion noted with a mixture of respect and loss. Although his sons had their faults, they were good men, decent, well educated and capable. The matter at hand returned swiftly to mind, and he hoped that he could depend upon one of them to do what was right.

"It seems we have a problem," he said without preamble. "You may remember that after Lady Marion arrived, I sent a ring belonging to her to court with the hope that someone there might identify it." Campion paused, noting, with approval, that he had their undivided attention.

"It was recognized by one Harold Peasely, who claims the ring belongs to his niece, Marion Warenne. The lady, who owns quite a bit of land to the south, has been missing since she undertook a pilgrimage in the fall. Peasely is her guardian, and he wants her back—immediately."

Campion looked about, assessing the reaction of his audience. Some faces, such as Reynold's, were taut and grim, while others showed anger and dismay. Good. Obviously, none of his sons wanted the girl to leave. Now, if only he could convince them to keep her here....

"But why does Marion not remember this?" Simon asked sharply. "When we found her in the roadway she knew nothing, and she still claims not to know her own name."

Campion rubbed his chin thoughtfully. "I do not think the lady *wants* to be restored to her former life," he answered slowly. "She has always seemed distressed by efforts to help her remember. I would speculate that she is happier here." Campion saw Robin nod in agreement, while the others released sighs, grunts and mutters as they mulled over that pronouncement.

"If she does not wish to return, do not send her back," Stephen said with a casual gesture that belied his concern.

"Unfortunately, we are in a rather awkward position," Campion said. "This Peasely has threatened to bring a force of arms against us if we do not return Marion to her home at once."

Robin whistled and shook his head.

"I would like to see him try to take Campion," Simon snarled.

"Who the devil is he?" Reynold asked.

"He is a minor landholder, brother to Marion's mother, but he holds sway over her extensive properties, her large fortune and her future, according to the messenger."

"I say let the bastard come and be damned. He shall know whom he threatens!" shouted Simon, slamming his fist against his palm for emphasis.

"'Tis not as simple as that, boys," Campion said, holding up a hand to stem the tide of angry voices. He glanced toward Dunstan, thinking that his eldest might contribute to the discussion, but Dunstan only lounged against the wall with a detached air and an expression of disgust on his face. Obviously, he had no interest in the lady's disposition and viewed his brothers' concern as a waste of energy. Campion sighed, for he would have no help from that quarter.

"We have no legal right to the girl," Campion explained. "Even if she *wants* to stay with us, we cannot keep her." Outraged mutters met his words, and he lifted his hand again for attention. "Peasely is Marion's guardian. There is naught we can do to change that, unless, of course, we were to *gain* the right to her in a perfectly lawful manner."

Campion paused to assess each man in the room, hoping that one of them would come to Marion's aid. They all looked at him expectantly, with the exception of Dunstan, who uttered a low snort and pushed off the wall with a grimace. Campion paid him no mind, for Dunstan did not even know the girl. One of his brothers would have to make the decision that Dunstan so rudely disdained.

"How?" piped up Nicholas.

"By marriage," Campion said simply. He studied them seriously. "Which one of you shall take her to wife?"

Dead silence met his question.

Campion's gaze swept the assembly, taking in each son, in turn, though none would meet his probing eyes now. Simon, the born warrior, scowled his denial, while Reynold grunted his dismay. Stephen, as was his way of late, immediately poured himself another cup of wine, Campion noted with a frown.

Robin was studying the tips of his boots with extreme concentration, while Nicholas fiddled with the knife in his belt, and Geoffrey looked torn, as always, between compassion and common sense.

"Will none of you have her?" Campion asked. He could not keep the disappointment from his voice, for he had come to care for the girl. He had hoped that this hastily formed plan would keep her with them, but no one said a word. "Are all my sons unnatural that they will not marry and give Campion heirs?"

Eyes downcast, they all refused to answer, except Simon, who flashed his silver-gray ones like steel. "Why is it that she is not already wed? She looks of an age."

"'Tis not difficult to imagine that her uncle covets her lands for himself. If so, he will never willingly let her marry. The messenger hinted as much. 'Tis more than likely that our Marion was little more than a prisoner in her own castle," Campion said, hoping that guilt might move his sons when duty and affection had failed to do so.

"He treated her badly," Nicholas said, his head hanging, his misery impossible to disguise.

"Why do you say that?" Simon asked sharply.

Nicholas shrugged. "Just things that she has said about how wonderful it is here and how she always feels safe and part of a family. She gives me that great smile of hers and says how lucky she is that we took her in."

Ashamed, furtive glances were exchanged, but still no one volunteered to wed Marion. It was his own fault, Campion decided. He should have remarried long ago, so that the boys would know the company of women. But after his second wife had died birthing Nicholas, a grief-stricken Campion had been loath to give his heart again.

Unfortunately, the result was that his sons had grown to manhood without the tender touch of female hands. Now he was cursed with a grown group of bachelors who thought nothing of easing themselves on a bit of bought flesh, but who would never give him grandchildren.

Could they not see the change in Campion and in themselves, wrought by Marion's presence? In a few short months, she had made herself indispensable to the household, improving the hall and the rooms and the meals. Campion thought of the girl's smile, so rich and full of warmth, and he felt a pang of loss.

He ought to marry her himself, Campion thought suddenly, and then sighed at his own foolishness. Although past the age when most girls were wed, Marion was far too young for him, and he was too old to begin a new family. The winter had not been kind to him, and his joints were bothersome. He did not let on to his sons, of course, but he was finding it harder to wield a sword with his previous skill. Fond as he was of Marion, that fondness made him want her to have a robust husband to give her many sons.

And he was looking at seven healthy candidates who refused to take her. Campion let them see his displeasure. "Very well, then. If none of you will have her to wife, she must go home. Who will take her back to Baddersly?"

Again, dead silence met his words. The toes of his boots still interested Robin, Nicholas still fiddled with his knife, and Stephen concentrated on the bottom of his cup. Reynold rubbed his bad leg, as he often did when he was disturbed, and Simon scowled out the window, as if an answer would strike him from the heavens.

"Well?" This time, Campion's tone left no doubt that he was angry.

Reynold glanced up. "Geoffrey is her favorite," he pointed out.

Geoffrey looked startled—and appalled. "Nay! I cannot. Make Simon go."

"Aye. He is best equipped to guard her," Stephen said, his lips curling into a smirk.

"Enough," Campion said, calling a halt to the bickering. Yet they muttered on, sending black looks at one another, none of them willing to do the deed. Campion felt his pride in them melt away. By the rood, he faced a room full of cowards! He was about to chastise them as such, when suddenly the voices trailed off. They all looked at one another, brows lifted in surprise. Then, six heads swiveled toward the wall behind him, as they spoke as one.

"Send Dunstan!" all of them cried at the same time.

"Aye! Dunstan is better equipped than I!" Simon said. His words made Campion pause, for normally Simon would rather have died than admit such a thing.

"Aye. He knows her not and would as likely feel nothing even if he did," Stephen added with a contemptuous sneer.

Campion glanced at Dunstan, who was watching the furor with a detached frown, and he wondered what the boy was thinking. When had his eldest son grown so distant? With a sigh, he turned his attention back to the matter at hand. "Dunstan is a good man on a journey," he noted.

"Aye! He knows his way throughout the whole country!" Nicholas said.

Campion ignored the youngest de Burgh's enthusiasm for his eldest brother and considered the idea further. Perhaps Dunstan would be the best man for the job. He was a fine knight and could easily handle any trouble that Peasely might serve him. He was also a baron in his own right, possessing some of the diplomacy that Simon so sorely lacked. And he was not involved with the girl's affections; it would cause him no suffering to give Marion over to her uncle.

Laying his palms upon the table, Campion made his decision. "If Dunstan is willing, then so be it."

"Aye, father." They answered as one, and Campion realized that for once his sons were in agreement, all relieved to escape the task that they had dreaded. Campion sighed, his disappointment heavy as they rose to their feet, eager to be gone, only to halt at the sound of Dunstan's low voice.

"Stay," he said, in a tone that brooked no argument. Although the boys rarely listened to one another, they were indebted to their sibling this day, so they deferred to him and remained where they were.

"Fetch the girl, and say your farewells, for we leave within the hour," Dunstan said.

Campion glanced at him in surprise. "But you just arrived. Surely, you will want to rest before beginning another journey." Campion felt a sting in his chest at the thought of Dunstan's swift departure. It had been a year since his firstborn had been home. Why would he go so quickly?

"If you wish me to take on this errand, I would hurry, for I am needed back in Wessex," Dunstan said tersely. He appeared none too happy to be saddled with the task, and yet he had accepted it readily enough. Campion eyed him closely, trying to see inside the man his boy had become, but Dunstan's dark eyes glinted dispassionately, revealing nothing. Campion felt another prick of sadness at the knowledge that Dunstan preferred his own castle, his own home now....

Campion turned back to his younger sons. "Have Wilda bring Marion to us," he said. Then he looked around the room. If the de Burghs had appeared uncomfortable before, they were practically squirming now. Not one of them wanted to face Marion—the cowards. Campion's shame for them was tempered with a bit of sympathy, for even he knew some trepidation at the coming confrontation. After all, he, too, had come to care for the lady he had taken in.

Now how, by the rood, was he going to tell her she had to leave?

Campion's summons stunned Marion. Panic such as she had not known since waking up bewildered in the roadway seized her, and for a long moment she could not even move. Slowly, firmly, she told herself that the earl only wanted to order a special feast in honor of Dunstan's visit or to introduce his eldest son to her, but her memory loss had forced Marion to rely on her senses. And they told her that something was amiss.

Marion tried to compose herself as she followed Wilda to the solar, but the sight that met her brought on a new rush of dread. Although all the de Burghs were there, the room was silent as a tomb, Campion's seven sons engaging in none of their usual boisterous banter. The six whom she had grown to love as brothers were arranged around their father, yet not one of them would meet her eyes. Only Dunstan, who was lounging against a wall like a dark, brooding presence, appeared to be watching her, his handsome face in shadow.

"Lady Marion. Please sit down," the earl said. Campion met her gaze openly, but something in it—a hint of sadness or regret—made her heart contract. She sat down on the edge of a settle, nodding calmly while her mind rushed ahead, pondering what harrowing news might be forthcoming.

"Marion," Campion began. "You know that we have been happy to have you with us. You have filled a need here, not only by acting as chatelaine, but by cheering us with your smiles. If we could, we would have you stay with us always."

Marion froze, her body immobile while the outcome that she feared most became a reality. He was sending her away! Where would she go? What would she do, a lone woman without friend or family to take her in, without even a memory of her own past?

"However, it appears that we are not the only people who care about you. Although you may not remember, you have at least one relative who has not forgotten you— your uncle."

Campion waited, as if expecting her to respond in some way, but how could she? Uncle? What uncle? "I know no uncle," Marion said finally, her words hardly audible above the pounding of her heart. Forcing her limbs to move, she folded her hands neatly in her lap, affecting an outward appearance of serenity.

"I know this all seems strange to you, my dear," Campion said. "But I am sure that your memory will return in time, perhaps more quickly when you are home."

Panic, renewed and ferocious, rushed through her, and Marion gripped her fingers together. It was one thing to be cast out, alone. It was quite another to be thrust into the custody of a stranger from a past that filled her only with dread.... Marion struggled for air while she sought to follow Campion's words.

"You are Marion Warenne, and you are quite an heiress," he was saying. He smiled slightly, as though he expected her to be cheered by the news, but she was not. The name meant nothing to her, the wealth even less.

"But, my lord, you told me that I might stay as long as I wish," she protested, trying to keep her voice steady.

Sympathy washed gently over the earl's face, frightening her far more than indifference. "I know that, my dear, and I am truly sorry. If you were still alone and unknown, I would most certainly extend my hospitality to you indefinitely. But you have a home of your own, and your uncle is most anxious for your return."

Through the blind haze of horror that had descended upon her, Marion tried to find words to deny the earl, but she could not. She could only stare at him wide-eyed, while she fought to keep her agitation in check. It came to her from nowhere, this knowledge that she must hide her fear, mask her emotions and keep her soul to herself. She had obviously learned it well, sometime back in the murky past that escaped her.

As if sensing her despair, Campion leaned forward. "Do not worry, Marion. We shall not let any harm come to you." Fixing his gaze steadily upon her, he spoke over his shoulder to where Dunstan leaned against the wall. "My eldest son, Dunstan, baron of Wessex, will escort you home, and he will make sure all is well."

Marion suspected that Campion was directing an order at his son, while trying to reassure her, but it mattered little. She knew that once she left the safety of these walls, the de Burghs, from the earl down to young Nicholas, would hold no sway in her life, and it would be foolish to pretend otherwise.

Her champions had deserted her.

Marion marshaled all her resources for one last effort. "You have me at a disadvantage, my lord, for I cannot plead my case very coherently. 'Tis true that my past is a mystery to me, but I know this much—something there was very wrong. I cannot even try to remember but that I am filled with dread. I beg you, my lord, do not send me back."

She let the plea hang in the air while Campion rubbed his chin and studied her thoughtfully. Although panic threatened to consume her, Marion betrayed nothing and made no movement. Her back remained straight as a rod while she perched on the edge of the settle, her hands in her lap.

Finally, the earl sighed regretfully. "I am sorry, Marion, but news of your stay here has reached your uncle, and he has threatened war if we do not return you to Baddersly at once."

War! Marion's heart sank, along with the very last of her hopes, for she could not blame Campion for his decision. Despite her distress, she had no wish to endanger the men who had taken her in and treated her so kindly. She could not see their blood spilled simply because she felt more at home here than at a castle she no longer recalled.

"Although I am not moved by his intimidation, I fear, my dear, that we have no legal right to you," Campion explained.

Marion listened, still and quiet, as she felt blackness descend, taking her to a place where she had not been for many months. When she spoke, it was from a distance, detached from them all. "I see," she said softly. She did not nod or smile, but only eyed the earl gravely. "When do we leave?"

For the first time since Marion had known him, the dignified Campion looked uncomfortable. "As soon as your things are packed," he answered. "Dunstan is eager to be off. He is well versed with the roadways, having served Edward for many years before receiving his own barony. He will see that you come to no harm."

As if in answer, Dunstan stepped out of the shadows, a huge, intimidating presence. He was as big as the bole of an oak tree, and right now he looked to be just about as feeling. He moved in front of the window, so that Marion blinked, unable to see him well. And in that instant, she hated him.

"Come, Lady Warenne," he said, eyeing her disdainfully. "We had best be on our way."

Marion rose to find the other de Burghs crowding around her. Robin and Geoffrey exchanged glances, both of them looking guilty and ill at ease.

"Dunstan will take good care of you," Geoffrey offered.

"Yes. He is the very best," Robin said. He held out his hands to take hers. "Godspeed."

"Keep well," Geoffrey added.

Marion nodded, then turned to Stephen, who raised his cup in salute. "Goodbye, Stephen," she said, surprised at the lump in her throat. She sought again the numbness that would shield her, reaching into the blackness for a place she had been to before coming to Campion.

"Marion." Simon's face was taut, his farewell terse.

Reynold did not even speak, but jerked his head and rubbed his bad leg. "Reynold," she said.

Nicholas stepped toward her then, hanging his head and looking miserable. "I am sorry, Marion," he muttered. "Dunstan will take care of you, though. He will not let any harm come to you!"

"Thank you for your kindness, all of you," she said evenly.

Campion took her hands. "Farewell for now, Lady Marion. I hope that we shall meet again soon."

Despite her best efforts, Marion felt a pressure behind her eyes as she pulled away. Then Dunstan moved forward to escort her out of the room, and she was spared the ignominy of losing her control. A swift glance at his hard features set her own, so that she left the others behind without a glance.

* * *

Since Marion did not turn back, she did not see the de Burghs fling themselves down in disgust. For long moments, silence reigned in the solar. Then Stephen finally spoke. "I would have preferred ranting and raving to that noble acceptance," he noted before taking a long drink from his replenished cup.

"Aye," said Campion, frowning thoughtfully. "'Twould have been easier if she had cursed you all for the cowards that you are."

"Aye," Geoffrey whispered softly. And for once, no argument ensued. The de Burghs were all in agreement again.

Chapter Three

Dunstan was not pleased. He had come to Campion for... well, he was not sure exactly why he had come, but it was not to be saddled with such a ridiculous errand. Not now, when there was so much to be done at Wessex. He rubbed the back of his neck and strode into the yard without even glancing at the woman at his side.

While the wench was packing, he had hastily washed, changed his travel-stained garments and devoured some food. Now, he looked toward a few of his father's men to supplement his own force before leaving. Although they would make only a few miles before sunset, that would put them a few miles closer to their destination—and the completion of his task.

"Dunstan!" He turned at the call from his vassal. Walter Avery, a beefy blond knight who had been with him since his first days serving King Edward, loped across the yard, looking decidedly annoyed to have been snatched from his leisure.

"Wait here," Dunstan curtly told the woman. Without staying for an answer, he walked over to meet his vassal.

"What is afoot?" Walter asked. "Have you news of Fitzhugh?"

"Nay," Dunstan said, frowning at the mention of his

bastard neighbor. "Campion would have me escort one of his guests back to her home," he explained curtly.

Walter's heavy brows lifted in surprise. "And you agreed?"

Dunstan glanced at the walls of the keep that rose behind them and realized, belatedly, that he could have refused his father. But that course had never even crossed his mind. As the eldest, he had always shouldered the most responsibility; as a de Burgh, he bore it without complaint.

"It should not take long, a few weeks, no more," Dunstan said absently. Walter shook his head. Obviously, he could not understand why a baron with his own property and its attendant problems would take on a commission from Campion—especially when there were at least five other brothers who could do the job.

Dunstan was wondering the same thing himself.

"See that we have sufficient men for the trip," he ordered. "I want to travel quickly and light, but most of all, I want this to be a safe, uneventful journey."

When Walter nodded grudgingly and stalked across the yard to see to the men, Dunstan turned back toward the girl, but she was not where he had left her. Unaccustomed to having his orders disobeyed, Dunstan clenched his jaw in annoyance and looked around. Although he soon spotted her not far away, surrounded by a group of urchins, his temper was unappeased. A lifetime of hard work, skilled fighting and book study, and he was playing nursemaid to a female!

And what a female! As Dunstan strode toward the brown daub of a creature, he wondered how she had ever wormed her way into his family's good graces. He had little use for women himself and had never known his brothers to claim aught but carnal interest in them, either. And yet he had witnessed the battle-hardened de

Burghs fawning over this one in wrenching farewells that had made his stomach turn.

As he approached her, she reached down to pat one of the children, and he studied her in earnest. The woman was not even beautiful! She was short and dark and too voluptuous for his taste, which ran more to willowy blondes. A certain widow from Edward's court, who had been free with her favors, came to mind. Yes, Melissande, pale and cool and glittering with expensive gems, was to his liking—not this moppet. He scowled at her.

She was stooping, making herself even smaller to speak to the children who crowded happily around her, when Dunstan reached her. He did not pause or wait for her to acknowledge his presence. He simply grabbed her by the arm and hauled her up. "I told you to stay put!" he snapped.

For an instant, she seemed startled, her big brown eyes growing huge in her delicate face. By faith, they were enormous, those eyes and rather... striking in their fashion. Was she frightened of him? Good, Dunstan thought smugly. Then perhaps she would listen to him in the future. "When I give an order I expect you to obey it," he said gruffly.

Her head bowed, and he thought she would nod submissively, but then she lifted her chin and spoke. "And I expect you to have better manners, Dunstan de Burgh!" she replied. Her voice was low and shaky, but the words were plain enough. They took him aback, and he stared at her. He could not recall the last time anyone had scolded him; no one possessed the audacity to talk back to him. The idea of this tiny female, this little wren, asserting herself, made him want to laugh. He released her arm none too gently.

"I want this journey to pass swiftly and uneventfully. Heed me, and we shall have no further problems. Now, please accompany me, my lady," he said. He snapped the polite phrases through clenched teeth and spread out an arm in an exaggerated gesture of cordiality. Although she shot him a brief look that hinted at barely suppressed outrage, she gracefully took her place in front of him.

Dunstan decided he had imagined the fierceness in her glance and smiled smugly at her back. Already he had the woman well in hand. The little wren might have thought she could run roughshod over him, as she had his brothers, but he had effectively put her in her place. He had no intention of playing nursemaid, nor did he plan on becoming besotted like the rest of his family by one small, insignificant female with huge eyes.

Marion let a faceless soldier help her mount her palfrey, then she gripped the reins tightly and waited for the train to get under way. Having seen her to her horse, Dunstan had gone about other business, and Marion was heartily glad to see his back, for she liked him not. Whatever appeal he had initially held for her had disappeared with his unfeeling handling of her departure. He had shown his true nature quickly enough!

Surprised to find her hands shaking with the force of her anger, Marion looked down at them, turning them over and over, as she assessed this unusual reaction. At Campion, she had never known such blood-coursing emotion, but somehow, it felt good. She let her hands tremble and her rage boil at the thought of Dunstan de Burgh's behavior.

On some level, Marion knew that Dunstan was not much different from his brothers. They had been gruff and rude and sometimes ill-mannered when she had arrived. Reynold still was difficult to reach, owing, she suspected, to his bad leg…and yet she knew that he cared for her.

Dunstan did not. There was no excuse for the way he had grabbed at her, bruising her tender arm with his huge hand and subduing her with his overpowering strength. Marion lifted her chin. For him she would make no allowances. He was the one who had brought the bad tidings. He would steal her from the people she loved and wrest her from the only home she had ever known. He would take her to a place she did not want to go.

Just the thought of this Baddersly made Marion stiffen. Happy at Campion, she had known no desire to discover her past, and whenever she tried to remember, she had been stricken with blinding headaches and cold, sweating dread that left her sick and shaken. How could she willingly travel back toward whatever horrors she had left behind?

Dunstan's sharp words came back to her, demanding in his smug, masculine way that she obey him, and Marion's will wavered. She knew what she *should* do.

She should remain in the middle of the train, riding her palfrey without complaint and avoiding any more confrontations with Dunstan. She should not disrupt the trip or call attention to herself. She should go calmly and quietly while he delivered her into the hands of her unknown guardian and into the dark mysteries of his castle.

That would be the wisest course, and she sensed that whoever Marion Warenne was, Marion would definitely have stayed out of the way, meekly meeting her fate.

But she was a different girl now. She had discovered a small spark of something in herself, something that had helped her bravely make a new life at Campion without a memory to call her own. She had nurtured that tiny flame, and it had helped her tame six de Burgh brothers, fierce as wolves, into accepting her into their home and their hearts.

That spark, infinitesimal as it seemed now, would not allow her to sit back and let Dunstan bully her. Nor was it going to let him take her back to whatever awaited her at . . . Baddersly. The very name of the place was fraught with foreboding.

Though she knew little enough about herself, Marion sensed that she was not an imaginative woman. Nothing else in her brief history had roused in her such tumultuous emotions as the mention of this purported holding of hers. Her entire being screamed a warning that she could not ignore.

She could not go there.

Her decision made, Marion felt an easing inside her, as if she had escaped the executioner's block but narrowly. Now, her only problem lay in getting away from her escort, and that, she realized, would be no easy task.

Dunstan would *not* be pleased.

Dunstan was pleased. They had traveled well their first day out and had camped peacefully off the road. He had seen little of the wench but a flutter of brown when she scurried to her tent to sleep, so he thought her well subdued.

This morning had dawned fair and mild, and he decided to stop to take the late-morning meal under some large oaks. This was, after all, not a military trek, but a journey with a lady, Dunstan told himself, even if the lady was hardly noticeable.

Eating his bread and cheese quickly, he quaffed some water and surveyed the train, checking the horses and carts and assessing the mood of his men. Accustomed to traveling with him, they were soon finished, too, and Dunstan had no intention of lingering. Although it was nearly summer, they could not count upon continued good weather. Today's warmth could turn suddenly cool, and rainstorms could reduce the already bad road into a mire of muck.

"Load up," he said to Walter, who echoed his order. Then he glanced around, watching with a practiced eye the swift dismantling of the makeshift camp. His men mounted their horses, and all seemed in order, but for something that nagged at the edge of his thoughts.

"Where is Lady Warenne?" he asked suddenly. Those who deigned to answer shook their heads. Dunstan stalked along the edge of the group until he found her palfrey. It stood, without its rider, next to another gentle beast ridden by an ancient servant. "Where is your mistress, old woman?" he snapped.

Shrewd eyes peered out at him from a wrinkled face, and he was met with a nearly toothless smile. "I know not, master! Have you lost her?" The crone laughed then, a high, cackling sound that grated against his ears. Dunstan silenced her with a swift glare.

"Walter, check the carts," he barked. Females! Lady Warenne probably was fetching some possession from storage and delaying them all with her thoughtlessness. Clenching his jaw in annoyance, he settled his hands on his hips and surveyed the area. When he had last noticed her, the wren had been eating her meal under one of the trees. She might have slipped into one of the carts, but he was beginning to doubt that. Something did not seem right, and Dunstan had not achieved his knighthood by ignoring his presentiments.

"She is not anywhere in the train, my lord," Walter answered briskly, confirming what Dunstan already felt in his gut.

Taking a long breath, Dunstan exhaled slowly and cleared his mind of the anger that threatened to cloud it. No brigands could have stolen her off with his small force surrounding her, and they were not deep enough into the forest to be threatened by wild beasts. If something had happened to the lady, Dunstan surmised, it was her own doing. With a scowl, he strode toward the oak where he had last seen her.

"Perhaps she wandered off to heed nature's call and became lost," Walter suggested, peering into the woods. It was a possibility, Dunstan agreed, for the little wren certainly looked witless enough to do such a thing. If so, he would have to stop and search for her, a course of action that did not please him in the least.

Dunstan followed Walter's gaze, but he could see no sign of passage through the brush. He dropped to one knee and studied the ground. Although the grass was trampled near the bole, there was no evidence of impressions away from the tree. A little thing like her would probably have a light step, though, Dunstan acknowledged.

"Lady Warenne!" Dunstan called out loudly, only to receive no answer. "Lady Warenne! Can you hear me? Are you hurt?" Silence met his words. With a low oath, Dunstan ordered his men to look in ever-widening circles until the stupid woman was found. She was, unfortunately, the sole reason for this trip, and he could not return to Wessex until she was delivered to her uncle.

As he mounted and turned his horse toward the woods, Dunstan tried not to think of the delay she was costing him. He tried not to think of how he would like to shake the foolish chit until her teeth rattled. He tried, valiantly, to control his temper.

After an hour, Dunstan was furious. They had combed the forest, the road and the fields, and had found nothing of Lady Warenne. It was as if she had disappeared without a trace. Gritting his teeth, Dunstan reined in his destrier near the spot where they had originally stopped and forced himself to admit the truth.

He did not like escorting foolhardy women to their homes, but even less did he like being bested by them. And that was what he was sure had happened. Somehow, the lady had fled of her own free will!

Dunstan chided himself for not taking his mission more seriously, for letting his thoughts drift to his own troubles at Wessex when they should have been focused solely on the business at hand. He knew the wench did not want to return to her uncle, so he should have kept a closer eye upon her. But who would have thought the little wren would rather brave the wilds of the countryside than go back to Baddersly?

Her flight had been so swiftly arranged that Dunstan could not even blame her success on outside assistance. No, he realized, the minx had outwitted him all by herself. Under normal circumstances, Dunstan might spare a fleeting moment of admiration for such a trick, but not today, when each minute spent looking for her delayed him further.

Instead, he stared at the now-familiar eating area, his eyes narrowing as he weighed the facts before him, trying to puzzle an answer from them. Finally, with one last glance at the clearing alongside the road, Dunstan shouted to Walter. "Come! Let us gather the train together and head toward Campion. Perhaps she is making her way there." Grim-faced, his men began turning the carts around and taking their places for the trek back.

Waiting while the others rode ahead, Dunstan caught the swift look that Walter sent him, a look that said, What will your father do when you return without the lady? But his vassal knew better than to voice such concerns, and Dunstan refused to consider them. He never failed in his tasks, and he did not intend to start now.

A mile down the road, Dunstan told his men to fan out again, while he turned back toward where they had camped. When he neared the site, Dunstan slipped from his horse and walked silently, making his way in a circle through the woods until he reached a point where he could see the tree under which Lady Warenne had taken her

meal. Then he leaned back against an oak, crossed his
arms against his chest and watched.

He did not have long to wait. Soon there was a pecu-
liar rustling up in the branches, and Dunstan moved forward soundlessly. By the time he saw a green slipper
descending, he was underneath the tree. A shapely ankle,
encased in dark hose, revealed itself, followed by a swish
of emerald skirts. With a rather gleeful malice, Dunstan
doffed his gauntlets, reached up and closed his fingers
about her calf.

"Eeeek!" Lady Warenne shrieked like a captured fowl,
lost her footing and tumbled directly into his arms.

Dunstan would never have believed that anyone so
small could put up such a fight, but the little wren struggled like a falcon. Finally, he was forced to pin her up
against the bole of the tree, her wrists pressed to her sides
and her body stilled by the pressure of his own. "Cease,
Lady Warenne," he ordered grimly.

Her large eyes flashed recognition, and she finally
stilled, but in that instant the shape of their encounter al-
tered subtly. Those incredibly huge eyes were not a dull
brown, as Dunstan had first thought, but the gentle, warm
hue of a doe's and fringed with the thickest dark lashes he
had ever seen. He found himself caught by them, and, at
the same time, he became aware of the feel of her against
him.

She was soft and lushly curved. Her abundant breasts
pressed into his chest, and his fingers grazed her generous hips. Her ever-present hood had fallen to release a
mass of heavy, mahogany curls that tumbled about her
shoulders as if she had just risen, tousled, from her bed.
Her cheeks were flushed, a compelling, deep rose, and her
lips, full and wide, were parted in silent startlement. A
pulse beat at the base of her throat, and Dunstan could
feel the rise and fall of her breath.

With vague surprise, he found himself spring to life against her belly. He looked down at her, trapped like a wild bird by his form, and he felt something indescribable. Without thought, he moved against her, and the tantalizing press of her body against his groin made him hot as a flame.

Dunstan closed his eyes against a realization that he would rather deny, but it formed nonetheless: he wanted her. He wanted her with a fierce desire that astonished him in its intensity. His head felt as if the blood was rushing from it, and like a man dazed, he released one of her wrists, sliding his hand along the sumptuous curve of her hip to her waist and then . . .

Day of God, he wanted to touch her! He wanted to slip his palm inside her bodice and cup her bare breasts, to feel the heft and weight of them. Dunstan smoothed his thumb along her ribs, underneath one fat mound, letting its heavy softness ride him, and he shuddered, his fingers poised but a hairbreadth from the taut material that covered her chest.

She made some sound, and he opened his eyes to gaze into hers, wide with some unnamed emotion. She was not afraid of him. He sensed that, but she was afraid nonetheless. Freeing her other wrist, he raised his left hand slowly, so as not to startle her. He wanted to curve it around her neck and take those parted lips with his mouth. . . .

With a growl, Dunstan stepped back, releasing her, and she slid down the bole of the tree to collapse at his feet. Refusing to look at her, he turned and whistled for his horse. By faith, he had never taken a woman against her will! He had rarely taken one outside of the confines of her own perfumed bed. What in God's name had possessed him to nearly force himself upon a lady his own father had entrusted to him?

Dunstan grimaced in disgust. Obviously, he had been too long without sex to react so heatedly... and to the wren, of all women! Instead of wanting to take her, he should want to strangle her after the dance she had led him!

Anger, long-suppressed, rushed through him, sluicing away the last vestiges of his desire. Just what had possessed her to try to escape him in the first place? The whole business was so ludicrous. Dunstan did not care to admit how close she had come to succeeding. He whirled on her suddenly.

"Why the devil were you up the tree?"

She stopped dusting herself off to gaze directly at him, and Dunstan noticed, not for the first time, that she possessed an oddly affecting grace. Even after such treatment as he had just given her, she held herself calmly, displaying no distress. The color in her cheeks was still high, but she gave no other sign of their strange encounter. "I... I saw a wild boar and climbed up to get out of its path."

For a moment, Dunstan just stood there staring at her, his mouth open in astonishment. Then he threw back his head and laughed uproariously. She watched him serenely the entire time, just as if her explanation had not been the most ridiculous thing he had ever heard.

"Perhaps you would care to tell me why no one else saw or heard this animal? Or why a lady such as yourself would not scream and run away, but instead crawl up a tree? A decidedly unladylike response, I would say," Dunstan said.

She was looking at him curiously, those enormous eyes of hers wide with something he could not identify, but that obviously had nothing whatsoever to do with what he was saying. "Well?" he prodded her.

"I was too afraid to scream," she answered without demur. The forthright manner in which she spoke nearly made him doubt his own presumptions, but Dunstan knew better. He put his hands on his hips and assessed her.

"And how is it that we spent a goodly time searching for you and calling for you, directly beneath this very same tree, and you made no response?"

"I believe I must have fainted dead away from sheer fright," she said, blithely meeting his gaze.

"I see." Dunstan eased out the words with no little effort. She was an audacious wench, if nothing else. "And you have been up there all this time, precariously balanced, but not awake—even to our cries?"

She nodded sweetly. What a liar! And she looked so innocent, too. No wonder she had easily gulled his brothers. From what Dunstan understood, she had convinced them she did not even know her own name. Who could tell what game the girl was playing? Dunstan fully admitted that he did not, nor was he particularly interested in discovering the truth. As tempting as it was to join in the play, he had neither the time nor the energy at this point in his life. He frowned as he studied her closely. "And this muteness that affects you occurs whenever you are frightened?"

"Oh, yes, my lord...Dunstan. May I call you Dunstan?" she asked, as nicely as if they were ensconced in a cozy solar exchanging sweetmeats and he had not just wasted precious hours dangling after her. He nodded curtly, then turned to his approaching horse.

He stood there for a moment, his feet apart, and then slanted a glance toward her. She was trying, uselessly, to better her hair, which he suspected resisted constraints of any kind. He grinned, certain she was not watching him, and let loose a battle cry that had been known to freeze the blood of his enemies.

His companion jumped and shrieked—loudly. With a smug smile, Dunstan mounted his horse and held out a hand to her. "It seems, my lady, that your voice has re-turned—in full force."

"That is hardly fair, Dunstan," she said, accepting his aid grudgingly. "I was not frightened by your mean-spirited gesture, merely startled."

He grinned wider. "Do not lie to me, my lady. And do not run away from me again, or I shall make you regret it," he warned. Then he grasped her fingers, lifting her up in front of him as easily as a child, and tucked her between his thighs.

He was going to elaborate on his threat, but she moved, settling herself comfortably against him, and desire flared again in his loins, much to his annoyance. With a grunt, he kicked his horse to a gallop along the road.

She must be some kind of witch, Dunstan told himself, for she was trying to enchant him as surely as she had his brothers. He could just picture her wiggling that gener-ous bottom like a lure, and all of them, led by the all-too-randy Stephen, jumping to the bait.

Suddenly Dunstan wondered if she were still a maid. She was, after all, past marriageable age, and she had been living with six robust males for the past winter.... With a grimace, Dunstan shook aside such thoughts as unimportant. It mattered not to him if she had bedded all of his brothers. His job was simply to return her to Bad-dersly.

At that moment, a movement of the horse brought his groin up against her even more tightly, and Dunstan grit-ted his teeth. So far his hopes for an uneventful journey had been dashed, and now, from the *feel* of things, it was not going to be very peaceful trip, either.

Chapter Four

Marion could not get comfortable. Nestled in between Dunstan de Burgh's heavy thighs, her back bumping against his hard chest, she felt...disoriented. Although she could not remember her past, Marion suspected that she had never been pressed up against a man's body before. It was strange. It was disturbing.

It was exhilarating.

Leaning forward, she tried to ignore it. After all, she was not enamored of the man. Quite the contrary! Dunstan, with his arrogant attitude and bullying tactics, was responsible for all her misfortune. It was bad enough that he had found her, foiling her clever escape, but to taunt her and scare her with that ferocious roar...That was beyond pardon. And so, the fact that she was riding in front of him, his body touching hers until his presence surrounded her, enveloping her like a cloak, should have no effect upon her at all.

But it did. It would help if he were not so deliciously warm, Marion decided. Heat seemed to pour from the man like a forge. He smelled of it even—of warm skin, horses and leather, and some kind of soap. Marion, who was always cold and could ever be found in front of a fire, felt blessedly toasted for the first time in her life.

Suddenly pulled more tightly against him, Marion was

awed by the hardness of him, the steel of his thighs and
arms and alien form. Dark male strength was apparent in
every inch of him, in every breath he took. It was daunt-
ing. Almost frightening.

Definitely thrilling.

Like a swimmer about to dive beneath the surface,
Marion closed her eyes, took a deep draft of air and
leaned back into that massive chest. For a few brief moments, she seemed to merge with the eldest de Burgh,
drawn into his heat and scent and vigor as the great beast
beneath them surged forward. And then, like a fleeting
but vivid dream, it was over. Too quickly.

In what seemed like an instant, Dunstan's destrier
reached the others, and Marion found herself the object
of attention. Although none asked where she had been
found, she caught questioning looks from some of the
men and unkind glances from those who had not liked
searching for her.

Ignoring them, Marion lifted her chin, secure in the
protection of Dunstan's embrace. The eldest de Burgh
might be more her enemy than her friend, but who would
not feel safe before him? Despite their discord, Marion
sensed that he would let no harm come to her, and she
stayed where she was until the boy who served as Dunstan's squire darted forward to assist her down.

Marion told herself she was not disappointed to leave
the haven of Dunstan's arms, especially when he thrust
her away none too gently, just as if she were a hedgehog
that pricked him sorely. "Put her back on her palfrey.
And keep watch upon her," he ordered his squire curtly.
Then, without another word or glance, he was off, barking orders to his men, a remote, dark figure atop his
massive warhorse.

Annoyed that he could so quickly forget her when the
touch of him still lingered on her skin, Marion stared af-

ter him until the young squire touched her arm gently.
"Please, my lady, we had best hurry."

Yes, better hurry, better dance to Dunstan's tune,
Marion thought churlishly. When the boy helped her
mount, she concentrated very hard on just how much she
disliked the eldest de Burgh brother. The biggest and
fiercest of Campion's boys was nothing but a brute, she
told herself. And yet . . .

"Well, a fine chase you led us all!" said Agnes. Although Marion heard the elderly servant Campion had
sent along to attend her, she did not respond. Apparently, the old woman was the only female the earl could
recruit for the journey, but Marion thought them ill-
suited. Agnes seemed to doze most of the time, even while
riding, and she was far too outspoken for Marion's taste.
Disregarding the rude comment, Marion looked away.

But Agnes was not to be deterred. "You look no worse
for it. Did he not beat you?" she asked, in a shrill, pene-
trating voice.

Marion's eyes flew back to the servant. "Beat me?" she
squeaked.

"Aye! A big giant of a man, dark and fierce, is the
earl's eldest. He looks like he would give no quarter. Did
he beat you?"

Appalled by Agnes's loud questions, Marion tried to
put the conversation to rest. "My lord Wessex has no
right or reason to abuse me."

The old woman made a noise and then blew her nose.
"Mayhap he is not so ferocious as he looks then, if he let
a wee slip of a thing like you rile him so and did not lay a
hand on you."

Lay a hand on you. The words hung in the air, making
Marion turn her face away, for Dunstan had put his hand
on her. Color, bright and hot, raced up from her throat at
the memory. He had touched her, had gripped her wrists

and pinned her up against the tree with his body, and then...

Marion's breath came quickly at the recollection of his palm skimming her waist and his hard thighs rubbing against her stomach. Mercy, but when his hand had moved, his thumb had brushed underneath her breast!

For one, long, incredible instant she had thought he might kiss her. Had she ever seen the hot flash of desire in a man's eyes? Marion doubted it, but she suspected that was exactly what had darkened Dunstan's green gaze, holding her in thrall. She could not have moved or protested if she had wanted to, and she had not wanted the moment to end. Ever. Marion shut her eyes against the wave of strange, restless yearning that consumed her.

"Ah, so he did do something!" Agnes's cackling laugh brought Marion out of her thoughts abruptly.

"Enough!" she said, blushing even more brightly at the old woman's astute guess. "Tend to your business and leave me in peace."

The cackling became a gravelly chuckle. "Many a maid's head has been turned by that one," Agnes said. "'Tis said at court that they call him the Wolf of Wessex, and not just because of his family's device."

Marion drew in a deep breath. This was something she did not care to hear!

"Why, a man that big—"

"Enough!" Marion's voice rose. "I am not interested in Lord Wessex's reputation or aught else about him! He is a mannerless brute, and he will not bend me to his will!" Just saying the words aloud seemed to strengthen Marion's resolve.

And why not? She was not chattel to be driven before him. The loss of her memory did not make her stupid. She had been clever enough to nearly escape him once. Just because she had failed this time did not mean she must meekly accept her fate.

She would try again. And again and again—until she succeeded. Marion felt that small spark in her ignite as new plans, half-formed, danced before her. She glanced over at Agnes. Apparently, her sharp words had been heeded, for the old woman was slumped in the saddle, as if dozing again. Marion relaxed—until she heard Agnes speak again.

"Do not tell me what you are about, lady, for I do not wish to know," the old woman said. She opened one eye to gaze at Marion cannily, then closed it again, a smile cracking her lips.

Biting back a sound of dismay, Marion looked away, ruing the day that Campion had given her such a companion. Apparently, Agnes saw much more than she should have. But the servant would not stand in her way, Marion told herself firmly. Despite Agnes's often astute comments, the old woman knew nothing and could not inform anyone of her schemes.

And scheme Marion did. Unfortunately, she had lost the advantage of surprise, so she would have to manage her escape under more attentive escorts. At the thought of those green wolf's eyes following her, Marion nearly shivered. But Dunstan had already forgotten her. She need only worry about the squire, and she knew that somehow she would manage to elude him.

Once away, she would find the nearest convent. For some reason, Our Lady of All Sorrows sprang to mind. Was it not close to Baddersly? The thought made her pause. If only she could remember! Closing her eyes, Marion tried again to see into the well of her memory, but she was met only with blackness, and the harder she concentrated, the faster her heart began to pound.

Her palms grew moist, and, although she was cold, Marion could feel sweat beading on her temple. Her mind thrummed, her head throbbing with the effort to concentrate as she sought an answer in the emptiness. *Bad-*

dersly. The dire name rang like a death knell, and a chill sense of dread washed over her, drowning her, sucking her down....

With a start, Marion opened her eyes and drew in a ragged breath. She lifted a trembling hand and pressed her fingers to her aching forehead. They were becoming more grueling, these attempts of hers to remember, with each one worse than the last, until she was forced to admit that her history was closed, unavailable to her whether for good or ill. All she ever came away with was a confirmation of her own fears of Baddersly—and a grim determination that to go there would be to risk her life.

Sighing soundlessly, Marion straightened and told herself that she must get along without her memory. Whether Our Lady of All Sorrows or some other convent, the good sisters would no doubt take her in, especially if she presented them with the fat purse of money and jewels that she had carried with her since the day the de Burghs had found her.

If they did not, well, then she would simply disappear into a city, creating a new life for herself—as a widow perhaps. The thought made Marion's lips curve in amusement, for surely few maids of her age knew less about being a wife than she did. Her smile faded as Dunstan de Burgh suddenly invaded her thoughts.

The Wolf of Wessex they called him, and Marion acknowledged that the name fit him well. She suspected that he could teach her much of what transpired between a man and a woman, married or not. Absently rubbing her wrist where he had bruised her with his fierce grip, Marion told herself that she did not such crave such knowledge.

All she wanted of Dunstan de Burgh was to be away from him. And soon.

"Well? Where was she?" Walter asked.

Hearing the barely restrained humor in his vassal's

voice, Dunstan scowled. "You do not want to know," he answered curtly, urging his mount to the head of the train.

Walter's laugh followed him, and soon his most skilled knight was riding alongside. "Admit it, Dunstan. The Wolf of Wessex has been bested by a mere wench." Walter's loud guffaws grated on Dunstan's sorely tested temper.

"Nay, Walter," Dunstan argued. "I was *nearly* bested by a woman. 'Tis not quite the same thing."

"Oh, aye," Walter said, snorting.

"I found her, did I not?" Dunstan demanded angrily. "'Tis more than I can say for my vassal."

Walter's laughter abruptly ceased. He looked as if he might say something further, but stopped, his mouth curving into a sneer. "I stand rebuked, my lord," he mocked. Then he shrugged carelessly. "But I am still curious. Where did she go, and why? Did she lose her way?"

"No," Dunstan answered. "She hid from us because she does not want to return home."

"What?" Walter looked genuinely surprised—and intrigued. "I thought she was some sort of heiress."

"She is, but apparently she was happier at Campion." *Weaving her spells around my brothers,* Dunstan thought to himself. "She does not fancy going back to a guardian, who might keep her to heel. 'Tis my opinion that 'twould do her good."

Walter chuckled, his blue gaze turning back toward where Marion rode. "An unusual woman," he mused aloud.

Dunstan did not like the way Walter's eyes gleamed with interest. Disinclined to whet that interest further, he did not concur. Nor did he add that Marion Warenne could look as innocent as a child while spouting lies worthy of a hardened jade. And what lies! If all were as transparent as those she had given him this day, Dunstan would have no difficulty seeing through them.

In fact, Dunstan suspected he could find a great deal of pleasure in trying to coax the truth from her. His thoughts strayed to the feel of her against him, and he promptly turned them back to the roadway. Marion Warenne was nothing to him but a package to be delivered, soft and luxuriantly curved, perhaps, but a package nonetheless. He pitied the poor fool who thought of her as aught else.

With an angry grunt, Dunstan urged his destrier forward, content to leave the woman under the watchful eye of his squire, Cedric. She had brought him naught but trouble since he had first set eyes upon her at Campion, staring at him from across his father's hall. By faith, he should have never accepted this task! He had his own problems, and right now they preyed upon his mind more fiercely than ever.

Two years ago when Edward had gifted him with the Wessex property, Dunstan had thought himself finally rooted after years on the road, making his bed wherever he might find it. But disputes with his greedy neighbor, Clarence Fitzhugh, had kept him from his hall. Now, it seemed that he was always on the borders, fending off raids and thefts. Yet Dunstan had no proof that Fitzhugh was behind his problems, and he could not retaliate against his neighbor's holdings without drawing the king's ire. He was neatly cornered.

Wessex itself had needed improvements and further defenses that had badly depleted Dunstan's coffers, and the small number of villeins had forced him to supplement their labor with that of his own soldiers. Last year's crops had been poor, stretching his resources to the limit....

With a grimace, Dunstan realized that his visions of taking his ease in his own hall, like his father, were but a youth's foolish dream. His life seemed destined to be that of a knight struggling to keep his lands, forever on the move, forever watching his back. Rubbing his neck in a reflexive movement, Dunstan sought to ease the weight that rested there, trying to crush him.

By faith, but he could use the help of his brothers and a loan of men or money from his father! But Dunstan would rather be damned than beg. He had gone to Campion, hoping for an offer of aid, and look where it had gotten him! Instead of returning to Wessex with reinforcements, he was wasting his precious time playing nursemaid to a runaway wench.

At the thought of Marion Warenne, Dunstan knew an urge to rein in and find her among the train. He told himself he would be wise to check upon her himself, and for a moment he hesitated, then he grunted angrily and rode ahead, determined to keep both his body and his mind away from his charge.

Dunstan avoided her all day. When it came time for supper, he glanced in her direction—just to make sure that she was there, he told himself firmly—but all he saw was a flash of brown cloak as she slipped into her tent to eat alone. What cared he? Dunstan thought with a surly scowl. By faith, just the sight of her would probably put him off his food!

He was able to finish his meal quickly, and in peace, but he returned later, seating himself not far away. Absently, he watched her lair for signs of movement, even though Cedric was stationed at the entrance, keeping guard.

"Why does she hide herself away?" his squire asked, and Dunstan jerked his head, annoyed to be caught staring.

"Mayhap she is ashamed of wasting our time this day in our merry chase after her," Dunstan growled. As rightfully she should be, he thought. Ridiculous wench!

"She ate but little," Cedric noted. It took a moment for the words to sink into Dunstan's distracted mind. Then, with slow deliberation, he lifted his head and gave his squire a look that questioned the significance of such news.

Coloring brightly, Cedric hurriedly glanced away, while Dunstan's eyes narrowed at the discovery of his squire's weakness. Already the boy showed signs of succumbing to Lady Warenne's mysterious spell. Did Cedric think the woman was in danger of wasting away? Dunstan snorted. From the looks of her lush form, Lady Warenne was in little danger of becoming skinny—like some of those bony women at court....

With another snort, Dunstan realized that he was actually comparing those ladies unfavorably to a runaway wench.

And yet, there was more to the little brown wren than one might expect, Dunstan mused. Just what would make such a dab of a female climb a tree? And why would anyone brave the dangers of the wild rather than return as mistress of a rich household? Foolishness, that was the only answer, Dunstan thought. Shaking his head at the senseless foibles of women, he settled himself more firmly in the saddle and fought the memory of soft curves pressing into his body and huge doelike eyes framed by a wild mane of dark hair.

For the next couple of days Dunstan saw little of his charge, though she plagued his thoughts. She and the old serving woman were quiet and kept to themselves, a situation that could not have pleased him more. No doubt the lady regretted her ridiculous stunt in the tree and was becoming reconciled to the journey.

Dunstan had lost none of his personal resentment at his task, however, for he was still anxious to return to Wessex. They were making good progress now, even over the poor roads, and he had to admit that all was, once again, going smoothly. At this rate, they should reach Baddersly in only a few more days. But his absence from his holdings still chafed at him, and the errand could not be finished swiftly enough for his taste.

So he drove the train on, stopping only for the mid-morning meal. Dunstan caught sight of her then, accidentally, as she sat alone with Cedric, the sunlight gleaming on her unbound hair. For a moment, he stared after her, wondering why she seemed to grow lovelier each time that he saw her.

Then, snorting in disgust, Dunstan turned on his heel to nearly run headlong into his vassal. Stopping just short of collision, Dunstan glared at the knight, who assessed his lord with a speculative gleam in his eye.

"Why do you not simply join her, or ride with her? Or perhaps 'twould be better just to ride *her*," Walter said with a smirk.

"What?" Dunstan looked at his trusted knight as if the man had spoken some foreign tongue.

Walter smiled slowly. "The lady, Dunstan. You have been avoiding her for days, while you snarl at everyone. Why not simply draw her out so that you may satisfy your...curiosity?" The words were spoken with sly innuendo, and Dunstan growled menacingly.

"I have no interest in Lady Warenne other than to make certain she reaches her home, Walter."

This time, his vassal laughed outright. "Then why the bristling, my friend? Everyone is talking about how the lady is making our lord testy as a boar with a toothache." He grinned wickedly. "Or is the pain located elsewhere?"

Dunstan's eyes narrowed. "That female has naught to do with my mood," he replied through gritted teeth. "I like not this errand and would rather be at home, keeping Wessex safe from the bastard Fitzhugh."

Walter's smile fled. "Wessex is in good hands."

"Aye," Dunstan said softly, thinking of the head of the castle guard, Leonard Collins. Leonard and Walter had been with Dunstan a long time, going back to the days of their youth when they served Edward together. Dunstan trusted them both, but he still felt a deep desire to be at Wessex, protecting his own, instead of on the road with a exasperating wench.

"Come," said Walter, banging him roughly on the back. "Sit and take your meal with me, and I shall ease your mind."

Dunstan nodded curtly, and the two ate companionably together, as they had countless times before. They spoke of Fitzhugh and Wessex's defenses, but Dunstan did not mention the crops that he hoped were being well tended in his absence. Strictly a soldier, with no head for farming, Walter would not understand. Dunstan had more to concern him than his next battle, however, and he felt the weight of his own responsibilities distance him from his old friend.

Perhaps because his mind was occupied with thoughts of Wessex, or perhaps because he had taken Walter's gibes to heart, Dunstan did not so much as glance toward Lady Warenne during the meal. It was only afterwards, when the train was again preparing to leave, that he looked to her palfrey. When he did not see her, Dunstan felt a vague apprehension.

He quelled it immediately, thinking that he might be acting testy after all—simply because of the insufferable woman he was forced to escort. Dunstan did not see Cedric either, so, obviously, the two had not rejoined the group yet. Their absence was probably easily explained, but Dunstan felt an odd sense of foreboding. Where were they? Slowly he turned, his eyes raking the area for his squire, but when he found the boy, he was not encouraged. Cedric stood near the edge of some bushes with a worried look on his thin countenance.

And Lady Warenne was nowhere in sight.

Chapter Five

By the time Dunstan reached him, Cedric was red-faced and stammering. "She...she said she needed to...to take a few moments to...to attend to herself, but it has been some time, my lord. Should I..."

In no mood to take pity on the youth, Dunstan gave him a furious glare that halted his speech. "Come, then, and help me look for her!"

At least she could not have gotten far this time, Dunstan told himself. He was in no mood to spend the rest of the afternoon searching for her again. A hot rush of anger swept through him, and he set his jaw hard. He always kept a cool head in battle and never lashed out at his servants or villeins, but this slip of a woman was sorely pressing him.

Dunstan glanced up at the trees, looking for the telltale flash of a slipper or gown, but he doubted that she would try the same trick. While his eyes flicked over the surrounding area, he tried to make himself think along the convoluted lines that the lady's mind followed.

She would not just walk through the woods; she had proved that before. Would she double back and sneak around the wagons? Was she, even now, on the other side of the roadway? No, Dunstan swore his men would not be that remiss. He had placed guards all around the perimeter of the camp, and she would truly have to be a witch to weave her way among them.

With the swift judgment that was his ally in battle, Dunstan decided his course and moved deeper into the forest as quietly as possible. He was certain that he would find her somewhere up ahead, but he was just as certain that she would use her wiles to try to hide from any pursuit.

Dunstan's long strides ate up the ground, giving him an advantage, if only she did not veer off in another direction. A straight, fast walk carried him through a dry riverbed where a broken branch made him smile grimly. He was on her trail, all right, and would soon overtake her.

He was surprised by the strange thrill of victory that rushed through him at the knowledge. It was as if he had won a skirmish through strategy alone, and yet there was something more to it, an unknown component that added heady pleasure to his triumph. Ignoring the strange pulsing of his blood, Dunstan concentrated on the ground, which ended abruptly in a great outcropping of rock. It rose before him, barring his way and forcing him to choose a new path.

Cedric came up behind him, breathing fast, but saying nothing while Dunstan surveyed the landscape. In a glance, he took in the surface of the stone, and rather than strike left or right, Dunstan continued on, moving closer to the face. Slowly, he began to walk along in front of the ridge, a sly smile lifting his mouth just as a certain suspicion entered his mind.

"Caves. There must be caves here," he murmured.

"Caves?" Cedric echoed.

"Aye. There will be caves," Dunstan said. *And she will be in one of them.* Knowing what he did of the lady, he suspected this was just the sort of trick she would try. Dunstan moved forward, his practiced gaze running along the rock until he found the branches of a bush that had obviously been disturbed, with the deep black of a telltale hole behind it. "There," he said softly to a dumbfounded Cedric. "She will be there."

Pushing the growth aside, Dunstan stooped to peer into the darkness, but he could see nothing. The foolish chit, to crawl around in there without even a light! Caves could be dangerous places, liable to drop off into fathomless caverns without warning, not to mention the vermin, vipers and beasts that might be harbored there. Dunstan shut out a sudden vision of the little wren lying broken or mauled upon the cold stone.

"Make me a torch," Dunstan ordered curtly, and Cedric quickly gathered a fistful of rushes and bound them together. While Dunstan peered into the hole, the squire produced a piece of flint from the supplies at his belt and struck a spark against the steel of his dagger.

"Lady Warenne?" Dunstan shouted into the space. Nothing greeted him but silence. With a grimace, he took the makeshift light from his squire and pushed aside the bush.

"Wait here," he told Cedric over his shoulder. "If I do not return, summon Walter, but do not follow me." He thrust the fire inside the cave and saw that the floor was solid. "Lady Warenne, I am coming in after you," he announced. Stepping inside, Dunstan finally heard a sound ahead, and he moved toward it impatiently, determined to beat the woman soundly when he found her.

"Dunstan! Watch out for the—" Smiling grimly as he recognized her voice, Dunstan lunged forward, banging his forehead firmly against a jagged ledge. "Overhang," Lady Warenne finished lamely.

Dunstan staggered back a moment, fury blazing as pain shot through his head. He would kill her. *He was going to kill her.* Righting himself, he stretched out an arm to lean against the cave wall and tried to contain his rage. He had never lifted his hand to a woman in his life, had never even been tempted, but Lady Warenne was something else entirely. "Come here now," he said through gritted teeth.

"I am sorry, Dunstan, but I cannot," she answered, her voice musical in the enclosed chamber.

He counted to ten, something he had not done since he had lived at home and his younger brothers' pranks had driven him beyond endurance. "Why not?" he growled.

"I am afraid that I have twisted my ankle and cannot walk very well. I suppose I could crawl..." Her words trailed off forlornly just as though she were put upon, and Dunstan let astonishment wash over him for a moment before he swallowed the worst of his ire.

With a grunt, he stepped forward, stooping until he was nearly bent double and all the time cursing her under his breath. The cave dipped and turned and then there she was, a huddled heap in the glow of the torch, only a few yards from the entrance really, but hidden by the twist of the tunnel. She was seated upon the floor of the cave backed up against the wall, looking pale and anxious, and Dunstan felt more of his anger slip away.

For a moment, he considered handing her the fire, but something told him that she would probably set his hair ablaze—accidentally, of course—should she gain possession of it. Giving the tight quarters one last look, Dunstan dropped the flame and reached for her. She was light and warm in his arms, like a wounded bird.

He was surprised to feel the wild beating of her heart, which gave away her distress even though her manner did not. So, the lady was not so calm as she pretended! That discovery did something to Dunstan's insides, but he ignored it, and, crouching low, made his way the short distance back to the entrance, remembering to duck especially deeply at the outcropping.

Fighting past the bushy growth, Dunstan finally straightened, glad to see the light of day once more.

Without sparing a glance at his squire, he pulled the form in his arms up closer to his chest and studied her with a fierce glare. She looked perfectly composed, if a bit dusty, and she had the gall to assess him in return.

Before he could launch into a diatribe about reckless, runaway women, her gaze lifted to his brow. "You are injured!" she cried softly. He felt her fingers, infinitely gentle, against his skin, and without thought, Dunstan leaned into the touch. Her face was but inches from his own, her huge eyes fixed on his forehead, her wide mouth parted, and Dunstan felt an ache that had nothing to do with his injury.

He noticed the curve of her cheek and the way her pale skin glowed with a slight rosy flush. Only when she lifted up her cloak to dab at the blood, did Dunstan realize he was staring. "'Tis but a scratch," he grunted.

"Nay. You must let me tend it," she protested. Her voice was low and melodious, like the purr of a kitten he had once held as a boy, and Dunstan was drawn by it. The hood of her cloak had fallen, revealing that wild riot of dark curls as a perfect frame for a heart-shaped face that was so vivid, so remarkable.... *She is not beautiful,* he told himself.

Or was she? Dunstan found her as intoxicating as spiced wine, an interesting mixture of sweet and tangy and heady. He pulled her closer, enjoying the soft roundness of her small body, and saw her take in a sharp breath in response. Her eyes flew to his own, the concern in them changing to surprise, then something dark and alluring, like wanting.... He pressed her hip against his groin, where he had grown suddenly hard, and watched her gaze drop to his lips. Day of God!

Some sound from Cedric drew Dunstan out of his daze, and he deposited the lady on the ground just as though she were a thorny branch that threatened to prick him. By faith, she was weaving some sort of spell upon him!

"Run on ahead, Cedric," he snapped at his squire. The boy scrambled to do his bidding, spurred on by the tone of Dunstan's voice, no doubt, but Dunstan wasted no more thought on his squire. It was time to settle accounts with the world's most troublesome female.

Taking a step forward, he towered over her with a scowl that had frightened more than one man, but Lady Warenne did not seem one whit intimidated. She simply looked up at him with those great, wide eyes as though she were as dazed as he had been. Dunstan shook his head, realizing suddenly that it throbbed, as did his groin, and he grunted in annoyance.

"Do not tell me. Let me guess," he said, resting his hands on his hips. "The self-same boar that sent you up a tree chased you out of camp and all the way into this cave."

She actually frowned at him. "Do not be silly, Dunstan. 'Twas a man who grabbed me and dragged me here against my will," she said, her brown eyes guileless as they gazed directly into his own. "He forced me into the cave and bade me not to leave or call out for fear of my life."

Dunstan stared at her for a long moment, then threw back his head and laughed so hard it hurt. "Do not jest with me," he said, grimacing, as he lifted a hand to his brow.

"You *are* hurt," she said, rising to her feet.

"No," he said shortly. "Now, describe this man to me."

"What man?" she asked, appearing genuinely, innocently puzzled.

Dunstan's eyes narrowed, and his mouth twisted. "The man who abducted you, wren."

"Wren? I am told it is Warenne, not Wren."

Dunstan swallowed back an exasperated growl. "Describe him."

"He was short and dark," she answered, her eyes meeting his own without hesitation. "Perhaps he is my uncle's man, up to some devilry."

"What nonsense!" Dunstan snorted. "If you wish to have me believe that your guardian threatens you in some way, you must give me facts, not vague conjecture."

"I cannot! Do you think I have not tried to remember, Dunstan?" she asked, poking a tiny finger at his chest. "I have tried! I have tried so hard that the dread overwhelms me, but that is all there is—dread. I cannot tell you what awaits me at Baddersly, only that 'tis not the life of a pampered heiress that you de Burghs would have for me!"

The fire that sparked from her was becoming, and Dunstan realized he much preferred this lively creature to the little wren. Her words, however, were as ridiculous as usual. Female whimsy at best—more probably lies. And if they were not? Dunstan did not care to consider that possibility, for if she told the truth, what then of his errand?

"My dear lady Warenne," he said in a tone that brooked no argument. "I have had enough of your tales and tricks. So, unless you want to travel the rest of the way home in chains, I suggest you cease your foolish antics and stay where I can see you at all times."

Obviously her brief show of spirit was spent, because she stepped back from him until she was pressed against a rock. Dunstan eyed her up and down and then suddenly noticed what had somehow escaped his attention during their heated exchange. Fresh anger at being duped once again by the wench came on him so swiftly that he felt his face flush with it.

"There is naught wrong with your ankle!" he growled. He raised his hand, an involuntary gesture, and she grew still—absolutely still.

It pained him, that stillness. It was as if she were no longer there, and he realized, standing there holding his arm in the air, that she thought he would strike her. Muttering a profanity, he dropped his hand. As if he would ever hit a woman! "I have never abused a woman in my life and never will—no matter how sorely tempted."

The lady did not answer. Those great brown eyes were empty, and she was far away. Dunstan cursed again, feeling an absurd sense of loss. "Come!" he snapped. "I am in a hurry, and each hour you delay us costs me dearly."

She moved then, walking in front of him with that quiet grace of hers, and Dunstan stared after her, feeling sorely disgruntled. The lying witch had led him a merry dance through the woods and deserved to be beaten soundly for her mischief. Why, then, did it seem as if he were the one who had taken a blow?

He grunted, urging her on, but it was not long before the rhythmic sway of her hips moving in front of him made his mouth water. He had been too long without a woman, that was the problem, and it would be easily remedied once he finished this errand, Dunstan told himself. He moved beside her in an effort to change his view, but she stumbled at the sight of him. He steadied her with an arm around her waist, and she looked up at him with eyes so wide and startled that he stepped back to follow her again.

By faith, Dunstan thought with a scowl, the camp seemed to be leagues away! They had only now reached the dry riverbed. The wren had a stride the length of a bird's, Dunstan noted, convinced that such dainty legs could not carry her far. Studying her walk a bit too closely, he caught a glimpse of a shapely ankle at just the moment that the lady, having pushed aside some brush, let it fall back.

It struck him directly in the face.

Dunstan erupted with a thunderous roar that made Marion jump and shriek. "Dunstan!" she gasped, backing away from him, her hand at her throat. "What? Oh! Did I do that? Oh, I am sorry."

If she had laughed, he might very well have strangled her and let his high-minded ideas about ladies go hang. But she did not laugh. She did not even smile. She rushed toward him with eyes so bright with concern that Dunstan was momentarily transfixed. Had anyone ever looked at him that way before?

The sounds of shouts and movement from the direction of the camp made him break whatever spell held him in her gaze. With a grunt, he grabbed her arm and stalked toward the noise. An anxious and breathless Cedric appeared, followed by a grinning and definitely unworried Walter.

"I heard the screams, my lord, and thought you were being set upon," Cedric explained nervously.

"I *am* being set upon," Dunstan muttered. Dragging the wren along beside him, he strode back toward camp.

"You found her in a cave?" Walter asked, amusement evident in his tone.

Dunstan sent his vassal a look that told him to save his breath, but Walter, never too good at obeying orders, merely chuckled. "What happened to your face? Did she attack you?"

Dunstan grunted in annoyance while Marion gasped. "Your face, Dunstan! You simply must let me tend it!" She continued babbling in such a vein as she ran to keep up with him.

"'Tis nothing but a few scratches," Dunstan finally growled. Thankfully, they had reached camp, and hopefully, an end to all arguments.

"Perhaps," Marion answered when they stopped. She gazed up at his bloody forehead dubiously. "But even scratches fester. Why, think, Dunstan, what would hap-

pen if it should putrefy! It might even swell your brain,"
she warned ominously. "And then your poor brothers
would be saddled with a great witless man to take care of.
Surely, you would not wish that upon them."

Did the wren have the audacity to toy with him? Dunstan eyed her sharply, but she simply stared directly at him
with those huge brown eyes, innocence plastered all over
her heart-shaped face. Something tugged at the edges of
his mind, out of reach. By faith! He did not believe that
a small head wound could lead to madness, but he was
rapidly becoming convinced that Marion Warenne could
drive a man to the brink.

"Get to your mount," he said through gritted teeth.
Then he turned on his heel and strode away from her as
rapidly as possible.

Walter sidled up to him immediately. "A little rude, are
we not? 'Tis not like you, Dunstan!" his vassal teased.

"That woman is a menace!" Dunstan growled, lifting
a hand to his throbbing head.

Walter laughed. "Because she wants to see to your
wounds? I wish that I were menaced so terribly!"

Dunstan snorted and gave his vassal a threatening look.
"Perhaps I shall set you to watch her then."

Walter smiled and shrugged. "'Twould suit me well
enough."

Dunstan's eyes narrowed. Somehow the idea of his
vassal fawning over Marion did not sit well with him.
Walter had been with him for years before rising to his
right hand; he was a good soldier and a friend. However,
the wren's property was rich enough to tempt a saint, let
alone a landless knight. With a grimace, Dunstan pictured Walter seducing the heiress and presenting himself
to her uncle as the father of her child.

"No," Dunstan said, finally. "'Tis bad enough that we
must all serve as errand boys for my father. I will not have

my best man act as nursemaid to the parcel. Let Cedric do it."

The boy was at his side, stammering apologies in an instant. "Enough," Dunstan said, cutting him off. "I will give you another chance, Cedric, but do not fail me this time. Keep watch upon the lady at all times. If she wants to attend to herself, as before, make sure that you keep a part of her in sight, and do not let her stick her cloak upon a bush and leave you staring at it!" Dunstan advised. "Make sure you see the top of her head and her hair. We are dealing with a very clever lady here."

Cedric listened, his face a study of surprise and awe. Obviously, the youth was not accustomed to hearing a woman described in such terms, and Dunstan realized that he had never used them. But the wren was something altogether different. "Have Benedict spell you," Dunstan ordered, glancing toward an elderly knight whom he trusted to keep his hands off Marion.

"Yes, my lord," Cedric said, and he rushed after his charge, his face somber and alert.

Dunstan turned away and strode toward his waiting horse. He did not fault Cedric for being fooled. Day of God! She had tricked them all—twice now! But once stung, a wise man would beware the bee. Dunstan decided he had better keep an eye on Marion, too. He had no intention of letting her flee again or of seeing her work her wiles upon his men to their detriment.

And, keeping wiles in mind, Dunstan judged that it might be well to post an extra watch this night, just in case her uncle really did present a threat. Of course, the woman spouted nothing but nonsense, yet it could not hurt to be more vigilant.

Rubbing the back of his neck, Dunstan sighed. The simple errand his father had entrusted to him was becoming more complicated than he could ever have imagined.

* * *

"Back again, are you?" Agnes cackled with glee when Marion mounted her palfrey. "What did the Wolf do to you this time?"

Despite all that had happened between Dunstan and herself in the past hour, Marion's mind, directed perhaps by Agnes's chortling, dredged up only one image. Her face flooded with color as she remembered, all too vividly, when Dunstan had held her in his arms. Warmth and strength had surrounded her, and his face had been so close to her own that she could see the darkening of his eyes—as deep and green as the thickest forest. For a moment, he had seemed to devour her with his gaze, and Marion could have sworn that he took a hungry glance at her lips. But then he had practically dropped her to the ground in his haste to be rid of her!

Marion sighed at her own foolishness. Surely, it was only her imagination that had Dunstan looking as if he might kiss her, for why would the Wolf of Wessex be interested in her? The great, handsome brute probably had his pick of lovely ladies....

As if in answer to her unspoken question, Agnes chuckled beside her. "You have captured his attention, lady. There is no doubt of that," she said, grinning crookedly to display several missing teeth. "You are a puzzle to him, and he has not known the like before. It makes you prey on his mind—more than any other female, I will warrant."

Agnes nodded sagely before continuing. "Yes, you are getting under his skin. The question is—what will he do when the itch strikes him? Will he scratch it?" Just as though she had made some hearty jest, Agnes threw back her head and let out a coarse peal of laughter, which Marion tried hard to ignore.

Although she had been listening with only half an ear to the old woman's rambling, Marion decided she did not care to know what would happen when she got under the Wolf's skin. Although he had not hurt her, she suspected that he was nearly at the end of his tether, and she would not like his temper loosed upon her.

He was such a surly, bullying wretch! All he ever did was shout and grunt and growl at her like some great wild beast. At one point, she had even thought he might strike her, but she should have known better. Even Dunstan, with all his faults, would not do that, for Campion would not raise a son to violence.

Marion was wary, though. When he had lifted his fist something inside her made her seek to protect herself— even from a de Burgh. What that something was, Marion did not care to examine, but she had an eerie feeling that the answer lay in the veiled mystery of her past.

And that was another thing, she thought, suddenly fuming. Dunstan did not even have the courtesy to hear her out about her uncle; he made it plain that he did not believe a word she told him of Baddersly. Of course, his reaction was no surprise to her, for she had seen enough of his behavior to know it well. The man constantly treated her like a child who had no life of her own, and no thoughts, no hopes, no dreams worth considering.

Well, she would show him! What had once existed only as a tiny spark inside of her was now a small blaze, fed by Dunstan's scorn, and Marion felt it—and herself—growing stronger each day. Twice now she had nearly outwitted the Wolf of Wessex. Today he must truly have sniffed her out like the beast that he was, but in the future she would cover her tracks more thoroughly. The third time was often the charm, Marion told herself.

If he would not save her, she must save herself. No matter what smug Dunstan de Burgh might think, Marion *knew* that her life was in danger, and she refused to be led to her death like some lamb to slaughter.

She had only to make a new plan for escape and leave the Wolf behind. Forever.

Chapter Six

Dunstan woke early. He had slept sitting up against a tree trunk, as was his way upon the road, and when he opened his eyes the first thing he saw was Lady Warenne's tent. Uttering a sharp oath, Dunstan stood quickly and went to rinse off his face in the cold running stream. In a moment, he had stripped off his clothes and doused his entire body instead.

When he had finished and dressed anew, Dunstan felt better than he had in days. Telling himself that he had rid the Lady Marion from his thoughts, he roused everyone with a vengeance in order to get the train off to an early start. The weather was holding and he wanted to take advantage of it.

Once they were off, he tried to maintain his improved mood, but the rest of the day stretched before him with all the appeal of a stay in the dungeon, and Dunstan decided he was getting too old for this nomadic life.

At one time a new journey would have thrilled him; now, he found that he longed far more for a good meal and a soft bed—mayhap even a wife with whom to share them. The idea of marriage, which would have startled him not so long ago, suddenly seemed long overdue. Perhaps it was time to get himself an heir.

Dunstan gazed behind him, toward a certain dark-haired female, and he found himself watching her, noting little details about her that had escaped his attention before.

Like the way she held herself, consummate grace exhibited in her every movement.

Like the way her body's generous curves were visible even under the relatively shapeless gown she wore and the cloak that covered it.

Like the way her hair curled against her throat under her hood, begging to be set free.

When Dunstan felt himself longing to jerk away the material, letting the rich, dark locks fall loose, he knew he was not himself. With a low curse, he reminded himself of the lady's sins. They were plentiful! She was reckless, willful, argumentative, thoughtless, fanciful and untruthful. She was delaying not only this errand with her antics, but his presence at Wessex, as well.

Dunstan was a man who liked his world as plain and simple as possible, while she had more facets than Hydra had heads! And he had not the patience to sort through them all. Ruing his own wayward thoughts, Dunstan resolved that although he might take a bride someday soon, the wren was definitely not worth considering for the position. Then he wheeled his destrier to the head of the column—well away from her.

Dunstan stayed there for most of the day. Although they passed only a few other travelers and some farmers, he remained alert. Despite their number, attack on the roadways was always a possibility, and his job was to see that nothing happened to his charge or his men.

As they approached a village, Dunstan fell back, searching for Marion. Although he did not think her so foolish as to try to flee again, he knew passing by gawking peasants would make a good diversion for her to try to escape, and he had no desire for any further delays.

When he did not immediately spy her or his squire, Dunstan felt a prick of uneasiness. Although he knew not how she could escape on horseback in full view of all, he was beginning to think that Marion was possessed of extraordinary abilities not associated with the typical female.

His jaw clenched tightly, Dunstan reined in and waited, eyeing the soldiers, servants and carts that passed him for a sign of her form. Despite his best efforts, his agitation grew—until he heard something that heralded her approach as nothing else could. Laughter such as Dunstan had never known danced across the air to him, rich as good earth and warm as summer sunshine, though what made him liken a sound to such, he was not sure. His mind, Dunstan decided, with grim humor, had been too much on husbandry of late.

Of course, it was *her* laughter, Dunstan noted with wry appreciation. When he noticed the source of the wren's delight, however, his amusement fled, for it was Walter who rode beside her, coaxing the most amazing smiles from her and engaging her in easy banter. As Dunstan watched, she laughed again, deep and full-throated, and he felt something inside himself stir and reach toward the sound like a plant to the light.

But it was Walter who basked in the glow of her brightness, and Dunstan felt his gut twist at that knowledge. He scowled blackly at his vassal before his attention was drawn to his squire, who rode behind the merry duo, easy prey for any outlaw and pathetic protection for Marion.

Dunstan's anger easily fixed upon his vassal, who knew better than to place the most vulnerable riders at the rear. What was Walter thinking? Dunstan wondered, before he realized that in all probability, Walter was not thinking at all—except with his nether regions.

"Walter." Dunstan's tone made his vassal swivel toward him immediately. "Scout up ahead," he ordered curtly. Not trusting himself to say more, Dunstan saved his rebuke for later and simply urged the knight on with a jerk of his head. For a moment, Dunstan thought he saw anger pass across his vassal's face, but so quickly was it replaced by a mocking smile that Dunstan deemed himself mistaken.

With an insolent nod, Walter sent him a look that plainly asked him if he was jealous. *Jealous?* Dunstan gritted his teeth as raw fury rushed through him at the ridiculous accusation. Walter knew very well that Dunstan could not care less about Marion Warenne. She was naught but a package to be delivered, but delivered she would be—in one piece and untouched by his men—to Baddersly.

While Walter rode away, Dunstan narrowed his eyes suspiciously and pondered his vassal's sudden interest in the woman. Aside from a few sly comments, Walter had never shown her the slightest notice, yet today he was playing the gallant, drawing her out, chatting with her and moving her to the end of the train.... It was passing strange.

"What be you about, my lord? Am I barred from any discourse with my companions?" Dunstan was dragged from his thoughts by the sound of Marion's soft voice. Turning to face her, he saw that she had donned her most composed manner, which, in light of her behavior with Walter, pricked sorely at Dunstan's already black temper.

"Perhaps you should be, if your intention is to work your womanly wiles upon my men until they are so addled that they are of no use to me," he snapped.

Her lovely eyes widened in response, as if his accusation stunned her, and Dunstan might have been taken in, had he not known her for a lying trickster. He began to wonder if her speech with his vassal hid ulterior motives. Surely she would not try to engage Walter to her cause. Even she would not attempt another flight alone into the woods...would she? Dunstan felt an uneasiness settle upon him that had nothing to do with her discourse with Walter.

"Cedric," he said in quiet admonition. "My lady's place is not at the end of the train. She is in danger here."

Cedric jerked upright in the saddle. "Yes, my lord!"

"Let us ride on till we are in the midst of the men," Dunstan instructed, sliding a glance toward Marion. She darted a look behind her, as if expecting to see outlaws pressing down upon them.

"Yea, my lady. The roads are dangerous," Dunstan said grimly. His disquiet grew at the thought of something happening to her, and an alien sort of fear washed over him, followed swiftly by anger at her foibles. By faith, he wanted to shake some sense into her! Had she no notion of the dangers that stalked abroad?

"We travel with a good band of armed men, and yet we must constantly be alert," Dunstan told her through gritted teeth. "All manner of brigand would fain kill us for our purse and ransom you—or worse. Have you no idea what can happen to you, a beautiful woman, at the hands of lawless men?" he asked.

She did not answer, but regarded him with those huge eyes, wide with surprise—and innocence. Dunstan clenched his jaw tighter against the need to make her heed him.

"There are those who kill for the sheer thrill of it, but at least the end would be swift. Some things, I suspect, are worse than death. Ladies, especially, can be ill-used beyond imagination." Dunstan broke off, torn between wanting her to see the folly of flight and wishing to protect her sensibilities.

Was she even listening to him? Her head was bent, her dark curls tumbling about her face in wild disarray, and her hands were still upon the reins. Dunstan longed to shatter that composure, to grab her by the shoulders and force her to listen until she swore never to endanger herself again. But he was not so uncivilized. He had learned restraint from his father, who rarely raised a hand to anyone. Campion had earned respect through his fairness, his leadership and the rewards he bestowed on those who served him well, and Dunstan tried hard to follow in his footsteps.

Sometimes it was harder than others, Dunstan thought as he glared at the lady beside him. How could he reach her? Beneath her sometimes foolish behavior was a clever mind, as he well knew. Why would she not be sensible? Had she not been attacked before? "The world is full of threats, Marion, but then, you must know this, for is that not how you came to meet my brothers?" he asked.

Dunstan saw his taunt hit its mark, for Marion blanched, her great eyes darting toward him in horror. "I...I do not know," she answered.

"Ah, yes, the infamous memory lapse," Dunstan muttered.

Marion drew herself up then, the pain he had briefly glimpsed swiftly replaced by the cool, unreachable mask he well recognized. Dunstan suddenly regretted his mockery. Clenching his jaw, he told himself that the advice he gave was for her own good, and yet he felt as wretched as if he had kicked her in the teeth for no good reason.

"I really do not remember," she said suddenly. She was staring off into the distance, and somehow, she seemed more truthful now than when she was looking him directly in the eye.

Dunstan felt something stir again inside him. The urge to take her into his arms, to protect this maddening woman from all of the world's hurts, was overwhelming. He grunted, disgusted, but unable to stop himself from offering whatever feeble comfort he could. "I have heard of such things," he said finally. "Back when I was a young knight, I saw a man with a head wound wander for days without his senses."

She looked at him, and he felt as if those wonderful wide eyes would swallow him up, taking him into their depths forever. "Thank you, Dunstan," she said. It was only a few words, gently spoken, but they touched him down to the bone. Strange, far too strange for his blood, he thought with a grimace.

"You frown too much, Dunstan."

Dunstan glanced at her in surprise to find her smiling at him. And the world dimmed in the face of it.

Speechless, Dunstan stared at that smile. Bright with life and accompanied by two deep dimples, it was like none he had ever seen before. It seemed to encompass him, cloaking him in its warmth and lightening his heart. How would he feel to have that smile turned upon him again and again? It made him want to move his lips in return, to reach for something he had long forgotten.

Dunstan decided a man would have to be as cold as stone to be unaffected by it, and he was not made of stone. Gad, but he felt himself go all soft inside. He straightened in the saddle. "I have had little enough to please me upon this journey," he answered.

Undiminished by his reference to her troublesome behavior, Marion's grin deepened, and Dunstan swore he saw a sparkle in her eye. In spite of himself—in spite of all he knew of this exasperating female—he felt himself drawn to her. She seemed the embodiment of so many things he had been lacking: warmth and comfort and caring. Caring? Dunstan frowned at his own foolish thoughts. Perhaps his brain *was* swelling!

"My lady, I would not have us be enemies," he said politely. "If you and I had met under other circumstances, I might have found you pleasing. And I can assure you, you would have found me much more accommodating. But I have business that requires my attention, and this journey is wearing on me sorely."

"What weighs upon you so?" Marion tilted her head slightly to train her great dark gaze upon him, and Dunstan felt its gentle touch like a caress.

You. Dunstan almost spoke the word aloud. You and your foolish escapades, from scaling trees to burrowing into caves. You and that bewitching smile of yours. You and the way you look and act and sound, filling my thoughts as no other woman ever has.... He stared off into the forest that rose in the distance. "I am needed at Wessex," he said gruffly.

"What is it? Have you problems there?"

The concern in her big brown eyes tempted Dunstan to speak, but being the eldest of Campion's sons, he had always borne the most responsibility. Long ago, he had learned to rely solely on himself in his efforts to meet his father's standards, and he had never deigned to share his burdens with another.

"There are difficulties, yes," he said abruptly.

"Surely 'tis not so bad," she murmured. Her voice, low and gentle, invited confidence. Dunstan felt himself drawn to her again, as if Marion could somehow lighten his load, free him from the weight of his worries, ease him....

"My neighbor, Fitzhugh, tries me sorely," he said slowly. "He constantly harries my people and attacks my property under the guise of outlawry. Many had fled before I came to the holding, so there are few villeins to work the soil. I would see they put in their proper days of service, so that we have a good harvest this year and do not all starve. Beyond the field work, there are ditches to be cleared, banks to be rebuilt...." The lady must be an enchantress, Dunstan mused, for he was voicing concerns he had not even shared with Walter.

"What does your father say?"

"Of what?" Dunstan asked, surprised by her question.

"Of your burdens. I cannot believe that he would send you away from your holdings when you are so needed there." Her heart-shaped face was tilted toward him, and the sun glowed on the heavy curls that escaped her hood.

"I doubt that he knows of them," Dunstan replied. "'Tis not his land, but mine own that is threatened."

"But he is your sire, and loves you well!" Marion protested. "Surely he can help you. And what of your brothers? Why are they not watching out for your interests?"

Dunstan frowned. "They have their own concerns."

"Nay! They have not," she argued. "They are six grown, healthy men with little enough to do at Campion. They would welcome a change."

"They have not been overly eager to lend me their arms," Dunstan said.

"Have you ever asked them?"

"Nay! I beg not," Dunstan replied, his eyes narrowing.

"Mercy! You are a stubborn fool!" Marion said, pushing a long, thick strand of hair from her face. Dunstan wondered what it would feel like between his fingers. A man could bury his hands in a mane like that....

"They would never step in to help you without being asked, Dunstan de Burgh! They think you are invincible and need them not. Do you know how thrilled Simon would be to aid you?"

Dunstan tore his gaze from her curls and looked at her earnest face, astounded that the little wren was working herself up in such a fashion.

"He is always trying to live up to your example, yet he finds no chance for glory in serving Campion, for it is well defended. I know that he has asked to join King Edward's forces, but your father is reluctant to let him go. Although your sire would admit it not, he likes having his sons around him. Simon needs a chance to prove himself, and what better way than by your side? Then, mayhap, he would see you are no god, but only mortal man, like himself."

Dunstan struggled to take it all in. Simon, cold and competent beyond reason, saw him as a god? Dunstan found that hard to believe, just as he did the notion of his father hoarding his brothers.

"And Stephen and Reynold, too," Marion added. "They need challenges. They have become less than they should be, kicking their heels at Campion. Stephen gets himself into mischief while Reynold broods in bitterness. Yet they are good men, brave knights all, who would be proud to stand by you. With such men as these, who would dare harry you?"

Dunstan shook his head, wary of her words, and yet, amazing as it might seem, they made sense. He imagined Simon, clearheaded and capable of fending off the most vicious threat, standing guard at his gates, and Geoffrey...Marion had not mentioned him, but Geoffrey had more sense than all of them. Geoffrey could see that the fallow land at Wessex produced double its measure.

Perhaps she was right. What good would come of remaining aloof and alone? Would he rather lose Wessex than ask his own family for assistance? He had already proved himself aplenty to his sire and his siblings. Mayhap it was time they proved themselves to him.

"When you return, you must confide in your father," Marion said. "'Tis no sign of weakness to call upon your brothers. They need you as much as you need them, Dunstan."

"I will consider it," Dunstan promised as he looked at Marion with new respect. She answered his regard with that beautiful, open smile that dimpled both her cheeks, and for an instant, Dunstan felt a dizzy sort of longing that had nothing to do with sex. Then his jaw tightened.

"You will excuse me, lady," he said abruptly, wheeling his horse out of the line and forward. Suddenly, he was overwhelmed with the need to get away from the only woman who had the power to twist and turn his thoughts into directions he found too disturbing for his comfort.

Marion passed the rest of the day in peace, glad to be left alone. Although she had enjoyed her brief conversation with Walter Avery, she found his sudden attention dismaying, and she had no desire for further complications. The fewer people interested in her the better. And she certainly had not cared to hear Dunstan's dire warnings, especially when she was planning to disregard them soon enough.

Although he did not seek her out again, Marion often sensed the Wolf's eyes upon her. Sometimes she would look up only to catch him quickly glancing away, that perpetual scowl marring his handsome features. Presumably, he was simply guarding her well, Marion thought, with no little disgruntlement.

When she had ridden beside him, Marion had briefly thought she saw longing in those green eyes of his, but it must have been indigestion—or loathing, she decided. Dunstan had no cause to like her, that was certain, especially since she had delayed this trip more than once.

No wonder he was so grumpy. Even though she did not understand why he had accepted this errand, Marion could see what drove him to hurry. Dunstan was worried about his lands and his people, and she could not fault him for that.

Watching his mounted figure, Marion felt a twinge of admiration for the man she had once despised so thoroughly. Could the feeling be mutual? Dunstan had always treated her as less than nothing, but today she had sensed a change in him. Had she imagined it, or had the Wolf of Wessex finally eyed her with some respect? At least he believed her about her memory loss—a small step that, but a significant one. Perhaps there was hope for the eldest de Burgh, after all, Marion thought with a smile.

With some surprise, Marion realized that she would not mind getting to know him better, to discover exactly what lay beneath that rough hide of his perhaps to change his snarls to smiles. She nearly laughed at the absurdity of such a scheme. Surely, it would be doomed to failure, for a wolf could no more change his nature than a leopard his spots.

No matter. She would have to ignore Dunstan's increasing appeal, for, though he might more readily believe some of her words, he was still intent upon returning her to Baddersly. And Marion had no intention of being left behind in that dark and dreadful place while the Wolf went on to resume his life.

Escape was never far from her thoughts. All day she had watched for a chance to ease her mount away from the rest of the train, but no opportunity had arisen. The men stayed close to her for her own protection, as did Cedric, who seemed doubly attentive after receiving his reprimand from Dunstan. And Marion's small but sturdy horse would be no match for the huge destriers ridden by the Wolf and his men.

No, Marion knew that she must somehow gain time, enough time to get far ahead of any pursuit. Longingly, she looked at the forest that rose upon the hills to their right, dipping closer here and farther there as the road curved and twisted. She could lose herself in those woods, if only she could slip away undetected. She had but to find her chance.

It came at supper.

It seemed the Wolf was avoiding her again, so she was spared his company. Eating but little, she excused herself early from Cedric's company. "But, my lady, 'tis not even dark yet," the boy protested, glancing up at the setting sun.

"I know, but I am tired," Marion explained with an apologetic smile. Would the boy forgive her deception? She felt sadly regretful for getting Cedric into trouble yet again, but she had to think of herself. And she knew that Dunstan was a fair master; he would not hurt the boy.

"Good night," she whispered.

"Good night, my lady," he answered, too kind and open to suspect her of anything but weariness.

And in truth, Marion was weary, but it was not to rest that she entered her tent. She knew that once she was inside it, Cedric would relax his guard, and that was when she planned to escape. She waited patiently, hoping that Agnes would stay out by the fire until late, helping the men with their meal. Of Dunstan, she had seen little, but she suspected that he, too, would leave her be, for had he not lectured her long and vehemently against the follies of fleeing? He did not think she would, and that was exactly how she would manage to, once again.

Peeking out from under the edge of the tent, Marion saw that Cedric had, indeed, left for the companionable glow of the fire, where most of the men still gathered. Agnes and Dunstan, too, must be there, for no one was near her tent. Wrapping the servant's tattered cloak around her, Marion slipped out from under the other side and moved calmly toward the trees.

She was nearly under the first heavy shadows of their leaves when a voice called after her, "Hey, old woman, don't go far."

Without turning, Marion attempted an imitation of Agnes's loud cackling laugh and limped into the woods, holding the worn garment closer about her. Praying that the sentry would take her for Agnes making her evening ablutions, Marion stepped into the shelter of the forest. Once there, she did not dally, however. This time, she intended to put as much ground between her and the Wolf as she could.

She hurried forward, not daring to run over the uneven undergrowth, but moving as fast as she could. Already night was gathering under the oaks, and Marion knew it would be her ally. Slipping in and out of clumps of trees she came upon a path of sorts and decided to follow it, simply because she did not want to travel in circles. She moved off the trail at times, but kept close to it until darkness forced her to stay upon the narrow track.

And darkness came soon, blanketing the world in a disconcerting blackness when the leaves above blocked out the moon and the stars. Marion lost some of her boldness. The rustling of small animals in the brush and the flap of wings overhead would make her freeze in her place, breathless. At first, it was pursuit from camp that she feared, but later, the strange sounds conveyed their own dangers.

Trying not to think of all that Dunstan had warned her about—wild beasts and desperate outlaws—Marion clutched her small dagger close and stepped carefully. Breathing evenly through her nostrils, she focused on her freedom and a life without threat of a dreaded past. Safety lay ahead of her, and she could not let the night noises cause her to veer from it.

Telling herself that no one could possibly be deep in the woods at this hour, Marion had herself convinced—until she heard a low rumble ahead that heralded the unmistakable movements of men.

Chapter Seven

Dunstan stood staring into the trees and listened distractedly to Walter's report. They had made good time today and had halted early enough to scare up some fresh game for the evening meal. The weather might hold another day, and they were that much closer to his mission's end. Why did he not feel better?

Glancing around the fire, Dunstan rubbed the back of his neck, where the muscles had tightened uncomfortably. The men seemed to be in good spirits, and even old Benedict was teasing that strange crone who served Marion.... Marion... Dunstan had tried to ignore her since this morning, but as if possessed by its own will, his gaze traveled toward her tent, seeking her out.

His eyes narrowed when he did not immediately see her. When he could not find his squire, either, his jaw clenched, and when he caught sight of Cedric picking at the last bits of meat on the bones of the night's supper, Dunstan felt a chill right to his own marrow.

"Cedric!" Startled by the force of his master's voice, the youth dropped a morsel onto the ground and jerked to attention. Dunstan closed the distance between them in two strides. "Why are you not with Lady Warenne?"

"She is bedded down for the night," the boy answered, flushing beneath Dunstan's glare.

"And who gave you leave to desert your post?"

"Uh, no one, my lord. I just thought that since she was sleeping . . ."

Dunstan tried to control his impatience even as raw fury, mixed with some foreign emotion, threatened to lay claim to him. "Is Benedict watching her?" he asked through gritted teeth.

"No, my lord." Cedric was staring at him, wide-eyed, apparently too witless to comprehend the enormity of his misdeed. Not trusting himself to speak, Dunstan turned and made for the lady's tent, Cedric at his heels.

"But, my lord, she was tired," the boy protested.

Dunstan marched on, hoping that his instinct was wrong and that the wren would not be so foolish. By the Lord's grace, let her not be so foolish. . . . Without preamble, Dunstan jerked aside the flap to the accompaniment of Cedric's gasp. Inside the dark cocoon, a form lay upon the ground, seeming undisturbed by his entry, and Dunstan felt his blood go cold.

Although Cedric breathed a soft sigh of relief at the sight of the heaped blankets, Dunstan was no empty-headed youth. A grim knowledge moved him to action, and with a swift flick of his boot, he tossed away the blanket to reveal to his astonished squire the mound of clothing and pillows that lay underneath.

"She is gone!" Cedric squeaked. "But I never thought—"

"Yes, she is gone! Heed you this, boy," Dunstan growled. "When I give an order I expect it to be obeyed without question. You were not given leave to think!"

"My lord, forgive me!" Cedric fell upon his knees.

"Get up!" Dunstan hissed. "And forgive yourself should we find her dead."

With a startled look, Cedric glanced at the woods, and Dunstan followed, staring into the fields and forest that lined the roadway. The sun was setting behind a hill, casting the ghostly glow of twilight all around them and heralding the coming night. It would be upon them soon, with only the moon and the stars to guide any search.

Dunstan's heart sank down to his toes as he realized the enormity of the situation. She could be anywhere—up a tree, hiding in a cave or fallen into a ravine—and he had not the resources to find her. It was too late. To divide up his men and send them off into the darkness would be just as foolhardy as her own recklessness. He could not do it.

Walter's voice broke through whatever force was gripping Dunstan, holding him stock-still. "She has fled again?" the vassal asked without surprise.

"Yes."

"We had better hurry," Walter said. Surprised, Dunstan shot a swift questioning glance at his vassal. Walter's eyes were hooded in the twilight, and, when Dunstan said nothing, they turned to him, strangely bright. "We shall spread out and find her."

"No," Dunstan said wearily. "It is too dangerous. I cannot risk separating the men and sending them off into the woods in the night to look for a needle in a haystack."

Walter opened his mouth as if to argue and then closed it again. "The road is quiet, and naught is abroad but one lone female," he reasoned. "If we began now—"

Dunstan shook his head, cutting off his vassal's words. "You have fought beside me long enough to know the folly of such a course. Yes, in all probability there is no threat among these hills, but I did not stay alive this long by taking such chances."

A muscle in Walter's cheek jumped at the implied reprimand, but Dunstan paid it no heed. He stared off into the trees, trying to decide what to do. He ought to abandon the foolish chit to her fate, but the thought of the wren alone out there did something to his chest, making it constrict painfully.

"But the lady! Surely, you cannot mean to let her run away," Walter argued. "What will your father say?"

Something in Walter's voice made Dunstan lift his head and look closely at his vassal. Was that scorn he heard? Contempt? Walter's face showed nothing but taut lines of concentration in the vanishing light.

Dunstan rubbed the back of his neck. On top of everything else, he was imagining things. Perhaps he was hearing taunts where there were none because of his own sense of frustration and helplessness. What was he to do? "I will go alone," he said finally. "And I will find her." Or what is left of her, he thought grimly.

In truth, he had not considered his father's reaction should he fail in his mission or, worse yet, if the woman his family adored came up dead or missing when in his charge. Campion's disapproval or Simon's scorn suddenly seemed a lot less important than they once might have. Right now, Dunstan just wanted to find her alive.

Then he would kill her himself.

Stopping only to grab up his pack, Dunstan headed toward the woods. Cedric begged to come along, but knowing the boy would slow him down, Dunstan bade him stay. He wanted no distractions as he sought her trail in the dusk. He spared a moment to consider the workings of her mind, but decided that was beyond any sane man. Instead, he simply took the most likely route away from the camp toward the cover of the trees.

Dunstan trod softly, taking the easiest way and hoping she did not veer off in her cleverness. If she hoped no one would discover her missing until morning, she was probably putting as much distance between herself and the camp as possible. Dunstan suspected that was her course, but the knowledge gave him no comfort, for moving as swiftly as he could to catch up, he might never find her in the blackness.

It was full dark under the trees, the moon casting its light but faintly through the branches overhead. Dunstan stepped more carefully, afraid that he might miss her form huddled off the track he had discovered. It twisted and turned over fallen logs and slippery ditches, which made him wonder if she would break her neck in some gully.

Actually, that was the least of the possible fates that disturbed him. There were so many other dangers, so many threats to a woman alone in a strange forest in the dark, that Dunstan could not even consider them. He concentrated solely on following her—on a muddy footprint, glimpsed in an open glade, or a bush, visibly disturbed—while he tried to ignore the weight that pressed down upon him, making him feel powerless for the first time in many long years.

Although Dunstan was not a superstitious man, what finally kept him going was a blind faith that she was ahead of him. And with no other clues to guide him, Dunstan did not stop to question whence the alien feeling sprung. He simply heeded it, moving forward with increasing urgency.

He went swiftly because something was not right. He could feel it as surely as a man sensed a coming battle—or an ambush. The woods were too quiet, the normal noises of night animals stilled, and even the air hushed with danger. Dunstan paused to listen, his very soul reaching out into the blackness.

And through the silence, she spoke to him, though it would not have been the call that he desired. The sound that rent the night was a scream that made his blood run cold, for it was a woman's scream of terror and pain and it belonged to Marion. His body flew to life in response.

Afterward, Dunstan cursed himself as ten times a fool for charging off like a madman, but at the time he could do nothing else. He saw red, his own blood seeming to burst through his brain to cloud his vision. All his soldier's training and years of caution went by the wayside as he rushed toward her.

Another scream was cut off, muffled somehow, but the first still rang in his ears, driving him onward, and, unsheathing his sword, Dunstan burst into a clearing. In less than a second, his mind took in the scene before him, lit by a small fire: Marion stretched out between two men, one holding her arms, while the other bent over her, pushing up her skirts. In less than a second, Dunstan had raised his blade, overwhelmed by a blood lust such as he had never known, and bellowed his rage.

The one between her legs looked up, his face registering a startled expression before Dunstan severed his head from his body in one blow. Blood showered through the air, making the other man shriek and fall back, fumbling for a weapon. But Dunstan was too fast. Leaping over Marion's body, Dunstan sliced the man's arm where it reached for a sword and then ran him through.

For a long moment Dunstan stood there, breathing heavily, his heart thundering, his body still tense, his eyes raking the area for more enemies. But the clearing was empty. Nothing moved but the flickering flames of the low fire, and the only sound was the bubble of life's blood leaving the fallen.

Dunstan drew in a deep, shaky breath as he tried to bring himself back to normalcy. It was not easy. He had fought fiercer battles many times, had been in more danger more often than he could count and had even been wounded several times, as his body's scars could attest. But never had he known such killing lust—unreasoning, overwhelming and still unappeased. When he realized that he longed to hack the corpses to pieces, Dunstan let the air out of his lungs in a low hiss and turned.

Spattered with blood, Marion was lying in the dirt with her gown bunched around her hips and one pale limb resting against the headless body of one of her attackers.

Her beautiful dark hair was spread out around her face in wild disarray, framing delicate features that were as white and still as death. Dunstan fell to his knees beside her and forced himself to speak evenly.

His voice came out a ragged whisper. "Wren! Wren... are you hurt?" Now that the threat to her was vanquished, Dunstan felt at a loss. What if she was injured? He knew naught of healing and even less of succoring the wounded. "Marion, 'tis I, Dunstan," he said louder.

When she did not respond, he removed his gauntlets slowly, afraid to startle her, and put a hand to her forehead. Her long lashes fluttered open. "Dunstan..." She murmured his name like a caress.

The pain in his chest eased a little, and he held out a hand toward her. She took it, rising to a sitting position, and he arranged her skirts to cover shapely legs made visible in the firelight. When he had finished, she was looking up at him with an expression he had never seen before. Something akin to dazed wonder shone out of those huge brown eyes, and then she threw her arms around his neck, buried her face in the warm curve of his throat above his mail coat and wept.

Dunstan grudgingly embraced her, hugging her close as he had not held another human being since Nicholas was a babe. He felt ridiculously ill-equipped to give comfort. What did he know of it? His years as a soldier had taught him to disdain such things, and women who took him to their beds knew better than to ask for more than a friendly tumble. But the wren needed him.

Awkwardly, Dunstan put a palm to the tangled softness of her hair, glad to feel the life pulsing beneath it. She was all right. By God's good grace, she was all right. Dunstan felt a shudder and told himself that Marion was reacting normally to all that had happened. It was certainly not his own body that was trembling like a newly weaned babe at the sight of a little blood. Thank God that it was not her blood. . . .

Dunstan's fingers drifted through curls silky and rich as the finest cloth. And thick! By faith, he could feel the weight of the mass tumbling over his fist. A man could bury his hand in hair like that, anchoring himself, he thought, before removing his own hand abruptly and laying it gingerly upon her shoulder.

He told himself she had nearly been raped. He told himself that she was frightened out of her mind and clinging to him for solace. He told himself that she was a troublesome piece of baggage who was here because of her own recklessness and that he had no liking for her.

But no matter what he told himself, Dunstan was becoming all too aware of the woman in his arms. The tears she had shed upon his neck were caught by a breeze, cooling the surface of his skin in a tantalizing sensation. Her breath was soft and warm upon his throat, and she carried some elusive scent of rich earth and fertile flowers. Her lush breasts were nestled against his chest, and her hips were nearly touching his own. Cursing himself for a fiend, Dunstan felt himself spring to life.

As if sensing his perfidy, she lifted her head, but her heart-shaped face held no accusation. Those great brown eyes of hers looked at him as no one had ever looked at him before—that strange sort of wonder mixed with something else. Could it be desire? Dunstan felt the spark between them ignite, heating the air, burning away all else. His hands went to her shoulders. She parted her lips. Shuddering with need, he leaned closer—and swore softly.

Pushing her away, Dunstan got to his feet before he took her himself, making him little better than the corpses that surrounded them. After a brush with death, a man often craved life, or the best use he could make of it, but that was no excuse. The wren was no whore, and they were not safely ensconced in any camp. With another low curse, Dunstan whirled around, half-expecting to see himself surrounded. What kind of a randy, witless fool was he to lie about as if they were on a pleasure outing?

From the looks of the camp, the two dead men had not been alone, and their companions might return at any moment. "We must go," Dunstan snapped without regard to Marion's sensibilities. His brain was working quickly now, and he was cursing himself for his vainglorious charge into the clearing. Why had he not left one of the men alive, at least long enough to discover who they were and what they were about?

Dunstan rubbed the back of his neck. Never, since learning the rules of combat at his father's knee, had he been so rash. The blood lust that had seized him now seemed a disturbing thing, robbing him of his senses and taking control of his body. With a low oath, Dunstan glanced down at the corpse, wishing, too late, that the dead could speak. Unfortunately, this fellow would tell him nothing, so Dunstan turned on his heel to go. But something made him swing back around to look more closely at the wretch at his feet.

The man was dressed poorly in plain rough wool, and yet he carried a sword. Unusual, that. Something niggled at the back of Dunstan's mind. Something familiar. Leaning down, he searched the body, but found nothing except a purse with a few coins. If the man was a robber, he had yet to win his gold—or be paid. Dunstan's eyes narrowed.

"Wh-what are you doing?" The wren's shaky voice brought him upright.

"Nothing," Dunstan answered abruptly. "Can you walk?"

She looked up at him, her great eyes awash with confusion, reminding him of nothing so much as a little lost fawn. He felt like cursing. He did not want to hurt her, but he had wasted enough time coddling her. Danger was in the air. He could almost smell it.

"Can you walk?" he asked again. She nodded dully, and he reached out a hand, pulling her to her feet. "Come then. We must be off." He glanced around the site and decided to let the low fire burn itself out. If it served as a beacon for other outlaws, he did not want to draw their attention by extinguishing it.

"What of...them?" Marion asked. Her voice was shaky, and he looked down to see her hugging herself tightly as she stared at the bodies. Anger pulsed through him—anger at the men who had reduced his little wren to this, and anger at himself for not reaching her sooner, for not being able to give her what she needed, and for not having his own wits about him.

"Leave them for carrion," Dunstan answered gruffly. He strode swiftly toward the trees, taking note of the footprints that marked the passage of more than those two. He stifled a curse. They needed to get away from the clearing and the path and find a resting place. Others, obviously, were abroad this night, and few men roamed the dark woods with good intentions.

"Dunstan." She was tugging on his sleeve, and when he turned to her, she let her hand slide down to his, apparently taking some comfort from his touch. Awkwardly, he squeezed her fingers. Then he strode from the clearing, one hand pulling her along with him, the other resting on his sword hilt.

Once under the trees, he paused to let his eyes adjust to the blackness, then he pushed on, far enough from the path to be out of the way of any travelers. When he finally paused, Dunstan stood looking up at several tall oaks, assessing them as well as he could in the dark. Moving to a large one with a split trunk, he said, "We shall bed down here."

Marion's small palm jerked in his. "Can we not go back to the train?"

"No. Others are abroad this night, and in this light, I can little judge what they are about. We know that some of them, at least, are not above attacking a woman."

She clutched his hand tighter, and the answering squeeze he gave hers came more naturally now. "Since you sleep like a babe in a tree, this spot should suit you perfectly," he noted wryly.

"But—but…" Marion stammered, and Dunstan's lips curved upward. Then he put his hands about her waist and lifted her up, setting her in the crook of the giant tree. She was still sputtering when he climbed up beside her and leaned back against the sturdy trunk.

"But what?" Dunstan asked easily. Despite having found her hiding in a large oak after her first escape, he assumed that she would object to spending the night on a branch. After all, he could imagine few ladies finding a comfortable berth up here.

"But… you do not really expect me to sleep here, do you?"

"Why not?" Dunstan asked. Although he had one ear tuned to the forest, he was beginning to enjoy himself. The wren was recovered enough to endure some teasing. He could not wait to hear her admit that her story about falling asleep in the tree had been a fantastic lie. Perhaps then he could get some other truths from her, as well. He listened, suddenly eager to hear her confession, but when she spoke, it was not to complain about the bed, but the company.

"Why, 'twould not be seemly to stay here alone with you," she protested.

Dunstan threw back his head and guffawed before he caught himself. "Do not make me laugh. We must be quiet. Now hush, and try to rest." He could make out the dark shape of her form and smiled.

By faith, what kind of woman thought nothing of running into the woods alone, but felt threatened by spending the night with him? A bit of moonlight danced through the leaves, illuminating Marion's face, and Dunstan caught a glimpse of her licking her lips before she was again cast in shadow.

In that instant, his smile died. Perhaps Marion was right, he thought grimly. She might be in more danger than either of them suspected.

Chapter Eight

Marion glared at the great dark form that disappeared into the blackness of the tree trunk, and did not know what to think. When she had first seen him, when he had held out his hand to her, dragging her back from the horror that had gripped her, Marion had been so happy that she had wept with relief.

When he had held her, comforting her in his own awkward way, she had felt something for Dunstan de Burgh that she had never known before, a welling of emotion so profound that she hardly dared trust her own senses. When he had stroked her hair and that odd look came over his handsome face, she had been breathless with anticipation—and wanting.

Marion blushed to admit it even to herself. And yet, for just a moment, it had seemed as if nothing existed but Dunstan and herself. There were no filthy hands pawing at her, no death cries, no blood and no flights into the woods. There was not even a Baddersly, waiting like a giant, loathsome spider, ready to draw her into its web. There was only Dunstan and the way he made her body tingle and her heart trip over itself eagerly.

But, all too soon, that brief interlude was over, and Dunstan was back to his old, surly self, grunting and dragging her along as if she were naught but unwanted baggage. And now he had tossed her up in a tree and laughed at her. The man was impossible! Marion moved restlessly, the bark digging into her back. How could anyone actually sleep here?

Her gown had ridden up, and Marion tugged at the hem, bringing it down. Although the weather had been pleasant, the setting sun had brought a chill to the woods. Wrapping her arms around her legs, she rested her head on her knees and her eyes upon the black shape opposite.

And, as soon as she did, it came again—that sweet rush of emotion. Was it only because he had rescued her? Would she have greeted any savior with the depth of feeling that swelled now in her breast? Marion stared at his dark figure and knew not with certainty, but she suspected that whatever she felt was reserved for Dunstan de Burgh, pigheaded, sullen and handsome devil that he was. Closing her eyes to call up his visage, she smiled—because it was scowling.

At least he had not scolded her. Marion would not have been surprised if he had launched into a long lecture about her foolishness. Grudgingly, she admitted that he had the right, for his warning had been all too true; the forest was full of desperate men. With disconcerting haste, the image of Dunstan was replaced by others, with faces and hands that held her down and something worse. It was there at the edge of her mind, taunting her tonight, that great well of her memories, threatening to overwhelm her. And Marion wanted no part of them. She opened her eyes wide.

"It is there, so close I can almost feel it," she whispered.

"What?" Dunstan's low, urgent response told her that he was awake and alert for danger.

"My past."

He grunted, rather irritably, and Marion wondered if he was heartily sick of chasing after her. Who could blame him? He had a home and duties awaiting him, while she had only bleak nothingness. "I am afraid of it, Dunstan," she said. "I do not want to remember."

"Then, do not," he said gruffly, and suddenly Marion felt his arm around her, pulling her into the curve of his body. "Sleep," he ordered in a rough whisper.

She had forgotten how warm he was, but the reminder made her snuggle up against his side. His heat surrounded her immediately, driving away the chill in the air, the horrors of the night and the dread of a history that loomed over her like a black cloud. She rested her head on his shoulder, safe and content, and began to relax, slowly but surely. Dazedly, she knew that she should not be curled up so close to a man, alone in the night, but it felt so *right,* how could it be wrong? She slid a leg up over his thick thigh and sighed softly.

Drifting off in that haze between awareness and dreams, Marion was slow to recognize the subtle change in Dunstan's embrace. Dimly, she noticed the great muscles in the arm beneath her head become hard and tense, the body touching hers grow taut. She moved, snuggling tighter, but the low hiss of his indrawn breath made her open her eyes and freeze, suddenly alarmed.

Her first thought was that something threatened them, but Marion realized quickly that no forest danger made the heart beneath her hand quicken its pace. In an instant, she knew what the problem was, for in an instant she felt it, too. What had but a moment ago been an innocent caress had become something else entirely as that strange fire flared between them.

Although she could not see his eyes, Marion knew they had darkened to the green-black that marked his desire. Her own eyes widened in shock, but she remained still, afraid to move lest any motion acerbate the raw, hot feeling that was coursing through her and, she suspected, through him.

Dunstan burned her everywhere they met—where her knee rested casually on his thigh and where his hard chest, encased in mail, lay beneath her arm. Even her scalp tingled where it touched the thick muscle of his arm. Her breasts became absurdly sensitive, the linen of her shift seeming to rub against them. It felt deliciously good.

Marion stiffened in surprise. Although she knew little of her past, she thought herself innocent. Then why this wanton yearning? And why only with Dunstan? She had never lain in a man's arms before, as far as she knew, but she had touched all of the de Burghs at one time or another and had never felt this wrenching heat with any of them—except the eldest.

Her throat became dry, and her body began to ache from the effort it took to hold herself rigidly in place. Finally, when she could bear it no more, Marion shifted her weight, easing away from him a little, her leg sliding along his. Dunstan made a soft, strangled sound, and she glanced up at him swiftly, but she could see naught of his shadowed face in the darkness.

"Go to sleep," he ordered hoarsely. Sleep? Every humor in her body was alive and seeking Dunstan. It was the strangest experience, frightening and wonderful, exciting and terrible, all at the same time. Would he kiss her? Marion fought the urge to search his face with her fingers and beg him to do just that. If only she could see him! Was he scowling? Or were his green eyes glinting with that wolfish look that threatened to devour her?

She waited, tense with anticipation, but Dunstan made no move, no sound, and gradually she realized the foolishness of her behavior. She had heard enough of Stephen's ribald commentary to know that she should not be here, lying in Dunstan's embrace, and wanting more.

Shame colored her cheeks and made her roll over, but she was not free of Dunstan immediately. Her bottom brushed his hip, and he jerked as if she had scorched him before she could inch from his side. Now only the top of her head touched him, resting against his arm.

They both lay stiffly then, their breathing swift and shallow. Marion stared out into the blackness of the woods, feeling again the chill in the air and the bark of the tree digging into her. Her new position left something to be desired in the way of comfort, but what else could she do?

She could turn back over and put her arms around him, drawing him to her and melting into his heat. . . .

Marion had to bite back the sound that rushed up at the thought. She could not. There were names for women who gave their favors freely, and they were not nice. Did she really want a quick tumble from the Wolf? No, Marion's heart cried out. She wanted more. . . .

It was impossible. No matter what strange desires she might harbor for him, no matter what tender emotions she might feel for him, Dunstan was the man who was taking her, against her will, to Baddersly, where he would abandon her. Marion closed her eyes against a sudden ache and turned her mind to calming images, as she often did to maintain her composure. "Tell me of Wessex," she said softly.

"Wessex?" For a moment, Dunstan sounded as if he were the one with no memory, as if the name of his home ushered up naught but confusion in his mind. Then he began to talk, slowly at first, but soon warming to his subject, and Marion could almost see his holdings in her mind: the green valleys, the steep hillsides and the tall castle in the midst of it all.

Under the soft, low rhythm of his speech, the fire between them waned, and the exhaustion that had been working upon Marion since her ordeal drew her heavily into its grasp. The hard bed, the height of her perch, and the coolness of the night faded away under the lulling warmth of his voice, and she slept.

* * *

It was barely light when Dunstan woke her. He stood below her, a great, menacing presence, staring up at her with a scowl, and Marion sensed that the man who had spoken freely to her of his hopes for his home was gone with the darkness. Dunstan was back to his old surly self. She smiled at him, anyway, for she had grown accustomed to his moods.

"I would get back to the train as quickly as we can. 'Tis unwise to linger here," he said curtly.

Marion nodded, and he lifted her down. For a moment, his hands rested at her waist and his green eyes met hers, but then he drew back as if she had burned him. Was she only imagining this strange pull between them? Or perhaps she, naive fool that she was, was the only one of them who felt anything at all.

Reaching down to smooth out her clothes, Marion's suspicions were realized, for one look at herself told her that the Wolf of Wessex could not possibly be attracted to her. Her cloak and gown were filthy dirty and covered in dark splotches that could only be the blood of her attackers. With a sinking heart, she lifted a hand to her hair to find it curling about her wildly. She fished a piece of leaf and a small twig from the tangles and frowned at them, unaware that Dunstan was watching her.

"'Tis not so pleasant to be on the run, is it, Marion?" he said sharply.

Oh, here it comes. . . . The lecture she had expected last night would be delivered now, when he was obviously at his worst. *Remind me never to wake him early,* Marion thought, then wondered what had put such a ridiculous notion into her head. *She* certainly would never be called upon to rouse the Wolf!

None too pleased herself this morn, Marion turned away, intending to attend to her personal needs, but his big hand closed about her arm in a firm grip. Her first reaction was to shrink into herself, to lower her head and protect herself somehow from whatever angry tirade was coming, but a winter spent with Dunstan's brothers had hardened her, and after three escape attempts her small spark of independence was flaring brightly.

She had also weathered enough recently to put her into a mood foul enough to match his own. The attack upon her person and the ensuing battle had left her shaken, dirty and covered with blood, while the night spent in the tree had left her bruised and aching and nursing a stiff neck. She was thirsty, hungry and desperate to relieve herself, and right now, she did not want to hear Dunstan de Burgh yell at her.

The surge of temper gave her strength, and Marion swung around so swiftly that she managed to loose herself from his grasp. "Let go of me, Dunstan de Burgh!" she cried. "I am sick to death of your bullying!"

He stared down at her openmouthed, the stunned look on his face nearly comical. "Bullying? Bullying! By faith, I saved your life, you ungrateful wench!" Tall and broad as one of the surrounding oaks, he stood with his feet apart and both hands on his hips, the scowl on his face reaching a new level of ferocity.

Marion was unmoved. "Now, if you will excuse me!" She turned to go, but his hand shot out to stop her again.

"I will not!" Dunstan's eyes narrowed, and his fine lips tightened into a thin line. "For I cannot trust you to have the good sense not to run off again! Day of God, lady, are you witless? Know you not what those men were about last night? They would have used you and left you for dead!"

Gripping her arm tighter, Dunstan shook her roughly, as if to gain her attention, and Marion realized that she really ought to be frightened of this huge, threatening knight. She really ought to freeze where she was, uttering not a word, and hope that he tired of this game before he

truly hurt her. If she did anything at all, she ought to fall
to her knees and beg his forgiveness.

Marion knew what she ought to do. Instead, she spat a
curse at him and stomped on his foot. It was hard as a
rock and made her own ache. She hopped up and down
in a one-legged jig.

Dunstan swore to himself, grimacing at her antics. "By
faith, listen to me, Marion! I am trying to protect you!
Even if you are so foolish as to ignore what happened to
you last night, I am not! Do you know how I felt when I
saw you between those men?"

Although he was shouting and he still held her arm too
tightly, his words made her look up, and Marion stared in
surprise. Was something besides rage fueling this fit of
his? His green eyes held a hint of confusion, and Marion
felt her own anger fade.

"No, I do not know," she said softly. "What did you
feel, Dunstan?"

Releasing her so suddenly that she nearly stumbled, he
turned and strode restlessly away from her. "I would that
you see how dangerous it is to be out here alone." Although his voice was low and taut, the reply came too
easily, as if he hid the real answer not only from her, but
from himself.

Or perhaps her imagination ran away with her. Marion
rubbed her bruised arm and stared at the handsome man
who roamed like a wolf among the woods, avoiding her
gaze, avoiding anything that might tame him, and she
knew not what he really felt. "I want you to stop this
foolishness and go home willingly," he said gruffly.

"To what?" Marion asked softly. "What difference if
I die here or at Baddersly?"

He swung around to face her, and she stepped back
from his menacing form as he snarled at her. "Be reason-
able, woman! The difference is that you will die here—

and brutally—yet you do not know that death awaits you at your home."

"It does, and I know it, Dunstan," Marion answered calmly. Looking off into the distance, she tried to frame Baddersly in her mind, but failed. Slowly, quietly, she laid a hand over her breast. "I do not know it with my mind or my memory, but I know it with my heart. I sense it."

Dunstan snorted loudly.

"If you refuse to believe me, then I know not what to say to convince you." Marion disliked argument of any sort, and she knew that this exchange with the eldest de Burgh would change nothing. Obviously, he was not in a receptive mood. As filthy as herself, he had probably kept watch throughout the darkness. He was tired and surly and no doubt chafing at the delay the night had cost him.

His mouth twisted. "You try my patience, Marion. Have you no faith in Campion? He will see to it no harm comes to you."

"Will he?" Marion scoffed. "My champion has sent me from the safety of his walls to a place I do not know, where I will be at the mercy of a man I do not even remember!" The skeptical look on his face grated her temper again, and she pointed a finger at his massive chest.

"You can have no idea how I feel, Dunstan, because you have always been surrounded by your brothers. You have a loving family, trusted retainers and soldiers who would risk their lives for you. At Baddersly naught familiar awaits me. I know naught of that place but dread!"

"You are mad," he snarled, "either that or totally witless."

"Fine," Marion said with resignation. "Believe what you will. You always have. But, now, I *must* attend to myself." She stepped forward, but he was in front of her, halting her path, in a thrice, and she wondered how someone so big could move so quickly and so quietly.

"No." Dunstan's hands were on his hips again, his legs apart in his warrior stance as he glared down at her.

"What?" Marion's eyes flew to his in confusion.

"No," he said smugly. "I admit that you have tricked me more than once, wren, but I would be a fool to let you do it again. You may not have a care for that luscious body of yours, but I must. My father has charged me with returning you to Baddersly, alive and reasonably well, so I do not intend to let you out of my sight until I have delivered you into the hands of your uncle. I suggest that if you wish to relieve yourself, you had better lift your skirts, and do it. We have already wasted enough time this morn."

Marion was taken aback. Surely, he did not mean to watch her? "But... but..." she stammered, blushing furiously. "You cannot expect me to..." Her voice trailed off as she realized there was something positively malicious in the way his lips curved into a smile that was not quite a smile.

"I do," he said simply.

Marion flushed crimson. "How dare you? I am a gentlewoman!" she protested.

Instead of agreeing, Dunstan had the audacity to throw back his head and laugh. "You have yet to convince me of it," he said.

For the first time in her life, Marion felt like striking someone. She smoothed her hands upon her gown, instead, and searched for some semblance of composure. Obviously, she could not assault the Wolf of Wessex. She would have to reason with him. "You are being ridiculous. I can go nowhere in these woods, and you have proven that you can find me anyway," she said a bit bitterly.

"'Tis true," he said, "but I have no wish to dally further. Come, now, do what you will and let us be off." He glanced pointedly at the dawn breaking over the treetops.

Marion opened her mouth to protest further, but something in his stance told her that it would be futile. She was rapidly learning that arguing with Dunstan de Burgh was a useless endeavor, and while she did not think him vindictive, she suspected that he was enjoying her discomfiture. Not wishing to prolong the ignominious conversation any longer, Marion bent her head. "Turn around at least," she said softly.

"I will not."

"Dunstan!" Her eyes snapped up to forest-green ones.

"I will look away," he conceded. "I have no intention of watching you closely, wren, but I mean to keep a bit of your skirts in sight ere you climb up the nearest tree or lead me upon some new dance. Hear me now, Marion, you have made your last escape from me."

Utterly mortified, at first Marion simply gave him her back, but nature's call was too strong. Somehow, she managed to squat carefully, arranging her skirts as best she good, and go about her business. Of course, she knew he could not really *see* anything, but it was little comfort.

"I do not suppose there is a stream nearby in which to wash," she said as she turned again to face him.

"I do not suppose there is, Marion," he answered. "'Tis one of the disadvantages of running away into the wild."

He motioned for her to walk with him, back to camp, and Marion calmly did as he bade, wrapping her cloak tightly around her as if to ward off his ill humor. She lifted her chin and straightened her shoulders.

"I shall never forgive you for that, Dunstan de Burgh," she said as they moved forward.

He did not even grunt in response, and Marion concentrated on making her way through the heavy undergrowth. Really, the man was impossible! Obviously, Campion had spoiled him unforgivably and everyone let him run roughshod over them, but she would not!

Handsome and strong and vital he might be, but she could not excuse his behavior. Well, some of it was, of course, due to her penchant for tricking him. And some seemed to stem from the Wolf's concern for her—which she still found difficult to believe. But most of it was rudeness, plain and simple. The man really needed to be taken in hand....

Although outwardly composed, Marion was still out of sorts. While walking along, she recalled every bit of their conversation, adding pithy comments she wished she had thought of at the time. They had reached the path before she slanted a shocked look up at the man beside her and nearly stumbled.

Had the Wolf of Wessex really called her body "luscious"?

Chapter Nine

Marion trudged along the path, wondering what she had done in her life to deserve the trials she had recently undergone—especially the trial who strode easily beside her over the uneven ground. Despite being twice her size, Dunstan was much more graceful than she would ever be, which was another example of the injustice of the world, Marion decided. As if she needed another example to add to her already lengthy list! Losing her memory was bad enough. Then Campion had tossed her out, and now... Now she had done the most ridiculous thing she could recall.

Out of all seven of the de Burgh brothers, she had to pick the least likable, most recalcitrant one with whom to fall in love.

It was obvious to her now, although she was not quite sure when it had happened. Sometime during their days on the road together, she had begun to care for the huge, surly knight at her side. Last night, when he had come to her rescue, Marion had felt it—a warm, rush of feeling unlike anything she could remember. It had filled her up so completely that it threatened to spill out of her, perhaps onto Dunstan himself.

Foolishness. Marion slanted a glance at him and nearly stumbled. His hand shot out and gripped her arm—too tightly—but she did not protest. In his own way, he was trying his best to help her, even though he was scowling ferociously at her plodding, bumbling pace. Marion noted idly that she was in desperate straits. She was not only accustomed to his grimace; she had grown to like it.

Foolishness! None of it mattered because in a few days he would leave her to her fate, without a backward glance. And she . . . She had no business mooning over the Wolf; she had her very life to think about. The closer they drew to Baddersly, the more imperative it became that she manage to escape. Yet how could she, when Dunstan would not let her out of his sight even to relieve herself?

Would he continue to haunt her? What of tonight? Did he intend to sleep beside her in her small tent? Marion tried to ignore the heated rush of bodily humors that the very thought of such closeness engendered. She shut her eyes, suddenly, painfully aware of his presence beside her—and his touch.

"Dunstan, you are hurting me," she finally said softly. It struck her then as to just how truly she spoke, though her arm suffered the least of it. The Wolf was making her ache from her head right down to her heart.

"What?" He threw a sharp look at her and then loosened his grip, but he kept his hand upon her sleeve, and Marion felt the warmth all through her. He did not apologize, and she smiled, certain that he never would. He was Dunstan, beloved to her, despite all his rough edges, and she would cherish him, if she could.

But she could not.

They would have to part soon, and that would be best, for she knew as surely as she drew breath that the Wolf would never return her regard. Oh, he might think her body "luscious" and he might look at her at times with the flare of desire shining in his green eyes, but he could not give her what she wanted: love and a home and a family.

He would not even give her freedom.

The thought was sobering, and Marion went still for a moment before Dunstan urged her on with a jerk. He did not hurt her, though, until they finally neared the edge of the forest, when his fingers dug into her arm again with more pressure than was comfortable.

Glancing up in surprise, Marion saw the tenseness in his stance, and she realized he did not even know what he did. He was looking ahead and concentrating intently, as if scenting trouble in the very air. His eyes were narrowed and his jaw clenched, and Marion stiffened instantly in response.

"What is it?" she whispered.

"Shh," Dunstan said, his attention elsewhere. "'Tis too quiet for my liking. Stay here." Too quiet? Marion could hear the morning birds trilling their songs in the treetops and small animals foraging among the roots not far away. All seemed as it should be, but she remained where she was, watching, with admiration, as Dunstan walked ahead.

His long hair was surely darker and richer than that of his brothers, she thought wistfully. His shoulders were definitely wider, and his thighs... Well, she had never really looked at any of his brothers' legs, but Dunstan's were strong and thickly muscled, yet he moved silently, like a wolf.

Marion saw him disappear through the edge of the trees into the light that marked the campsite area, then she stood there, staring stupidly after him, dreamily musing on Dunstan de Burgh's attributes. It took her a full minute to realize just what he had done, and when she did, she froze.

The man who had sworn never to let her out of his sight had left her alone.

It took another moment for the knowledge to sink in, and Marion hardly dared breathe as the possibilities presented themselves to her dazed mind. She could flee. She could actually leave the Wolf, his men and his nearby camp, and proceed with her plans. Although last night's attack had left her wary, she told herself that it was morning now, and her chances of being set upon were surely fewer during the daylight hours. Were they not?

Ignoring the echo of Dunstan's warnings, Marion scanned the area around her, trying to make her decision swiftly. If she turned and made her way through the trees off the path and headed back toward Campion, Dunstan might not find her. Ever.

Although she stood perfectly still, Marion's heart raced, pounding so loudly that the sound seemed to rise above the raucous call of the birds. Suddenly aware of the number of dark wings flapping against the gray sky, Marion looked up and felt a chill omen, the kind of unearthly dread that she knew about Baddersly. She could not see the road, but she was sure that something was wrong. She could sense it.

And then it came to her—the reason for Dunstan's caution. The camp *was* too quiet. If it lay just ahead, why did she not hear Agnes's cackle or the voices of the men or the sounds of the horses? Although the group was not boisterous, the general noise of people and animals surrounded them wherever they went. And yet, Marion heard nothing but the birds. Uneasiness crept over her, along with concern for Dunstan.

If anything should happen to him... The thought rocked Marion with raw emotions so fierce that she nearly fell to her knees, and without hesitation, she stepped forward, determined to see for herself that he was all right. Then she stopped abruptly in her tracks. What of her plans to fly?

Now, Marion! You must go now! Turning to leave, she told herself to run, but her legs refused to move. How could she go without making sure he was well? She felt torn, pulled in two different directions, and with only a moment, perhaps less, to decide.

It was the hardest thing she had ever done. Finally, with a resignation that was painful, Marion closed her eyes tightly and discovered that she really had no choice. She loved Dunstan with a dizzying force that could not be denied, that seemed to engulf her body and her will.

She loved him more, perhaps, than her own freedom.

With calm determination, Marion pressed her hands to her skirts and walked to the edge of the woods. At the last line of trees, she took a deep breath and looked toward the roadway, afraid of what might meet her gaze.

The camp appeared peaceful enough, mocking her fears as foolishness. Perhaps Dunstan was right and she was overly sensitive, seeing threats where there were none. With a soft sigh of relief, she realized why it was so quiet. The men were still asleep. Perhaps it was earlier than she thought or mayhap they thought to lie about without Dunstan to rouse them.

Stepping out into the grassy area before the road, Marion walked to where the embers of the night's fire glowed and several of the men still huddled in their blankets. Dunstan was standing not far away, with his back to her, and it was then that she began to notice the deathly quiet. Why was he not shouting at them all? The hair on the back of her neck rose, and her throat shut tightly, cutting off her air.

She must have made some sound because Dunstan turned toward her, and the naked agony on his face struck her like a physical blow. Dread enveloped her, bearing down upon her very soul, and she closed her eyes. It was nearly overwhelming this time, and she struggled with it, pushing away that black well of memory that threatened to drag her into its depths. Fear of the past warred with fear of the present until she felt wrenched in two, until she had no choice but to open her eyes—and to look. And when she did, she saw that Dunstan's men were not really sleeping.

They were dead.

Those near the fire must have been killed as they slept, for their bodies still lay wrapped in their woolen blankets, stained red with blood. Others had risen to fight, for they had fallen near the carts, their eyes open and staring, their wounds already sending up a stench.

The unholy silence was broken only by the sound of a bit of tent flapping in the breeze. Not one single moan rose from the men, and Marion realized that there must be no survivors. No noise came from the animals, either, and a glance told her that the horses were all gone, leaving Dunstan and herself as the only living creatures in the entire camp—seemingly in all the world.

For a long moment, Marion stood transfixed, her brain registering the facts that met her eyes without emotion as something built inside of her. Each gruesome sight added to it, until she felt a great weight upon her, threatening to burst her heart. Then she chanced to see the battered corpse of young Cedric, and whatever had held her distant from the horror gave way, letting pain rush through her like floodwaters through a dike, drowning her senses and making it difficult to breathe.

And suddenly the terrible scene before her was replaced by another vision of carnage. Marion fell to her knees, covering her eyes, but it rose before her, erupting into her mind so vividly that she could neither stop it nor deny it.

She could only watch helplessly as outlaws charged forward like fiends from hell, bent upon killing them all without a single word of treaty. Young John, little older than Cedric, was cut down immediately. Marion saw him fall herself and heard Enid's screams. She pulled out her knife and turned to strike at the man who threatened her maid, but fear stayed her hand. And then it was too late.

The assassin's evil face rose before her, mottled and filthy, his eyes glinting with malice, the silver ring in his ear glittering coldly. He struck her, sending her off her palfrey to the ground, but before the pain exploded in her head, Marion felt the sharp sting of recognition. She had seen that earring before.

The man who wore it might masquerade as a common robber of the road, but she knew him as one of her uncle's men.

Marion shuddered, weeping silently and gasping for breath, until she felt a heavy hand upon her neck, pushing her head down to the ground so that she would not faint. Her dizziness passed then, and she simply cried silently, for the men who lay before her, for her own people, dead these past months, and for the memory that had returned to haunt her.

"We cannot stay here," Dunstan said. Marion heard the words but did not respond. Beyond her grief, fresh and wrenching, was the overwhelming sensation of remembering. Where once there had been nothing but a void, there was a lifetime, for all of it came back. Her uncle, her treacherous uncle, had sent his men to kill them all!

She heard Dunstan mumble a low oath, but remained still, retreating inside of herself. "Marion, Marion!" He crouched beside her, exasperation edging his voice, and took her arms in a fierce grip. "Marion! We cannot stay here, for this was no ordinary attack. The thieves took nothing from the train. They came in silently at night to do murder, and they may not be finished."

"My uncle." The words were a dry, hoarse croak struggling up from her throat.

"Forget your uncle!" Dunstan said, giving her a shake. "I know not who has slaughtered my men, though I suspect those two from last night were a part of it. I know only that it was not common thieves who did this, and whoever it was might still be about. We must fly and watch our backs!''

He loosed his fierce hold on her, his voice growing gentler. ''Take whatever you can—a change of clothing, money, valuables and food if you can find it. But hurry.''

He helped her to her feet, and moving as if in a dream, Marion crawled into the cart, her numb fingers making a bundle out of a blanket and some clothes. Even while she worked, images danced before her. She was a child again, sitting at her father's knee and smiling at her mother's sweet laugh. Oh, dear Lord, she had once had a family and a loving one! But they were gone—all but her mother's treacherous brother who, even now, reached out to kill her.

Jumping down from the cart, Marion lost her balance and nearly fell. She reached out for Dunstan and felt a moment's panic when she did not see him. It never occurred to her to try to flee from him now; she was too shattered to scheme of escape. And Dunstan was all she had.

Overwhelmed by terror and tragedy, she needed his strength, his warmth, to cling to, now more than ever. When she spotted him at the edge of the wood, pulling an arrow from the body of the sentry, her relief was palpable. Her love for him swelled and steadied her, dulling the sharp edges of her anguish.

She ran to him, weaving her way among the dead and scattering the carrion birds that had returned to feed upon them. And when she reached him, Marion flung herself heedlessly at him, throwing her arms around him. For once, he did not snarl at her or turn away, but pulled her to him, crushing her against his mail and lifting her from the ground.

''Ah...wren,'' he whispered brokenly, and in his voice, Marion heard the pain, the aching, crushing pain that he was carrying around inside.

His people had been slaughtered. Some he had known for years; some, surely, were his friends, but the Wolf of Wessex could not fall to the ground and cry like a maid. He was a knight, and he had to get them to safety. He was holding all that rage and hurt inside of his great body, and Marion wanted to weep anew—for him.

Slowly, he let her slide back down to the ground. "Without horses, it will be a difficult journey, but there is a town within a day's walk, I think. We shall get new mounts there." He glanced up at the sky, his eyes narrowing, and Marion followed his gaze. After so much clear weather, they were due for rain, and from the looks of the darkening clouds overhead, it would come soon. With a low oath, he led her into the woods.

They stayed among the trees near the edge of the forest, close enough to the road to keep their bearings, but under cover of the oaks and beeches. They walked along in silence, each brooding over what had happened, each grieving for their dead as they picked their way among the heavy undergrowth.

They had gone perhaps a mile before Marion's numbness finally wore off. One moment she was moving along, following Dunstan's long strides with her own smaller steps, and then suddenly, she was on her hands and knees in the dirt, retching.

Of course, there was naught that could rise from her empty stomach, but still she knelt there, heaving and crying until Dunstan crouched beside her. The touch of his hand, awkwardly stroking her brow, made her weep more piteously, for she knew that if not for her, he would not be suffering so.

"My fault," she gasped. "'Tis all my fault."

"Nay." His voice was low and gruff.

"Yes! They are all dead because of me."

"Nay," Dunstan countered, more insistent now, but Marion would not be comforted.

"You do not understand," she said. "My uncle did it. He killed them all."

"Stop it!" Dunstan's hands grasped her shoulders, and she lifted her head to look at the handsome features that were now twisted into a fierce grimace. "Stop this nonsense about your uncle. I know not who murdered my men, but your uncle would have no reason to do the deed. As far as I know, he has done nothing, to you or anyone else. And until you can prove aught else, give me no woman's prattle about vague dreads!"

"You do not understand," Marion said softly. She raised her hands to her face, burying her swollen eyes in her palms, trying desperately to regain control of herself. When she finally lifted her head, he was still there, his green eyes intent upon her, his mouth a tight line.

Nothing showed in his face, and yet, she could sense his concern for her. She knew, without seeing it, that something blazed inside of Dunstan de Burgh, something besides grief and anger and frustration. Hope, like some long-forgotten strain of music, threaded its way into her heart. Perhaps, if she told him . . .

"I remember now," she said brokenly. "I remember everything."

Why should he believe her?

Dunstan had listened to the wren as she sat with head bent, her eyes trained upon the hands folded neatly in her lap while she recounted the miraculous return of her missing memory. And he could not countenance it. By faith, the woman had lied to him time and time again. Why should this new, fantastic tale be any different? And yet something in her calm delivery made him more inclined to trust her—this time.

By faith, he did not need this nonsense! Dunstan rubbed the back of his neck, but the tension there seemed to have moved to his head, making it difficult to concentrate. And concentrate he must, for their very lives depended upon it. For the millionth time, he cursed this wretched errand and the woman he must escort home. His men were murdered, and he could not pursue the killers because he was burdened with a maddening female!

They were alone and defenseless in the middle of nowhere, without even mounts to make an escape. And since his train had been slaughtered by no ordinary robbers, Dunstan had to face the possibility that whoever had done it could be out for more blood. He looked over his shoulder, knowing full well that they might be followed, even now. Although he had a fairly good idea of where they were, he was not certain how far away Wisborough lay. The wren was doing her best, but they were not making good time, and if the rain started . . .

Dunstan closed his eyes against the throbbing in his temple. He needed to get her safely delivered to Baddersly as soon as possible so that he could go back to Wessex and avenge the deaths of his people. Now, more than ever, he worried about his absence from his holdings. And now, more than ever, he needed to be up and on the move instead of listening to fanciful stories from a troublesome piece of baggage.

"You do not believe me." The husky tone of her accusation pricked him, and he grunted.

"I will speak to your uncle myself, as soon as we arrive," he said, neither confirming nor denying her statement.

She rose angrily to her feet, that beautiful mane of dark curls flying about her, and Dunstan was pleased to see the fire in her spark to life again. He did not like it when she knelt upon the ground, weeping and retching. It bothered him at some level that he did not care to explore. And he had enough problems right now without feeling someone else's pain more acutely than his own.

"You do not understand, Dunstan," she said, pointing a dainty finger at him. "The man slaughtered my train, and now he has done the same to yours! If you take me there, he will kill me!"

"Show me the proof!" Dunstan growled, resting his hands upon his hips. "What evidence have you that he is responsible for what happened at the camp? Tell me what his arrows look like. I have the one that killed a sentry in my pack, and we shall see whether it matches."

Marion frowned, her lovely mouth tipping downward, and Dunstan realized he would much rather draw a smile from her than argue. But he had a mission to accomplish and murder to investigate, and he could hardly credit the charges of one foolish female, however appealing she might be.

She poked his mailed chest with her finger. "You are being as stupid and stubborn as the king when faced with your claims about your neighbor. You should know better than any that an enemy may take many guises."

Dunstan scowled at the mention of the bastard who harried him, and something niggled at his mind, just out of reach. He had no time for further disagreements, however. Reaching out, he grasped her arms tightly and opened his mouth to tell her to cease her prattle, but as soon as he touched her, the words failed him. She was flushed with anger, her cheeks rosy, her dark eyes wide, and her lips were parted slightly. Suddenly, he wanted her so badly that he could taste it.

He wanted to taste *her*. He wanted to thrust his tongue into her mouth and his fists into her hair. He wanted to pull her up against him and ease the ache in his loins. He wanted to see her eyes hazy with desire and feel her tremble beneath his hands.

He wanted her.

Dunstan told himself it was the memory of the camp, the brush with death, that made him want to seize life, however briefly. But as he stared down at her, he knew that the need plaguing him could be assuaged by no other woman. He wanted only this one. Now.

She was staring up at him like a trapped doe, and he could hear her breathing, quick and shallow. Dimly, he suspected that his own was coming loud and harsh. Tightening his grip on her arms, Dunstan tried to gain control of himself, but only when she flinched under his hold did his mind clear enough to return to him. In that instant, the flashing, hot moment was gone, the spell broken.

She blinked, as if suddenly released from some dark place—perhaps the same that had possessed him. "Dunstan de Burgh! Must you always bruise me?" she complained shakily.

He let go of her. "Come, we must be off," he said roughly. Turning away, he strode forward without even waiting to see if she followed. His groin ached so painfully that he felt like seeing to himself. That would certainly send the wren scurrying for cover, he thought grimly. His lips curved at the image of touching himself in front of her, but his amusement fled swiftly, to be replaced by a swift surge of blood rushing through his body, heating him anew. By faith, of all the women in the land, why did this single female affect him so?

Clenching his jaw, Dunstan marched forward. To him, this bizarre attraction to one insignificant female was simply one more complication for which he had no time. Mentally, he tried to calculate how many more days he would have to spend in her company. If they could just reach Wisborough today, then he could find horses for them and perhaps an inn where they could spend the night. He would welcome a warm, soft bed in which to rest his bones. Unbidden, an image of Marion stretched out upon a feather tick, with her body loosely gowned and her hair spread out around her, came to his mind.

Dunstan swore aloud and turned his head round to glare at her.

She was walking with head bent, despair etched across her usually composed features, and Dunstan felt a sharp pain inside himself, as if someone had lanced a wound he did not remember taking. He shuddered for a moment, uncharacteristic indecision making him pause. Then, with a growl of annoyance, he reached out, unable to stop himself from touching her.

He saw her swift glance of surprise, those great dark eyes of hers wide and rich as the finest velvet, as he took her hand. He had only meant to comfort her, but the moment his ungloved fingers contacted the butter-soft leather that covered her own, the air sizzled between them as if a storm were brewing. Her dark gaze flew to his again, startlement followed swiftly by a heart-stopping languor that made him want to toss her down upon a bed of grass and thrust into her.

She wanted him, too.

The thought sent his head reeling, but all the connotations were lost in the shrill call of a bird overhead. Distractions. Complications. Dunstan thought of his dead men and cursed himself for a randy fool. Like as not, he would find his pleasure followed by an arrow in the back when his enemies discovered him taking his leisure upon her. And the wren... As much as he desired her, he did not want her life lost because of his own carelessness.

Dunstan dropped her hand, swearing silently this time, and trudged on.

Chapter Ten

Marion huddled in her blanket, watching Dunstan under lowered lashes. They had spoken little during the day's long, tiring march. She had nursed her anger, and he had kept his thoughts to himself. Like a wolf, he had prowled restlessly forward, growling under his breath and maintaining his distance, except for a few odd occasions when he had suddenly reached out to her. At those moments, Marion could have sworn she saw dark desire flashing in his forest eyes.

She told herself she was imagining things.

The man had enough on his mind, between his grief and trying to keep them alive, without her putting dangerous thoughts in his head. Besides, he did not even like her. He did not even believe her. That stung, and Marion swallowed against a lump rising in her throat. His disbelief stood between them like one of Campion's walls—tall, cold and impregnable.

Although it pained her, Marion was not really surprised by the Wolf's attitude. That he had listened to her story at all was a small wonder. Dunstan de Burgh was not a man for half-truths or half measures. He liked things plain and simple, and with a sad smile, Marion knew her life could hardly be described in those terms.

Exhaustion rolled over her aching body in waves, threatening to drown her, but she struggled against it. Focusing on Dunstan, she watched him, marking with her eyes the dark spill of his hair, the high curve of his cheek, the muscled contours of his great body. And slowly, like a nameless fever, the strange heat that sparked between them roused her flagging body.

He would not light a fire, so they had eaten what food they had packed and made their bed at the foot of some trees. He sat leaning against a trunk, his legs spread before him and his eyes closed, and Marion felt a sweet familiarity at the sight. She concentrated on details to take with her when she left him: his thick lashes in repose against his skin and the shape of his hands, large but gentle, their backs dusted with hair.

Marion swallowed back a sound of shock at the sudden rise of her bodily humors. What was it about his hands that made her feel like shivering? She wondered if the rest of his body was covered with that fine coat of hair. She had never seen any part of his flesh uncovered, save for his hands. Perhaps that was why they seemed so exciting to her. They were naked without his gauntlets, and they had the power to daze her with one touch.

Tearing her gaze away from his fingers, Marion noted the rise and fall of his massive chest and wondered how soon he would be asleep. Despite her aching feet and tired body, she had to stay awake until she was certain that he slept, for it was then that she meant to make her escape.

The thought held no joy for her, only a numbing inevitability. Where once she would have been thrilled to outwit him, now Marion only felt an absurd longing for what could not be. Ironically, of all the pain that fought for a hold upon her, the impending loss of Dunstan was uppermost. The return of her memory made all her griefs fresh and new, from the deaths of her parents to the slaughter of her train, but her love for the Wolf was so overwhelming that to leave him would cut more deeply than aught else. Yet she could hardly stay with him just to be delivered to her enemy.

No matter how much she loved him, Marion refused to die needlessly for him.

And now, knowing the truth about her uncle, she was certain that death awaited her at Baddersly. Although she could not prove that Harold Peasely was responsible for last night's slaughter, she knew for certain that he had murdered her own train that autumn morn, a lifetime ago, when she had sought to leave him.

Closing her eyes, Marion called back those days after the death of her parents when she had been grief-stricken and lonely. In the bleak years that followed, she had become a shadow of herself, isolated and fearful of her uncle's increasingly difficult moods and violent behavior.

Like someone removed, Marion thought of the woman she had been then and wanted to weep for her. That woman could not have held her own against the de Burgh brothers, and she would never have had the courage to argue with the Wolf of Wessex. If he had slammed her up against a tree, pinning her with his body and his dark green gaze, she would have fainted away.

With a wry smile, Marion thought perhaps it was best that she had lost her memory, for how else would she have found this new woman inside herself? She closed her eyes to find an image of Dunstan forming in her mind, warming her even in the chill of the night. If she were truly brave, she would offer herself up to the Wolf and let him devour her. . . .

Marion jerked awake and stared across at Dunstan's shadowed form in the darkness. How long had she dozed? She cursed her weary body as she scanned the blackness that surrounded them, but perhaps it was not too late to make her escape. Listening to the Wolf's breathing, low and even, Marion waited, her own breath caught perilously, until she was sure he was asleep. Then she rose, slowly and stealthily, to make her departure.

Maybe this time he would not follow her. After all, he was needed back at Wessex, and had more pressing concerns than one wayward woman. If only he would just let her go and get on with his life... Marion turned as quietly as possible and took a step away from him.

"Going somewhere, wren?"

Marion jumped a good foot at the question, which emanated from the base of the tree where Dunstan lounged in the blackness. "I was...just thirsty," she said. "Where did you put the flagon of water?"

"'Tis beside you," he snapped, and Marion noted the underlying anger in his tone. Obviously, he did not believe her. She rooted noisily for the vessel, wondering how she was ever going to get away from him when he seemed never to sleep or let her out of his sight. Taking a long swallow, she put the drink away, and glared at him across the darkness. The man was infuriating.

"Remember, Marion—you have made your last escape from me," Dunstan said suddenly, his voice harsh with warning.

It was on the tip of her tongue to argue, but she had no desire to be trussed up and hauled back to Baddersly on the Wolf's shoulder. And she would put nothing past Dunstan when he was in one of his moods. Let him think that she heeded him well; then she would do as she pleased.

"Yes, Dunstan," she said meekly.

He grunted, incredulity evident in the sound, and Marion fought a smile. Apparently, he accepted her agreement, however, for when he spoke again his tone was gentler. "I shall judge myself just what kind of man this uncle of yours may be. You have no need to fear, wren, for I will not let anyone kill you."

The gruff assurance was a small concession, but Marion's heart swelled. She loved him so much that she was surprised he could not see it, rising up to overflow her and wash over him in the night. If only he would believe her... If only things were different...

"Now, come. Lie with me," Dunstan said softly, extending his hand.

Taking his words at face value, Marion made a small sound of startlement as her body responded with a dizzying assent. Although she had only vague ideas of what went on between a man and a woman, she felt helpless to deny such an invitation. The Wolf of Wessex wanted her? Marion leaned forward eagerly, her love for him overriding her modesty, her caution and her good sense.

The hiss of Dunstan's surprise rang out loudly in the stillness. "Make your bed here beside me, wren, and get some sleep," he ordered harshly. Disappointment flooded Marion as she realized her mistake. He did not want her to lie with him; he wanted her to lie near him—probably so he could prevent any further escapes. For some reason, the knowledge made the backs of her eyelids prick with pressure.

Of all the foolishness! She had seen enough death and destruction this day to last her a lifetime, and yet she would weep because Dunstan de Burgh was not going to kiss her? Marion smiled crookedly, glad that he could not see her features. It was too dark for that, but she could still make out his arm, reaching toward her.

Gathering up her blanket obediently, Marion inched forward, then hesitated. His hand was still outstretched, waiting, and without a thought about it, Marion stripped off her glove and placed her bare hand in his.

It was wonderful. His fingers were so warm and strong. She had known that, of course, but she could never have guessed at the way his skin would feel against her own—

delightfully rough and different, firm but gentle. She wanted to rub her palm against his in a soft caress.

He growled her name, so low and impatiently that it startled her, and Marion lifted her head, trying to see his face in the blackness. He said nothing more, but she could hear his breath, rapid as her own tripping heartbeat. A long minute passed by, and then another.

"Go to sleep," Dunstan finally ordered gruffly. He released her, and Marion knew a moment's regret, but she felt good, too. She had touched him, really touched him, her skin to his, and now she could take the memory of it with her when she left. Nestling down beside him as he leaned against the tree, Marion pulled the cover over her and closed her eyes.

Dunstan's heat reached out to her, and she fought the urge to doze once again in the warm shelter of his body, for she was still determined to escape. After all, the man had to sleep sometime, and when he did, she wanted to be ready. Stifling a great yawn, Marion told herself to stay awake, but before she knew it, her mind was drifting, the image of the Wolf's hand appearing before her eyes.

Was it only yesterday when she had been shocked at spending the night alone with him? Now, she would willingly go into his arms, if he would but ask her. Smiling, Marion dreamed of kissing the dark hairs that were scattered across his skin, the long fingers that held such strength and the roughened palm that had touched her own.

The rain woke her. It began dripping down through the leaves around dawn, striking her face until she opened her eyes. Still groggy with sleep, Marion took a few minutes to realize where she was, but when she glanced around, Dunstan was already up, hurriedly preparing for another march. Marion felt like groaning aloud—or throwing something at him.

The prospect of another day of walking filled her with loathing. Her body ached, her feet were blistered, and she longed for nothing more than a soft bed where she could lay her head. Instead, she was stuck in the middle of nowhere with the Wolf of Wessex, who, from the looks of him, was even grumpier than usual.

A steady drizzle continued, obscuring the line of the road and forcing them to leave the cover of the trees, which ill suited Dunstan. After a string of low oaths, he said they should reach Wisborough soon, but as every new hill rose and fell before them, Marion began to wonder. And even the promise of approaching a village could not raise her spirits, for each step took them closer to Baddersly.

Although she had not surrendered her hopes for escape, Marion did not know how to get away in the mess that the world had become. She could barely keep her footing on the slick grass and muddy hollows. As the morning wore on, she was soaked to the bone, wet through cloak and gown and shift and skin—wet, tired and miserable.

Knight that he was, Dunstan plodded on as though oblivious to the conditions that tortured her, and his stoic silence added to her frustration. The only time he even acknowledged her existence was when she slipped. Then a strong arm would shoot out to steady her, but gradually those gestures began to resemble impatient tugs rather than chivalrous assistance.

The temper that Marion had only recently discovered in herself began to make itself known, urging her to stomp along in an ungainly manner that could not match the Wolf's long, graceful strides. Naturally, she slid again, prevented from a tumble into a puddle only by a swift, bone-crunching grip on her elbow.

She shook it off, stopped still right where she was and let the rain pelt her sodden cloak. For a long moment, she stood watching as Dunstan trudged on ahead. Then, suddenly, he turned around to glare at her, a question in his shadowed eyes. Her first thought was that the insufferable man still looked as handsome as ever, even with water matting his dark hair to his head and dripping down his broad cheekbones past that incredible mouth.

Marion's anger dimmed somewhat as helpless, hopeless love for him welled up in her, but she tried on one of his infamous grimaces and held her ground. "I am surprised, Dunstan de Burgh, that you do not pull out a length of rope, tie me to you and drag me along like chattel."

His positively blank look told her that he was oblivious to his less than tender treatment of her. Against her will, Marion's heart melted some more. She had to force her lips into a scowl. "Dunstan, I am a mass of bruises from your rough handling! Despite what you may think of me, I am a woman, and I am not made of leather and stone."

A long silence followed in which his forest eyes seemed to burn into her. "Believe me, wren," he finally said, his voice low and rough. "I am well aware that you are a woman."

His tone made Marion catch her breath, but she told herself not to read anything into it. How often had she imagined that Dunstan de Burgh was noticing her? More times than she could count, and naught, so far, had come from it. She steeled herself against the darkening of his gaze. "Then quit grabbing me!"

His eyes narrowed, and he gave her that look that said she was a woman all right—a baffling one. "You want me to let you fall headfirst into a ditch?"

"No."

He put his hands on his hips. "Well, then, Marion, what exactly do you want?" The condescending tone that told her he thought her naught but a foolish female made her temper flare anew.

"What do I want? I will tell you what I want, Dunstan de Burgh, baron of Wessex. I want this to stop—all of this," she said, raising a hand to encompass the surrounding area. "And right now. Why should I trudge along in this rain on a march to my own death? It is bad enough that you are going to deliver me into the hands of a murderer, but must you torture me first?"

Marion could see the swift rise of irritation in the tightening of his mouth, but she went on. "Let us just turn around, Dunstan, for the love of God! Take me to Campion or to Wessex or the nearest village. Or just leave me here! Go on. Go on about your business," she said, moving her hand in a shooing gesture.

"Go on about your business and tell everyone that I died along with your train. It will hurt you naught to tell this small falsehood. And it will save my life!"

"My father—" Dunstan began, a grimace on his face, but Marion did not let him continue.

"Your father cares not what becomes of me. And my uncle will be overjoyed to learn of my demise. 'Twill save him the trouble of murdering me, and he will take all my lands in celebration. May he have joy of them." Worn-out and dejected, she stared at Dunstan, hoping against hope for some sign of agreement.

"Are you finished?" he growled at her, his jaw clenched.

"No, I am not." Marion plopped down upon a nearby rock. "I am staying right here. Go on, now," she said, shooing him away again as she would a pesky fly. "And leave me be."

He was not amused. "If you persist, Marion, I will be forced to carry you over my shoulder, and if you think you are miserable now, bumping along against my back is not going to be an improvement."

With a soft curse, borrowed from Dunstan's vast store, Marion rose and huffed past him as best she could. They had veered away from the road along some kind of sheep track, and her slippers were sticking in the ooze. It made a dignified display of contempt difficult, but she continued on, ignoring the towering figure that caught up with her effortlessly.

When they reached a small rise, Dunstan lifted his hand to his eyes, shielding them from the rain as was his habit, to have a look below. Marion did the same, and to her surprise, this time she saw something down in the hollow.

"Look there!" she said, pointing excitedly. "What is it?"

"A shepherd's hut, perhaps," Dunstan mused under his breath. "It does not look like much, but mayhap it will give us shelter from the storm."

Shelter! Marion rushed forward eagerly, but when she did, one slipper caught in the ooze and she fell, facefirst, onto the soggy ground. She came up sputtering to the sound of the Wolf's laughter. It rang out, deep and rich, and normally it would have touched her very heart. But as she lifted herself from the wet, clinging dirt of the path, Marion was in no mood to admire anything about Dunstan de Burgh.

"You . . . you bugger!" she cried, echoing a word she had heard from his brothers. Anger flaring brightly, she shoved at his mailed chest with all of her might. Of course, her puny efforts did little but leave muddy marks on the front of his tunic—and send her careening backward.

This time, between gulps of laughter, he reached out to halt her fall, but suddenly the ground upon which she stood gave way and Marion's feet dropped. She saw Dunstan's wide-eyed look of surprise, and then they were both rolling and sliding down the muddy slope to the bottom of the hill.

Unhurt, Marion ended up on her back in a puddle at the base of the rise, but before she could catch her breath, Dunstan landed with a thud on top of her, knocking the wind from her body. She opened her eyes to see his face above hers, the rain slashing down all around them and dripping from his face. His dark hair hung in wet ribbons, his green gaze focused intently upon her.

Marion's first thought was that he was crushing her, his great form bearing down on her with the weight of two men. Just as she opened her mouth to protest, however, she realized that he had shifted his mass somehow, allowing her to gulp in some air. He was up on his elbows, but still lying upon her. With that recognition came the discovery that his body felt extremely good just where it was. She shut her mouth.

Rather bewildered, she looked up at him, and Dunstan caught her gaze, his green eyes damp and compelling. For a long moment, neither of them breathed as whatever strange forces worked between them sprang to life. Marion stilled, her humors rising feverishly while he hovered over her, his massive figure covering her own tiny one. Dunstan's eyes darkened, unfathomable.

"'Tis time for the reckoning between us, Marion," he growled. And then he lowered his head.

Dunstan's mouth came down upon hers, hot and frantic. Her memory now intact, Marion knew that she had never been kissed before, and this was hardly what she had expected. Dunstan, true to his nature, was not tender but demanding, and she felt a tingle of fear that the Wolf would devour her.

She parted her lips to protest, but swallowed it in shocked surprise when his tongue thrust into her mouth. It swept over her teeth, searching, marking and claiming, until Marion was stunned, not only at the Wolf's actions, but at her own reaction. Her body tightened, her nipples hardening against his massive chest and her thighs lifting, as if endowed with a will of their own, toward his.

The rain pelted down, sluicing around her in its own wild fury, but it was nothing compared to the tempest raging between them. Marion felt as if she had spent her entire life sleepwalking, unaware of this whole world of passion and feeling, and now she was alive, every inch of her wet skin animated and seeking his.

Heat, welcome and wonderful, seeped through the water to rouse her body to a frenzied pitch, and Marion reveled in it. She clutched at his tunic, hanging on for her very life as he swept her away on a maelstrom of liquid fire. A moan escaped her, and he answered by pressing his lower body into hers. His hand wound into her hair, forcing her head back so that he could thrust more deeply into her mouth.

Tentatively, Marion ran her tongue along his lips, and Dunstan released a feral growl of pleasure that sent her reeling with breathless excitement. Lost in the tumult of sensation, she did not even notice the lightning cracking above them, followed by an answering boom of thunder, but suddenly Dunstan tore his mouth from hers to look up at the sky.

She whimpered, bereft at the loss of him until he glanced back down at her. "Come, we must get inside," he ordered roughly. Dazed, Marion simply lay there, staring up at him, unable to move while he rose swiftly. Then, with ridiculous ease, he lifted her into his arms and headed toward the shepherd's croft. Her heart pounded so furiously that she thought she might faint, but she knew that was something the old Marion would do.

The new Marion wrapped her arms around Dunstan's neck and clung shamelessly. The rain, which had been an uncomfortable nuisance all day, abruptly became exhilarating. Marion lifted her face toward the chill water that washed over them, cleansing them in a natural bath, while Dunstan's long strides carried them across the sodden grass.

A bolt of lightning streaked through the black sky, lighting the area with an eerie glow that heightened Marion's sense of unreality. Was she deep in a vivid dream, or was she really being carried by the Wolf through a savage storm, the wind pounding drops against them, soaking their skin and sliding off their wet bodies in great rivulets?

Thunder reverberated with a ferocity that seemed to shake the very earth, and Marion looked up at the Wolf's handsome face. His jaw was clenched, his features set with an intensity she had never seen, and she wondered if the warring elements were but a pale echo of what raged between the two of them. She fought back a shudder of anxiety.

The hut looked deserted, and the plot of land beside it overgrown. Marion caught a glimpse of an old well, and then she was whisked inside, where a rotting stack of wood stood in a corner near a blackened fireplace, promising warmth, and a straw bed took up half of the space. Although it smelled dank and musty, the place was relatively clean, and, more important, it was dry. At one time, Marion might have protested such a tiny, dusty and smelly abode, but right now, anything with a roof seemed like heaven.

"Abandoned," Dunstan muttered. Then he flashed her a genuine, one-of-a-kind smile that made her grateful that he still carried her. Otherwise, she was certain her bones would have dissolved at the sight of those fine, white teeth, displayed so wickedly. He let her down slowly, sliding her against his body in an exotic motion that threatened her ability to stand, but when she tested her legs, she was astounded to find that they could support her.

Leaving her with a burning look, Dunstan knelt to make a fire, and, suddenly cold without him, Marion rubbed her arms futilely as water dripped from her to the thirsty packed earth below.

"You had better get out of those wet clothes," he said over his shoulder. "We will lay them out as best we can here to dry." He was right, of course; the sodden material was already chilling her. And yet the idea of removing her gown in the presence of Dunstan de Burgh was dismaying, to say the least, especially in the closeness of the hut. Even the new Marion could not do it.

With a sigh, she struggled out of her clinging cloak and hung it on a rough spot in the wall. Although she immediately felt lighter, her gown was still hanging on her heavily, its damp folds pressing into her and making the drafts in the croft bite more sharply.

Hearing the welcome hiss of wood catching, Marion turned toward the promise of a blaze. Instead of greeting it readily, however, she froze where she stood, a small shocked noise escaping her tightened throat.

Apparently, Dunstan moved much faster than she, for he had already hung up his cloak and his tunic. His sword and his mail were set aside, and as Marion watched in stunned surprise, he calmly removed his braies.

The sight of the his broad back, gleaming with moisture, and his buttocks below, narrow and steely, made her sway on her feet. Pressing hands to her scalded cheeks, she gasped in alarm when he turned to face her, and the sound became a strangled moan as the Wolf of Wessex stood before her totally, utterly naked.

For long moments, Marion could only stare at his gigantic male body. She had never seen so much skin in her life. It stretched taut over bulging muscles, glistened with the remnants of the downpour and puckered in places where fiendish-looking scars marked him. His shoulders alone were massive, his chest, too. It was incredibly wide and covered with dark hair that trailed down to his groin, where his man part lay in a thicket.

As Marion gaped, astonished, it rose up, growing before her eyes, as if gifted with a life of its own, until it was huge and erect. Mercy! Her gaze flew to his face, and she saw that smile that was not quite a smile, lifting the corners of Dunstan's mouth while his eyes darkened ominously.

No little afraid of the look in those eyes, and of the bare form of the man who possessed them, Marion backed away until she was pressed against the side of the hut and leaned into it, grateful for support. With difficulty, she found her voice.

"Dunstan! What are you about?" she squeaked.

"I was about getting myself warm and dry," he answered in a low, rough voice, "until you distracted me, wren." Totally unashamed of his nudity, Dunstan put his hands on his narrow hips and assessed her slowly, his gaze glinting hotly over every inch of her in a way that made her burn with an answering fire.

"And I guess I shall have to take you in hand so that you may do the same."

Chapter Eleven

Marion found herself staring at the moist whorl of hair on Dunstan's massive chest, which led downward, inexorably, to the dark thatch at his thighs and the huge member that was rooted there. Breathless and weak, she wrenched her gaze up to his face, only to find his eyes gleaming with a feral light, his lips curved in a wicked smile.

He reminded her forcibly of a wolf contemplating its prey.

He took a step forward. Shaking her head, Marion tried to back away but she felt the rough wall of the hut behind her. "I cannot undress here...with you," she choked.

"Then I shall have to do it for you," he said, grinning at her in that smug de Burgh manner that she had come to know so well from his brothers. He took another step, moving perilously close in the small confines of the hut.

"No!" Marion shifted aside. She looked around frantically, knowing that there was nowhere to go, nowhere on earth that the Wolf could not find her, and then she felt a strange sense of resignation. To run was ridiculous, to argue futile. Dunstan had stripped her of choices; she did not wish him to take her clothes, as well. "I shall do it."

"Good," he said simply. As if to give her the strength

to begin, he turned away and knelt to feed the budding fire. Marion noticed how the glow cast his smooth, muscled body in gold and she was forced to admit that he was more beautiful than any man had the right to be. Although Marion knew she had no business admiring him, she could not help it. Her mind told her to glance away; her body had other ideas.

It leaned forward as if reaching for him of its own accord. Her breasts grew taut, her nipples hard as they strained against the wet linen of her shift. The sodden heaviness of her clothes, a miserable nuisance only moments before, now seemed an exotic weight, rubbing and clinging to her flesh. Abruptly she wondered how it would feel to run her fingers down the contours of his back. A sound escaped her, of shame or torment or desire, she was not quite sure. His eyes flicked up to her.

"Well?" The word held a wealth of impatience, and Marion hurried to keep the Wolf at bay. Turning around, she fumbled clumsily with her bodice, fingers shaking. She pulled at her gown, tugging at the wet material helplessly until it was whisked over her head with sudden ease. Whirling, she found Dunstan standing only a handbreadth from her, his eyes alive with green fire, his mouth wearing that smile that was not a smile, his chest so close she could reach out and touch it—if she dared.

"Dunstan...please..." she whispered, uncomfortable with the proximity of his naked body, yet, paradoxically, wanting him nearer.

"Do you need more help?" he asked, his normally husky voice even deeper and rougher than usual. Although Marion shook her head slowly, he knelt before her and put his hand on her leg.

Mercy! When his fingers brushed against the bare flesh at the top of her hose, Marion nearly jumped. Although she was astonished by his boldness, Dunstan bent to his task as if it were not a shocking intimacy. After rolling down the wet material, his callused hands slid down her calf, lifted her foot and ran over her toes.

It was such a simple thing really, a kindly service that one person would perform for another, Marion told herself, and yet she found her knees growing weak. Although Dunstan's movements were measured and controlled, she sensed the intensity in him. It was there, just below the civilized surface... waiting. Dizzily, Marion wondered if he would again unleash the beast that she had seen outside, fierce and plundering. And if he did, would she recoil or rejoice?

Just when Marion thought she might collapse from the heady thrill of his touch, Dunstan straightened slowly, his hands skimming to the hem of her shift. "No! Not that, too!" she cried. In embarrassed panic, Marion struggled to hold on to it, but her paltry efforts were useless. In an instant, her arms were lifted over her head and her only covering was gone. She was naked, and Dunstan, clutching her undergarment in his hand, was staring at her.

It was not so much the lack of clothing that disturbed her, for she was used to sleeping nude, as was the norm. However, it was one thing to crawl between the sheets in this state; it was quite another to stand before a man in nothing but her flesh.

But she did, and she did not cringe. There was nowhere to hide, and nothing to drape over herself, for she knew all her things were soaking wet. If Dunstan wished to see her, there was naught she could do about it. Painfully aware of all her faults, Marion suspected that the Wolf would soon tire of his view, anyway.

In the meantime, Marion became absurdly concerned with her hair drying in its unruly waves. She lifted a hand to her head, but the sharp hiss of the Wolf's indrawn breath made her drop it back to her side.

He was gazing at her with an fierceness that was nearly frightening. His eyes had darkened in that manner she had come to associate with desire, but Marion sensed it was something stronger than that. He looked . . . hungry. Uneasiness trickled up her spine, along with a budding excitement. She rubbed her arms warily.

"Day of God, wren. You are beautiful." The words rushed from his wonderful mouth in a soft torrent, stunning her, for Dunstan spoke little. And Dunstan never lied. "Are you cold?"

Dazed by the compliment, Marion just stared at him. When she did not answer, he put aside her shift and moved toward his leather pouch. To her amazement, he pulled out a cover and threw it across her shoulders.

Released from her trance, Marion found her voice and used it. "Dunstan de Burgh! You had a dry blanket, and you made me stand here with nothing on!" Outraged, she balled a hand into a fist and thumped his chest. It was hard as stone.

Smiling wickedly, Dunstan caught her hand. "In truth, 'tis only a loan, for we must use it on the bed," he said with a nod toward the straw mattress. "I would not vouch for the cleanliness of our nest."

Marion stilled, stunned by the notion that Dunstan planned to take the blanket from her—and by his reference to "our nest." Were they to share the bed? Surely he did not want to sleep now. Although the hut was dim because of the storm that howled around it, she judged it to be morning still. "But 'tis broad day!" she protested.

Although Dunstan did not reply, his lips turned up at the corners, and his eyes gleamed like a deep forest, lush and welcoming. Glancing nervously at the narrow bed, Marion stepped back, but he followed, his fingers tightening upon her wrist. She bumped into the hut, and the blanket slipped, exposing her shoulders.

Dunstan stared at them. "I care not for the time," he said roughly. Even though Marion could move no farther, he came closer, stopping only when his huge body nearly touched her own. Putting a hand to the wall beside her head, he leaned forward and bent his head, that de Burgh hair, darker and richer than sable, falling forward.

"'Tis time for our reckoning, Marion," he whispered. He loomed over her, so big, so beautiful and so assured that she could only stare up at him wide-eyed. "I have wanted you ever since you fell out of that tree into my arms. You have bewitched me, wren, just as surely as you did my brothers, and I can resist you no more. Enchantress..."

Alarmed by his speech, Marion felt compelled to protest. "I am no enchantress, Dunstan!" she said. "I am but a simple female—short, rather plain and past marriageable age."

"Tell that to my brothers," Dunstan replied with sudden ferocity, his eyes glinting brightly.

"Your brothers think upon me as a sister!" Marion cried.

Smiling in a manner that told her that, as usual, he did not quite believe her, Dunstan released her wrist and lifted his hand to her shoulder. Extending one finger, he ran it slowly along the edge of the blanket, across her arm and over the uppermost curve of her chest. The blanket drifted slightly, and Marion drew in a breath, then watched in fascination as his dark skin slid across hers again. His finger made its way over the swelling of one breast, then the other, before it slipped underneath the fabric.

Marion shivered.

"Ah, yes. Tremble for me, wren," Dunstan said, his face suddenly dark with passion. "I want you trembling beneath me as I fill you." His eyes took on a feral gleam, his lips parting slightly as if he could already taste his prey, and Marion realized that whatever he wanted, she could not gainsay him.

Whether a convent or death or exile awaited her, what use to keep her maiden's virtue? She loved Dunstan de Burgh with every breath of her body, and whether sinful or no, she would take this chance to know him as a woman. Any moment now she might wake up to find this all a dream, a frenzied fantasy brought on by the long, wet march and her love for the man before her. Why not glory in it?

Marion was disinclined to let go of this vision without savoring each moment. Gathering her courage, she reached out and laid her palm against the soft matting of hair upon his chest.

The Wolf growled a low sound of encouragement as his hand moved into her hair to drag her face to his. He thrust his tongue into her mouth, deep and hot, in a kiss that acknowledged her surrender. Between them, the blanket slipped from her lifeless fingers, and their naked bodies came together.

It was incredible. The same wild, drowning sensation that Dunstan had conjured out in the rain, rushed through her, and Marion welcomed it. She lifted her arms and circled his neck, enjoying the strange feel of her bare breasts pressing into his hard chest. His hands ran down her back, closed over her buttocks and then lifted her to meet him.

Marion felt the floor drop away and the dizzying pressure of his manhood as he fitted her to him at the same time that he deepened his kiss, his mouth hot and open upon hers, devouring her. She had no idea how long she clung to him breathlessly, adrift in a maelstrom of passion, but eventually she became aware that Dunstan was lifting her legs to his hips. Then, he slid an arm around her and bent, with amazing ease, to pick up the blanket.

Still holding her, Dunstan tossed the material over the straw and fell onto the mattress. With a gasp, Marion took some of his great weight before he settled himself over her.

Then he was upon her, his heat torching her skin, his callused palms running over her as his lips reclaimed hers. He cupped her breasts, kneading and lifting, rubbing the nipples with his thumbs until Marion whimpered and shivered.

"Ah, wren. Ah, yes," Dunstan muttered before his hand moved lower, caressing her thighs and closing tightly around her buttocks. Blinking up at him, Marion saw that his handsome face looked dark and fierce in the dim glow of the fire. It gleamed off a lock of drying hair that fell across his cheek, and her blood sang in her ears at the sight of him, beautiful and untamed.

When he touched her between her legs, Marion flinched at the contact, but he murmured a rough assurance in her ear. "Yes, wren, I must... Ah, God, you are already wet." And it was true, though where the moisture came from, Marion had no idea. It was there, and he was spreading it on her, stroking her with his great, callused hand. Who would ever have imagined such a thing? As if of their own accord, Marion's hips lifted to his questing touch, and then one of his large, long fingers slipped inside her.

Marion gasped at the bizarre intimacy. He probed her, and she let him, but just as she was becoming accustomed to the foreign presence, Dunstan removed it and settled himself between her thighs. With a shock, she realized that he was guiding himself into her now, and she was dizzy with a mixture of shock and forbidden pleasure.

To think of Dunstan de Burgh inside her body. It was as startling as it was seductive, and then he was entering her, huge and hard, and Marion felt too full of him. She cried out, and he stopped his uncomfortable progress. His breath was a harsh rhythm above her, his face taut, his eyes closed. Had she done something wrong? She had no idea how to ease this increasingly painful union.

"Ah, Marion, Marion," he said, his voice catching oddly. "You are a maid."

"Of course," she murmured, confused by his words.

"Ah, God, I did not…" Dunstan sucked in air in a low hiss. "I must go deeper, wren," he muttered, and she realized that he was gritting his teeth, as if he, too, were suffering.

"No!" Marion protested, alarmed.

"Yes. Yes, take all of me, wren." The speech seemed torn from his throat, then he surged forward, and pain seared through her like a hot lance. Marion cried out with the force of it, sure that he had rent her asunder.

"Day of God," Dunstan muttered. As she stared up at him in mute horror, he opened his eyes and met her accusing gaze. "Ah, wren, do not look at me like that. I would make you tremble again." He lifted a handful of her hair and ran his fingers through its thickness. "I *will* make you tremble again for me. Only me."

Growling out the promise, Dunstan moved inside of her, and Marion would have balked but for the rapturous expression on his face. Small beads of sweat formed on his brow as he withdrew and then thrust, slowly at first, and then faster. He made wonderful sounds that made her feel all weak and warm inside, and yet she sensed the Wolf was tightly reined. Then, abruptly, he slid a big hand to her buttocks and lifted her to meet him, straining, in a gesture of fierce possession.

He would devour her. Marion felt again that thin thread of alarm at his ferocious plundering, but her body knew no fear. It rose to greet him, and passion returned with a vengeance. Suddenly, she was as wild and desperate as the Wolf himself. When his fingers dug into her, forcing her closer while he thrust deeper, Marion answered by sobbing his name.

"Dunstan!" she screamed as piercing pleasure so sharp as to be painful shattered her, and then, as if through a haze, she saw the Wolf's great body shudder violently before it fell heavily on top of her. She was nearly crushed for a moment before he seemed to come back to his senses and rolled to the side, taking her with him.

"Ah, wren, so good. So good..." he whispered against the top of her head.

Marion tried to reply, but she could find no words to describe what had happened between them, the passion and the glory and the wonder.... *I love you, Dunstan de Burgh,* she wanted to say, but instead she blinked back tears and snuggled closer to the amazing heat of him.

For once, Marion did not worry about tomorrow or escape or Baddersly. She thought only of Dunstan, and she let the even sound of his breathing lull her to sleep.

Marion was dreaming of butterflies. They fluttered across her skin as she lay naked in the sun, blessedly warm and fascinated by the sensation of their wings touching her bare flesh. Bare flesh? Confused, Marion felt the dream fade, to be replaced by a reality even more delightful: tender, moist kisses were being placed all over her body.

She opened her eyes, startled to see the dark head of Dunstan de Burgh poised over her until remembrance flooded back, heating her blood and her cheeks. The fire cast his features in gold and shadow, making him look fierce, as usual, but Marion was surprised to see his green eyes were narrowed and his jaw clenched.

"I did that," he said. Marion was at a loss as to his meaning until she followed his intent gaze to her upper arms, marked with bruises that were of his making.

"Not... recently," she whispered, her face flushing crimson.

He grunted in response, and Marion would have admitted that her skin bruised easily, but the words stopped in her throat. As she watched, the Wolf lowered his head and placed his lips to the discolored flesh. His kiss was utterly gentle, warm and tantalizing, and then she felt the slow sweep of sensation when he touched his tongue to her.

Marion sighed as all her senses reawakened, clamoring to life for the Wolf. He lavished his attention first on one arm, then the other, and then he returned to hover over her chest, a secretive smile, full of dark promise, curving his lips before he leaned forward and put his mouth to her breast.

She shivered, although her body was aflame, alive and wanting. Dunstan growled in triumph, his tongue darting out to taste her, and its touch seemed to delve beyond the surface of her skin to reach deep inside of her. Helplessly, Marion entwined her fingers in his hair and arched upward until he took her nipple into his mouth, suckling her like an infant.

Just when she thought she could stand no more, he took her other breast, and Marion moved against him restlessly, hungry for the surcease she had known before. If all this was designed to make her want him inside of her again, it was working, she thought, for she wanted him, needed him, had to have him....

When his lips left her breast, Marion was bereft, but he moved down her stomach, teasing her flesh, fueling her desire. She felt him part her legs, and he kissed the inside of her thighs, drifting closer and closer to the apex. And then he took her bottom in his big hands and lifted her to his mouth.

Marion gasped when his tongue touched her so intimately. It stroked her, flicking against her secrets and making forays inside her until she was shivering uncontrollably at this strange, new torment. "Mercy!" she cried, breathlessly.

"Yes, love, *yes!* Tremble for me," Dunstan whispered heatedly. The rough stubble of his cheeks rasped against her skin wickedly as he spoke, and his fingers tightened upon her buttocks. He lifted his head to look at her, and Marion, through the dark mane of his hair, saw his eyes glinting with a feral light. His parted lips glistened with a sheen of moisture before he bent his head to her again.

Suddenly, everything seemed to converge in that spot between her legs: each breath, each beat of her heart, each drop of blood, each fiber of muscle. Closing her eyes, Marion threw back her head, and gasping wildly, pushed against the mouth that eagerly met her. Then she came apart, shattering into a million pieces even as she clutched at Dunstan and cried out at the unimaginable pleasure that rent her flesh.

Vaguely, Marion became aware of him nudging at her body, gaining entrance, and filling her with his great member as she became whole again. This time there was no pain, only a biting hot sensation of fullness, and then Dunstan was moving, sliding nearly out of her until she demanded his return and he buried himself deep again. It felt so good that Marion was soon wild, so consumed with new passion that she did not even know she had spoken aloud until Dunstan echoed her.

"Yes. So good, my wren. *So good,*" he growled. Wrapping a fist in her hair, he bent down to kiss her, his tongue plundering as she tasted herself upon his lips. He devoured her, eating her mouth in a fierce and frantic communion until finally, gasping, he loosed her to move faster and sink farther. "I shall never have my fill of you, wren," he whispered hoarsely. "No matter how deep I go, 'tis never enough."

He slid a hand along her thigh, lifting it, and, because it seemed the thing to do, Marion wrapped her legs around him. He responded with another low growl and pushed harder, as if he truly could not reach his goal. His breathing was loud and ragged and he grunted his pleasure until the sound alone made Marion feverish and frantic.

She dug her nails into his muscles, wanting him to do something, anything, to ease the fires raging inside her. In response, she felt his palms slide down her arms to pin her hands against the mattress just as everything was coalescing. Entwining his fingers in hers, he thrust home, and Marion came apart again while he groaned and shuddered, spilling his seed into her.

This time, Dunstan said nothing in the aftermath of their union, but he again pulled her close, fitting her back to his massive chest and wrapping his strong arms around her until she felt as though she were in a cocoon, safe and blessedly warm. Marion was so accustomed to seeing him resting upright against a tree that this nestling position seemed strangely at odds with his usual behavior.

Perhaps he only curled up this way when he had a woman with him, Marion thought, and felt immediate regret at the notion. She did not want to imagine Dunstan de Burgh with any other female, but she could not fool herself. She knew from his reputation that he had known his share of ladies. And yet, maybe today had been different for him, Marion thought, with a glimmer of defiant hope. She had been amazed at the selfless way the Wolf had pleasured her this last time, and she colored to remember just how he had done so. He had seemed different somehow, more tender and giving.

Swallowing back a thickness in her throat, Marion listened to his even breathing, and then smiled when she heard him emit a low snore. Apparently, the man did sleep sometimes! The unguarded intimacy of the sound made her blink back tears. Foolishness, she knew, but how she loved him! The passion they had shared only made that love more wonderful, more powerful and...more painful. For no matter what she felt, they would part—and soon.

And now, when she knew that he well and truly slept, would be as good a time as any for her to make her escape. Marion realized that, and yet she could not force her limbs, still heavy with lethargy, to move. She wanted to stay in the heavenly heat of him forever.

Heaving a great sigh of regret, Marion finally wiggled free of his embrace. She sat up on their makeshift bed and looked down at him, still deep in slumber, and her heart swelled with yearning. Without his perpetual scowl, his handsome face was softer, his lips gently curved in repose. His dark lashes were long and thick, a perfect compliment to the dark de Burgh hair that fell across his forehead.

If only she could stay.

Perhaps she would remain just long enough to eat, Marion considered. After all, there was no sense in running off into the wilds and starving to death. And she was thirsty, too. Climbing out of the cozy bower where Dunstan de Burgh had taught her the meaning of passion, she looked around the small, dim hut.

She needed a bath. Standing, Marion realized how sticky and sore she was. Mayhap she would stay long enough to wash. With a slow smile she remembered the well, and dressing in her dry clothes, she grabbed up a bucket by the fireplace and opened the door.

The afternoon was as sparkling and bright as a newly minted coin, and Marion blinked in the sunlight. All around her the wet grass gleamed, and the air itself smelled fresh and clean. Was it only a coincidence that the gloominess of the past few days had vanished in the sweet consummation of her love? With a giddiness she had not known since girlhood, Marion ran across the shining green carpet to her destination.

She was busy trying to lower the bucket when the sound of hoofbeats froze her in her spot. She stood silently, her hand upon the rope while she glanced around, realizing all too quickly that there was no place to hide. The hut was set in what had obviously been a clearing, and both it and the nearest grove of trees were too far away for her to reach running.

Letting the bucket fall, Marion slowly turned, memories of mounted marauders flashing vividly in her mind. Should she scream? Would Dunstan hear her? Counting six riders, she clamped her mouth shut, for even the Wolf could do nothing against that many men. Her fear shifted its focus to Dunstan then, and Marion silently willed him to continue his slumber, for worse than anything that might happen to her was the thought that he might be cut down, like the Miller boys, before her eyes.

It never crossed her mind that the riders could be harmless or lost or fellow travelers; Marion had learned to expect the worst. And as if to confirm her beliefs, the worst appeared in front of her as she spotted the black and gold colors that marked the riders as her uncle's men.

They had come for her at last. Panic nearly blinded her, but Marion sucked in deep breaths, trying to think, to scheme, to lose the dazed contentment that had clouded her sharp mind.

Bryan Goodson, the head of her uncle's guard, rode at the lead, and when Marion recognized him, her very heart stilled. Half-formed plans to brazen out the meeting by posing as a peasant wench died a quick death, for Goodson would know her, even dressed as she was in wrinkled and stained clothing, her hair loose and tangled.

She was lost.

Perhaps it was best this way, Marion thought a bit wildly. She would not have to suffer any sad goodbyes or strained words with Dunstan; she would take only the glory of the past few hours with her. She sought it out,

clutching it tightly as she turned to face them and re-
treated deep within herself.

"Lady Warenne!" She heard the shocked surprise in
Goodson's voice and saw the thinly veiled disdain for her
appearance. How well her uncle had turned them all
against her! "What are you about? How came you here?"

"My escort was slain," Marion said, her eyes narrowing. Or do you know that only too well, Goodson? Did
you kill them all? she wondered, her throat tightening as
she choked back the unformed words.

Marion waited, wondering if he intended to finish his
bloody job right now and murder her where she stood. A
small part of her longed for a swift end, but that tena-
cious flame that had begun burning inside her at Campion would not go out. It urged her to practice deceit and
regain her freedom. "And how is it that you are here on
this road, heading toward Baddersly?" she asked.

"We were sent out to meet your party, but finding the
carnage back there, we feared you were...dead, and
turned around," Goodson said slowly. "How did you escape the slaughter? Are you alone?" he asked, his sharp
glance raking the area and lighting upon the hut.

Marion's heart stopped in her chest. Dunstan! She
could not trust her uncle's men with the life of the Wolf.
Her own fate abruptly faded in significance at the thought
of her love cut down, the heat stolen from his great,
beautiful body.

"Yes. I am alone," she lied, looking Goodson directly
in the eye. "I was attending to myself in the woods when
the attack came, and I hid myself away until it was long
over. Everyone was dead. Even the horses were gone. So
I began walking. What else could I do?" She waved a
hand in the air. "I took shelter here from the storm."

Staring up at the head of the guard, Marion read no
guilt in his face, and for the first time since regaining her

memory, she knew some doubt. Goodson did not look like a man who had but recently missed finding her corpse. But, if her uncle was not responsible for the raid upon Dunstan's camp, then who was? And for what purpose?

Marion knew she had no time to waste in such contemplation. At any moment, Dunstan might waken and charge out of the hut to be killed by her uncle's men. Perhaps they would not attack him, but she could not take that chance. She was familiar with Goodson and his ilk; they knew no honor, no rules but their own. She had heard dark rumors of torture and innocent blood spilled by their hands. Marion would not risk the Wolf.

"You are to be commended, Goodson. No doubt you have saved my life, for I could not have gone on much longer, alone and afraid, prey to all manner of beast and ruffian," she said, lowering her head in a submissive pose. "I am sure my uncle will reward you greatly."

Peeking up at him from under her lashes, Marion caught the flash of Goodson's ugly smile. Her words had the desired effect, for he lost all interest in his surroundings, puffed out his chest and barked an order to his men. Perhaps he had not been sent to kill her after all, Marion mused, for why then would he be so pleased to take her home?

Marion had no time to pursue the thought, for she was soon riding pillion behind a surly-looking fellow who smelled of the strong drink that her uncle's men favored. The stench, so unlike Dunstan's appealing scent, made her dizzy, and she struggled for the rigid control she had learned so well in her uncle's household.

She found it deep within herself, and, staring straight ahead at the foul guard in front of her, did not blink as the horses wheeled around and struck for the road to Baddersly. Her uncle and, surely, her death waited ahead, but she did not flinch.

She did not even glance back at the small hut that held all that she loved.

Chapter Twelve

Something woke him. Dunstan tensed and eased his eyes open, alert for danger, but nothing threatened. He was alone in an empty hut with a cold fire and the fading scent of woman lingering in the air. Marion! Jerking upright, Dunstan leaped from the cot, but she was nowhere to be seen.

Day of God, the wench had bolted again! Dunstan reached for his clothes, the bitter taste of betrayal in his mouth. The knowledge that she had fled, after all that had passed between them, came perilously close to hurting him. Thrusting that odd ache firmly aside, Dunstan nurtured his anger instead. This time, by faith, he would throttle her. He would beat her soundly. Nay, he would strangle her with his bare hands!

Dunstan had yanked on his braies and his tunic before he noticed that Marion's cloak still hung by the fire. Turning swiftly, he saw her pouch lying on the floor where she had left it, and unease traveled up his spine as he rushed toward it. He pulled out a soggy blanket and clothing, some personal items and a small bag that held . . . jewels. Surely, the wren would not leave without these?

His anxiety increasing, Dunstan surveyed the rest of the tiny space. The bucket, too, was missing, so he told himself she was probably only fetching some water. But no sounds came from outside and he could not shake the feeling that something was not right.

When he was mailed and armed, Dunstan slipped out of the hut into the golden glow of late-afternoon sun. The area outside was deserted, the well standing alone, and something akin to panic jerked at his insides. Fighting it, Dunstan forced himself to look carefully for any signs of Marion's passing.

He had nearly reached the old structure when he saw the hoofprints. Feeling as though someone had just kicked him in the gut, Dunstan dropped to one knee to examine them closely. Horses, several of them, had been here.

Who? And why had they taken Marion? One answer came all too quickly as the memory of her stretched out between her two attackers struck him like a blow. "No!" he growled. Fear for her, along with something else— something deep and vulnerable—assailed him for a moment before he could school himself. He had a job to do, a job entrusted to him by his sire, and by faith, he would not fail.

Pausing only to take up Marion's meager possessions and his own leather pouch, Dunstan did the only thing that he could do. He gave chase on foot, thankful for the soft, wet earth that gave him an easy trail to follow.

And he blamed himself. As he trotted along the road, Dunstan cursed under his breath, for if he had not been sleeping in the middle of the day, Marion would still be safe. What was the matter with him? Had his soldier's training deserted him completely because of a satisfying tumble or two?

On second thought, satisfying did not begin to describe what had gone on in the hut. Grim-faced, Dunstan continued on, intent upon his task, but the memory of Marion's lush body and his response to it haunted him.

He had made her tremble and sob and scream, while she...she had wrung him dry, and yet, before long he had been eager as a lad again.

Dunstan's groin tightened as he recalled the fevered frenzy of their joining. Never before had it been so good for him. Why, he could not say. Perhaps their desperate circumstances gave impetus to their passions, or perhaps the days and nights spent fighting his attraction to her were responsible. Forbidden fruit always seemed to taste sweeter, and, of course, he had no business taking the lady's maidenhead.

The stab of guilt Dunstan felt was quickly overwhelmed by the heady pride of possession. Whatever her relationship with his brothers, the wren had lain only with him, and that pleased him mightily. *She* pleased him mightily. Dunstan had thought to put the lure of her to rest by bedding her, but even after having her twice, he could not deny that he still wanted her—now, more than ever.

Luck was with him, for he reached Wisborough within the hour. It was a small village, tucked under a hillside, but it had a manor house and a squire who attended the horses stabled there for his lord. Dunstan ended up with a costly nag that could never keep up with the beasts he was following, enough food to keep him alive for a while and some information.

"A group of riders came this way this day, with a dark-haired lady. Did you see them?"

"Aye," the man said slowly. He frowned slightly, obviously intimidated by an armed knight, but trying not to show it, so Dunstan tossed a bit of coin in the air as an added incentive. The fellow's eyes glinted avariciously. "They came through here. Soldiers from Baddersly, they were," he said, spitting out the words as if they soured his mouth.

Baddersly? Was he that close to Marion's home? Dunstan realized that he had lost track of time and distance since the attack on his camp. The gnawing suspicion that Marion had deliberately left him, fleeing without her belongings, died a quick and merciful death, for he knew she would never willingly go home. "Baddersly?" he asked aloud. "How far be it, and how might I reach it, good man?"

The fellow frowned as if talk of the castle ill-pleased him, but his eyes followed the coin that jumped in Dunstan's palm. "The quickest way lies over that rise," he said, pointing. "Take the old track behind it, and you shall find Baddersly soon enough. It lies a day's ride to the east, through the hills."

Dunstan flipped the coin, and the man reached out quickly to grab it, licking his lips with his good fortune. Then he glanced back at his benefactor, his hairy brows drawn together. "Go you there alone, my lord?"

Nodding, Dunstan mounted up, while the man backed away, shaking his head. As Dunstan spurred the horse to a gallop, he thought he heard the fellow yell, "Watch your back," but he was already riding away, heading toward the rise and on to the castle beyond.

It did not take Dunstan long to wonder why he was going to Baddersly at all. Marion was on her way home, where she belonged, escorted by her uncle's guards. Why should he trail after them? His own lands and people needed his attention, and he could ill afford more delays.

But Dunstan knew he could not simply abandon her without assuring himself of her safety. After all, he had naught but a lone villager's word as to the identity of the men who had taken her. And, knowing Marion as well as he did, Dunstan did not trust her to be a docile traveling companion. What if she escaped them? She might, even now, be lost and alone somewhere among these hills, without even a warm cloak to draw around her.

Dunstan felt a sharp pain in his chest at the thought, and fast on the heels of that grim image came another. What if these soldiers became impatient with her escapades and tied her up...or beat her? Ignoring his past vows to strangle her, Dunstan felt a venomous surge of anger for any who would lay a hand to her.

His thoughts wandered to the bruises he had unthinkingly given her, and Dunstan's jaw clenched tightly. Would that he find her safe, he would never mark her again. But what of her uncle and his men? Was there any truth to her accusations about Harold Peasely? From the freeman's expression, Peasely was not well liked, but such fellows were not always the best judge of their betters. Dunstan had a notion to see for himself just what kind of man the uncle was, and he considered staying at Baddersly for a few days, just to relieve his mind.

With a grimace, he rejected the notion. By faith, he had never listened to a woman before, let alone a lying, troublesome wench like Marion Warenne! Dunstan's eyes narrowed at the knowledge that the wren affected him in a variety of ways, not all of them physical. And yet...

He would stay at Baddersly, but only long enough to assure himself of her welfare. His sire had enjoined him to make sure the lady was safe, and he would do it. It was his duty, and he could not relinquish it in good faith until he saw for himself that Marion was unharmed and ensconced in her home.

And then what? The thought came, unbidden, to tease him, for he could hardly linger long at Baddersly when Wessex and his myriad responsibilities there called to him. What then of the woman who haunted his thoughts and flamed his blood? If he could but bed her one more time, mayhap he could quench his thirst for her, Dunstan decided. Then he forced the wren out of his mind, concentrating instead upon the trail ahead.

He followed it until nightfall, when it disappeared in the darkness. Then he ate some of the provisions he had purchased and rested briefly against a tree, sorely aware of how cold and solitary his bed, compared to the last place he had slept. At dawn, he was off again, cursing the poor beast under him and wishing for his battled-hardened destrier.

Although years of traveling had perfected his patience, Dunstan found that this time the miles dragged by at a frustrating pace. Concern for Marion kept him on edge in an odd way, as if he were fighting a losing war with useless weapons. He was so anxious to find her, he had to curb himself from driving the nag to its death in his impatience.

When the poor beast started puffing and blowing, Dunstan stopped by a small creek to water it. He cupped his hands and drank his fill, then rose to prowl restlessly along the stream's edge. He pulled out some bread and chewed it absently, but it tasted like dirt in his mouth. By faith, would nothing ease this unfamiliar ache? He sank down on the bank, feeling as though his chest were a bellows from which all the air had been sucked.

He missed her.

It was more than lust, Dunstan admitted. During the past week he had become accustomed to Marion's presence, and lately, he had grown quite used to touching her often—to keep her from falling, among other things. Her quiet strength, her sometimes foolish, ofttimes clever wit, her gentle pride—all these made up the lady known as Marion. And Dunstan missed them.

When she smiled, revealing those impish dimples, and turned those huge, dark eyes upon him, it seemed as if, somehow, something was right with the world. The knowledge gave him a queer feeling in the pit of his stomach. Telling himself it was hunger, Dunstan finished the rest of his bread with a low growl of annoyance.

But he was in trouble, and he knew it.

By the time Dunstan reached Baddersly, night had fallen again, and he was weary, not only in body, but in soul. Numberless times in his life, Dunstan had been bone-tired on the road, sick of sleeping in the open, chilled and hungry. This evening, there was something more to it. Anxiety had crept into his blood, tainting his every thought and action.

He told himself that it was only natural to worry about the wren, for she was his charge, entrusted to him by his sire. Once he saw that she was well and truly home, then this almost debilitating concern would ease. After all, it had nothing to do with taking his leave of her, with never seeing her again. . . .

Dunstan's name got him through the gates and into the great hall, but there was something about the castle that made the hair on the back of his neck rise in warning. From the first words of the surly guard to the atmosphere in the cold, dark building, Dunstan felt danger. It was as if he had walked, unarmed, into his neighbor's hold.

Grimacing, he told himself that Marion's deluded ramblings were affecting his perceptions. Harold Peasely could hardly wish him ill, for Dunstan had done naught but perform an errand for the man. Although Marion's uncle might not have been pleased to discover his niece was roaming the countryside by herself, still she was alive and well, with no harm done to her . . . except the loss of her maidenhead.

Dunstan had not stopped to think what might be in store for him if Marion related that choice bit of information to her uncle, but he knew that the theft of her virtue was not a killing offense. If worse came to worst, he could always marry the wench. A surprising thought that, but the more Dunstan considered it, the more palatable the idea seemed. After all, it was time he got himself an heir, and Marion would do as well as any other woman in producing one.

Smiling tightly, Dunstan mused upon the possibilities, not the least of which was the opportunity to bed Marion again, and decided to bide his time. First, he would see what her uncle had to say, and then, if need be, he would present his suit. Although he might not be as wealthy as she, Dunstan could not imagine Peasely turning away his proposal. He was a titled, landed knight, and though he usually did not dwell on it, he also stood to inherit the vast holdings of Campion one day.

Secure in his own worth, and with the mighty support of his family and King Edward behind him, Dunstan expected no trouble from Harold Peasely, but still the odd threatening feeling persisted. And Dunstan had lived too long and through too many battles to ignore his instincts. He kept both eyes open and his hand on the hilt of his sword.

Dunstan's gaze swept the room, and he felt more uneasiness. Peasely's men were drinking and dicing in one corner, their language foul, their voices loud. It was a far cry from his father's hall, where warmth and peace reigned. With a sudden pang, Dunstan realized just how much he admired his old home and his family. His own castle seemed cold and lifeless by comparison. What he needed was children of his own, boisterous boys racing through the hall and . . .

Collaring his errant thoughts, Dunstan concentrated on his surroundings. Now was not the time for woolgathering. He was alone with many long, treacherous miles to go before he reached Wessex. He had planned to ask Peasely for an escort, but from the looks of them, these were coarse, undisciplined men he would not trust at his back. They looked more like outlaws than soldiers, and the hair on Dunstan's neck rose again as he remembered Marion's tale of murder and mayhem on the road.

"This way," said a voice, and Dunstan turned to face an evil-looking fellow who sported a gold ring in his ear. Something nudged at the back of Dunstan's mind, making him tighten his grip on his hilt, as he followed the man forward for an audience with the master of Baddersly. But his attention was soon focused solely on Harold Peasely.

Marion's uncle sat in a huge, ornately carved chair on a dais at the end of the hall, just as though he had delusions of royalty, and Dunstan noticed that, like his men, he had been drinking. His face was flushed and puffy, suggesting that he made a habit of it, to his own detriment. Dunstan's eyes narrowed at the discovery, for too much wine dulled a man's wits. Before Peasely even spoke, Dunstan found him wanting.

To his surprise, Marion's uncle seemed to feel the same about him. Fixing Dunstan with a beady glare, Peasely grunted, "Who the devil are you?"

Dunstan's jaw clenched at the rude greeting. By what right did this...caretaker question him? With deliberate care, he framed his answer. "Dunstan de Burgh, baron of Wessex, son of Campion, earl of Campion."

To Dunstan's astonishment, Peasely burst out with a sharp laugh. Was the man so full of drink that he had forgotten Dunstan's errand? "Perhaps you will recall that I was charged by my father with the task of escorting Lady Warenne from Campion to Baddersly," Dunstan explained, hanging on to his temper with some effort.

"If that was your errand, then you have failed!" Peasely shouted.

Dunstan bit back a sharp retort and tried to think of how Geoffrey, the diplomat, would handle such a recalcitrant host. When he spoke again, his voice was level, despite his exasperation. "My train was set upon by assassins, with only myself and the lady escaping. We traveled on foot until—"

"Lies, lies, lies," Peasely said, his mouth curving into an evil smile. "Hear you this offal?" he cried to several of the rough fellows who stood nearby. When they murmured their agreement, Dunstan suddenly realized how dangerous the situation could become. He was alone in a roomful of hardened men who might turn upon him without a moment's notice.

As if to confirm Dunstan's impressions, Peasely lurched to his feet, shouting, "This is an outrage! This arrogant filth claims to be a de Burgh!" He laughed loudly, his men joining in, and Dunstan saw two females, an old woman and a younger one, back away from the dais, obviously anticipating the eruption of violence.

"I am Dunstan de Burgh," he affirmed, his voice even.

"Then get you back to your papa and tell him that I will have his neck for this! If he does not return my niece at once, I will march upon him," Peasely said, shaking a fist into the air.

Dunstan's chest constricted tightly. Marion was not here? The now-familiar panic for her struck him like a blow, and he drew a slow, shallow breath before he could speak. "Are you saying Lady Warenne is not here?"

"Why would you think so?" Peasely asked, sneering. Dunstan's eyes swept the room, taking in, with heightened unease, the suspended dice game. The drunken soldiers lounged against a wall, watching him insolently, and Dunstan looked behind Peasely for another exit, should he need one.

A movement in the shadows there caught his attention, and he saw the old woman he had noticed before. She stared at him, her eyes hollows in her white face, her mouth working soundlessly. And Dunstan knew in that moment that Peasely was lying. "She is here, and I wish to speak to her myself," he said with certainty.

"She is not here! Toss this peasant out upon his ear!" Peasely screamed. "You have not the look of even the lowest knight, let alone a baron, about you. Methinks you are naught but a common knave trying to stir up trouble. Begone with you!"

Dunstan could hardly contain his rage, but a look at the approaching group of soldiers told him that he had better keep it in check. If he could get his hands around Peasely's neck, by faith, he would wring the truth from the bastard! He took a step forward and halted. "If you hurt her, I will kill you," Dunstan warned evenly.

"Begone!" Peasely shrieked.

Turning on his heel, Dunstan strode across the hall, followed by Peasely's men, who rained taunts upon his head that made him clench his jaw in frustration. At the doorway he swung around, hand on his sword and fire in his eyes, and they stepped back, spitting and cursing, though none was brave enough to make good his threats.

Flushed with that small victory, Dunstan stepped outside into the bailey, blinked in the darkness and wondered what the devil he was going to do next.

"Pssst. My lord. My lord, here."

Turning toward the whisper, Dunstan saw a white hand beckoning him from the shadows. It was the old woman from the hall, and Dunstan was at her side swiftly, merging with the blackness himself.

"Where is she?" he hissed, without preliminaries.

"Hush, my lord." The woman's voice was strained with fear, her eyes darting like a cornered hare's. "She is locked in her room in the south tower, the second window up." Dunstan glanced around, picking the tower out of the night, but before he could ask how the devil he was supposed to breach it, the old woman had disappeared, seeming to fade into the very stones.

Biting back an oath, Dunstan surveyed the bailey. It was quiet but for the occasional bark of a dog or tramp of a sentry. Then, suddenly, the hall door opened, spilling light out around the entrance, and Dunstan flattened himself against the wall.

Two men stepped forward, one tall and lean, the other shorter and burlier, and Dunstan recognized both of them as Peasely's. "Where is he?" asked the tall one in a hushed, angry voice.

"Halfway to Campion, if he's smart," answered the shorter fellow in a low drawl, thick with drink. Dunstan's eyes narrowed as he realized they discussed him, and his instincts screamed afoul. Were it not for the old woman, he would have been headed toward the gate. What mischief would these two plan behind his back?

"Be still!" the tall one ordered. "Where is Aylmer?"

"Asleep. He has watch later."

"Good. At least he will be sober. Wake him. Take Aylmer and find our guest," the tall one said. "And make sure he never reaches his father."

Dunstan heard the guttural laugh of the burly fellow. "And how shall we do that, Goodson?"

Although he could see naught but figures from where he hid, Dunstan could swear he heard a smile in the tall one's voice. "The roads can be so treacherous at night, especially for one lone man. Brigands and the like would find our visitor easy prey," he answered. "See that they do."

The door closed, taking the light with it, and Dunstan loosed a low breath, harsh with fury. So they meant to murder him, did they? Perhaps they would find him not such an easy mark. He had half a mind to lie in wait for them and slit their throats, but he had more important business waiting. With the speed and silence of a battle-hardened warrior, Dunstan moved among the shadows until he stood below a square tower at the southern end of the building.

Was this where Marion was being held? He glanced upward, discerning the darker outline of a window, and higher, another. Although it was narrow, Dunstan suspected he could fit himself through, if only he could reach it. Clenching his jaw in frustration, he looked about him and then back to the hall. Most of Peasely's men seemed to be drinking and dicing, oblivious to a stranger in their midst, but just how lax were they? Stealthily, Dunstan moved toward the next building, intending to find out for himself.

Marion sat hugging herself in the darkness, wondering just how much time she had. All during the long ride home she had tried to think of a way to escape, but Goodson and his men kept a close watch upon her. He was her uncle's minion, hard and lean and cold as driving sleet, and he knew, more than Dunstan had ever dreamed, just how much she did not want to return to Baddersly.

There had been no opportunity on the way home, nor had there been a chance since her arrival, for her uncle had taken one look at her and had her locked away. How long would he keep her here? Marion froze in horror when she considered that he could starve her to death. But no. She would find a way out before then. She had escaped before, and she would do it again.

If only she were not so tired; she could barely think properly. The old fears that had been so much a part of her life at Baddersly crept back insidiously, and a keening grief at the loss of Dunstan waited to overwhelm her if she would but let it.

Just when her mind threatened to break, a silent and stiff Fenella brought her bathwater and some food, and Marion bathed and dressed in clean clothes. That small luxury revived her, and hunger forced her to eat, even though she wondered if each bite was laced with poison.

When no summons came from her uncle, Marion lay down upon the bed, fully dressed, intending to form a plan of escape, but her mind was soon crowded with thoughts of her long dead parents, the de Burgh brothers and Dunstan. At least he was alive and away from here, safe and well, she thought, taking her only comfort in that before she drifted into a restless slumber.

Chapter Thirteen

Disturbed by a noise, Marion awoke with a start, fear coursing through her as she remembered who she was and where she slept. Her first thought was that her uncle was at the door, ready to slip in and murder her in her bed, but then she heard it again, the rasping of metal against stone. She froze, her body immobile but for wide eyes that turned in the direction of the grating sound. In the utter darkness of her room, she found the lighter midnight of her window. Was something hanging over the sill?

Although she wanted to close her eyes and remain where she was, Marion knew that she could hardly lie prone, waiting for a possible attack. Forcing herself to move, she rose as silently as a wraith and crept along the wall toward the opening. Her heart thudded in her ears, threatening to deafen her when she realized that a pickax was slung through the open shutters. As Marion watched, it jerked, embedding itself more firmly, and she saw that a rope was tied securely around it, taut and swaying as if...

Marion stifled a gasp as a huge shape filled the window. Stiff with horror, she frantically glanced about for something to use against the intruder. Whoever managed to scale the smooth side of the tower could only mean to do her ill, she knew, and yet when she looked into the shadowed face of her assassin, she felt dizzy and uncertain.

"Marion?" The sound of that voice, calling her as if from her dreams, made her tremble so violently that her legs gave way and she sank to the floor, convinced that she had finally lost her mind. For how could *he* be here?

"Marion!" A soft thump announced that he was inside her room, and then he was kneeling before her, his deep tones husky with concern. Mad she might be, but she flung herself into his embrace in the hope that he was real.

"Dunstan!" Wrapping her arms around his neck, Marion buried her face against his throat. Warm and throbbing with his pulse beat, it proclaimed that he was no vision, but a living, breathing man. His scent, familiar and potent, surrounded her, along with his terrific heat, and she pressed her lips to his skin, tasting the salt there. He made an incoherent sound, took her face in his huge hands and kissed the very soul from her.

The Wolf was devouring her again, and Marion welcomed it, meeting his thrusting tongue with her own and twining her fingers in his long locks to tug him closer. Love for him surged through her, driving away all else— her heartache, her fear and whatever modesty she still possessed.

In some inner recess of her mind, Marion realized that she would happily mate with him upon the cold stone floor, so glad was she to see him again. She had thought never to look upon his beloved face, and yet here he was, bursting into her room and her world, a huge, vital presence, greater than ever.

When he broke the kiss, Marion clung to him so that he took her up with him as he rose to his feet. "Come, wren," he murmured, setting her forcibly from him. "We do not have much time. Your uncle's men are looking for me."

Why was he here? Where was he taking her? Endless questions leaped to her tongue, but Marion bit them back, for now was not the time to talk. As she watched in amazement, Dunstan slung a leg through the window in one graceful movement, gripped the rope that hung from the ax and lowered himself outside.

He beckoned her from his airy perch, but Marion remained where she was, her feet firmly planted on the floor. Although the bailey was lost in blackness below, she knew just how far up they were, and the knowledge was not comforting.

"Me?" she whispered. Pointing to her chest, Marion thought that she might have understood his gesture, but unfortunately, Dunstan nodded. He wanted her to climb out there with him. She felt faint.

"Come, wren. Put your arms around me. I will keep you safe." His gruff reassurance touched her heart, and drawing a deep breath, the new Marion stepped onto the ledge and locked her hands around his neck. "Put your legs around me, too," he directed, and somehow she managed to grip him with her thighs. Even through his mail, Marion could feel the heat of him seep into her, and she blushed to recall the last time she had been similarly positioned.

Then all such thoughts vanished as she hung on for dear life while he took them down the rope, bit by bit, hand over hand, kicking off from the side of the tower at intervals in a way that made her stomach lurch. By the time they reached the lower window, Marion was in awe of his strength. Although she had known that his muscles were massive, she was still amazed that he carried her as if she were naught but a bit of cloth against his chest.

When they finally dropped to the ground, Marion eased out a sigh of relief, which was stopped by Dunstan's finger upon her lips, warning her to silence. Although he had freed her from her locked room, they were still inside

Baddersly's walls, at the mercy of her uncle. She stilled, suitably cowed by his reminder, and yet her blood thrummed with the knowledge that the Wolf was here. *He had come for her.*

Pulling her into the black entrance of a nearby storage building, Dunstan whispered in her ear. ''Shall we brave our way through the gate?'' She looked up at his darkened features, uncertain whether he was asking her advice or questioning her courage. Either way, she could give him only one answer.

''Yes,'' she said softly. *He had come to take her away.*

A grunt of approval met her response. ''From what I have seen, most of the soldiers are drunk and security is lax. I doubt that anyone will question someone *leaving* the grounds. Know you any different?'' Dunstan asked.

Marion felt a jolt of pleasant surprise. Was Dunstan de Burgh actually consulting with her? ''I thought you said my uncle was searching for you,'' she whispered.

''Yes, but they plan to waylay me on the road.''

''Oh,'' Marion said softly, finding little comfort in his words.

''Come, wren,'' he said, his voice low and urgent. ''We must hurry before your absence is discovered.'' He pulled her along then, flitting from the shadows of one building to the next, stopping only when he heard a sound. They waited, in tense silence, behind one hut, until Marion wondered what was keeping them there. Then he leaned close. ''Is this the brewery?''

''Yes,'' Marion answered. She watched in surprise as he flung a leg through the low window and slipped inside. He was back in a moment, a vessel in hand, which he put to his lips. *He was thirsty?* Stepping back, Marion realized that the man positively reeked of ale. ''Did you fall in?'' she asked with a sniff.

She could have sworn she heard the low rumble of laughter in answer. ''Nay, wren, but I would douse us both. Wait, cover your finery," he said, and to Marion's amazement, he pulled out her old cloak from his pouch. After she had wrapped it about her, he sprinkled her liberally with the brew. "We are naught but two peasants returning home to our cot," he whispered fiercely.

For a moment, Marion did not understand, but when Dunstan began weaving drunkenly toward the gate, with her in tow, understanding dawned clearly. He had pulled his own cloak about him to hide his mail, and Marion only hoped that whoever manned the entrance would not look too closely in the darkness.

Marion's heart was pounding so loudly that she feared the soldiers would hear, but they barely looked up when Dunstan approached, singing a ribald ditty in a coarse voice. He was slouching in an attempt to hide his size, she realized, and she clung to his side, as if to hold him up when he staggered.

Each step was perilous, and Marion felt a bone-deep terror that she had never known in her other escape attempts. One swift glance at her companion told her the source of her newfound fear. *He was rescuing her. He was risking his life for her.* And although she was well used to her own being threatened, she could not bear to imagine anything happening to the Wolf.

The walk past the walls seemed endless, but Dunstan continued his charade, only lengthening his strides as they moved farther away from Baddersly. The cloud-covered moon lit their way faintly, making the road a dim line, and Marion was watching it closely, trying to keep up with Dunstan's long legs when he stumbled and fell, dragging her down on top of him with a low oath. Absolute panic knifed through her, along with the certainty that he had just been struck through the back with an arrow. Struggling for her voice, she cried out his name in a broken whisper.

"Hush," he warned. "For the benefit of anyone watching, we have just passed out upon the road. We will stay here for a while, then roll into the grass. When I tell you to run, we must go low, crouching, to avoid any chance sighting from a soldier on the battlements. We will head over that hill, bearing west for now to throw them off the scent."

Off the scent? Marion froze as the implication of his words became clear. "Think you that my uncle will send his men after us?"

"I am certain of it," he answered grimly. "I am sorry that I did not believe you sooner, wren, but I do now. Your uncle is, indeed, a murderer."

"How do you know?" Marion asked.

"Because he is out to kill me."

After silently walking for what seemed like hours in what to Marion's mind might as well be circles, they stopped by a river to bed down under the canopy of a overhanging tree. Luckily, the night was balmy and the ground dry, and when Dunstan rolled out the blankets, Marion sank down gratefully. When he handed her the pouch she had left in the shepherd's hut, she beamed in happy surprise.

"Dunstan, my things! How wonderful you are! And my... jewels?"

"Right here," he said. Flashing her a white-toothed smile, he patted the pouch at his waist.

Relief soared through her. Suddenly, after all that she had been through, Marion felt tears prick the back of her eyelids. She had not cried for him when she had left him, nor had she wept when locked in the tower, facing the prospect of her death, but now she had to blink several times as if to hold back a flood.

Love for the Wolf washed over her in waves, making it difficult to speak. She wanted to throw her arms around his neck and kiss his wonderful mouth. Her hands ached to stroke his skin as they had once before, and Marion felt a sweeping yearning to join with him, here in the stillness of the night under the cloud-covered moon.

The desire had none of the sharp awareness that came so suddenly upon her when he touched her unexpectedly. It was not that vivid, burning passion that sparked between them like a blaze, but rather a wish to express her love for him the only way she knew how, to give him pleasure such as he had given her....

Marion watched as he sat down near her, leaning against the tree and stretching his long legs out before him. When he tilted his head back in a gesture of weariness that she had never seen before, she realized that the Wolf was not made of iron, but flesh and blood. And in that instant, he revealed a vulnerable side Marion suspected he rarely showed anyone.

"Here, let me help you with your sword and your mail," she said when she found her voice. She sensed his eyes upon her in the darkness, questioning her, but Marion only stood and let memories of long-ago teachings help her as she laid aside his heavy war weaponry.

"Rest," she advised, kneeling beside him and pushing him back upon the blanket. She heard the sharp hiss of his breath as she placed her hands upon his chest, then she could wait no longer. She leaned over and put her lips to his.

They were soft and warm. Already, she could feel the heat of him, seeping up through his clothing to envelop her, along with his unique scent, very male and very compelling. Her tongue darted out to run along the seam of his mouth and then inside where it was so hot and moist and...dizzying.

Twining her hands in his hair to anchor herself, Marion felt a heady sense of power as she knelt over his great knight's body. She was naught but a portion of his size, and yet she knew she could make him groan and shudder. The knowledge made her bolder, and she thrust her tongue more forcefully over his.

One of his huge hands came up to grip her long locks and he groaned, making Marion become weak with her own strength. She trailed kisses along his jaw and down his throat as she moved lower and tugged at his tunic, anxious to bare his magnificent body to her questing touch.

He was so big and strong, a fearsome warrior, and yet he let her have her way, unresisting as she explored him. His acquiescence gave impetus to her passion, for the realization that the Wolf lay prone for her, his wildness momentarily leashed, gave the slow, easy meter of her love a new urgency.

Pushing up his tunic, Marion spread her palms across his massive chest and felt his heart pounding beneath her hand. It thrummed through her skin and into her blood like a drumbeat, primitive and wanton, urging her to its rhythms. Glancing at his face, she saw his eyes glinting in the faint light, and a rush of blood flooded her cheeks at her brazen behavior before she lowered her face and nuzzled the silky hair that covered him.

"Ah, wren..." Dunstan's voice, the low drawl of a man drunk or fogged with sleep, brought a smile to her lips.

"I want to pleasure you," she whispered, delight in the task making her words fierce. Then she bent over him again, and finding the hard nub of his nipple, took it into her mouth, as he had once done to her.

"Day of God!" he moaned, his hands reaching for her and roving over her with fevered urgency. But Marion would not let her attention be turned away. She was too intent upon the feel of him beneath her fingers, a wondrous combination of heat and texture and form that responded to her every touch. Pressing her mouth to his hot skin, she sent her tongue over thick muscles, across ribs and down to his taut stomach while he muttered low oaths in a harsh exhalation. The murmured curses became an endless chant as he strung one after another together so roughly that she could scarcely recognize a word.

Intoxicated by her discoveries and by her own burgeoning passions, Marion lost all modesty. Flinging her hair back over her shoulder, she tugged on his braies until his manhood sprang free, huge and erect, from the thicket of hair at his groin. A strangled sound escaped her throat as she stared, fresh exhilaration coursing through her at the sight.

A low growl of impatience told her that the Wolf was at the end of his tether, but she evaded his hands when he reached for her and moved to pull off his boots and his hose. Then she knelt between his legs, running her hands along his thick calves and upward to the steely muscles of his thighs. They were rock hard. Her fingers tingled at the touch, sending shivers all the way to the core of her and robbing her of breath. She was panting by the time she reached his manhood, her fingers trembling as they traced the smooth tip and the thick root with loving interest.

"Wren!" The harsh exhalation sounded like a warning.

"Hush," she answered. "I wish to pleasure you." Remembering the way he had kissed that most intimate part of her, she bent her head, letting her hair flow over his stomach and thighs as she touched her lips to the tip of him. With a low oath, he jerked upward, and Marion took him in her mouth. Then his hands wound in her hair, guiding her movements, until the Wolf was growling his pleasure and shuddering violently under her.

He took her swiftly and masterfully. One moment, Marion knelt between his legs, wide-eyed and breathless at his surrender, and then, with the speed of a predator, he had her on her back and was poised over her, covering her body with his massive one.

He consumed her mouth while his hands roamed her curves, stroking her through her clothes, then burrowing beneath her skirts to grip her buttocks. He bared her breasts and suckled them, and when Marion reached up to touch him, he pinned her hands to the ground, his eyes glittering, his white teeth a flash in the darkness.

Then, when she felt his manhood pressing hard against her once more, he knelt between her thighs and lifted her up to him, impaling her in one smooth motion. He thrust deeply and drew out slowly, again and again, until she writhed beneath him, sobbing.

"Hush, I would only *pleasure* you," he whispered in a half-wicked, half-teasing tone, and Marion sensed that he must show her his own power. He had let her play with him, but he remained an untamed creature, full of fire and strength. . . . When she came, she cried out so loudly that he covered her mouth with his own, but still he moved within her, driving her to yet another peak. Only after she had again cried out in ecstasy did he empty himself in her, his great body shuddering before it fell upon her own.

Dunstan roused himself with difficulty, his eyes narrowing as he glimpsed the first light of dawn. By faith, Marion wrung him out! He had slept like the dead, and now they must make haste to be on their way. His annoyance vanished as he looked down at her, rosy-cheeked and soft and warm, and he had to fight the temptation to take her again.

Easing himself away from her body, Dunstan decided that a quick bath would both waken him and cool off his burgeoning ardor. Pulling a sliver of soap from his pouch, he waded knee-deep into the stream and proceeded to wash himself.

Even under the chilling effects of the water, Dunstan found his gaze returning to the bank where Marion lay, and while he watched, she awoke, rising to lean on one elbow in an innocently sensual pose. His groin hardened painfully as she sat up and stared at him, her hair a wildly tousled mane, her cheeks flushed, her lips parted. He made a sound. It was definitely not good-morning, but Marion understood clearly enough. She rose and walked toward him.

Would he ever get his fill of her? "If you want a bath, you must hurry, for I would be off at once," Dunstan snapped, knowing full well that he should finish his own and get dressed instead of lingering in the stream like some randy peasant lad.

She took off her clothes.

"Marion! You rob me of my good sense!" he growled when she reached him. Instead of retreating, she gave him one of her glorious smiles, dimples and all, and he felt light-headed. "Quickly now, for we must go," he murmured, before taking her mouth with his own. He lifted her up in his arms, wrapped her legs around his hips and entered her swiftly as he stood knee-deep in the stream, the sun rising around them.

After only a few deep thrusts, she was crying out with pleasure, her body milking his seed, and Dunstan was shuddering violently in a protracted release that made him want to stay buried inside her always.

It was a long time before he breathed evenly again. By faith, he had never known the like before. Dunstan had thought their first experience together unusually good—a product of her innocence and the startling attraction between them—but last night had been even better. And now, in what amounted to only several minutes, he found himself more satisfied than after spending hours with the most experienced of harlots.

He felt as if he had been wrung inside out. Without pausing to examine the why or wherefore or how, Dunstan knew he had to have this—whatever it was—between them, again and again. He wanted to rock some soft bed every night with the incredible passion they shared, but he realized that even that would not be enough. He wanted the same driving, hot ecstasy under a tree or in a stream in broad daylight whenever he might sneak away from his duties.

By faith, he wanted it forever, for the rest of his days and nights. It was overwhelming. It was unbelievable.

He had to have it.

Dunstan seemed to know where they were going, so Marion followed as best she could behind him, along the edge of the river. Although the going was difficult, she was too euphoric to complain. After the past few weeks of unhappiness and terror, these idyllic hours spent with Dunstan were like a dream.

Although she flushed at the boldness she had displayed last night, obviously her eagerness had pleased the Wolf. And this morning, their tryst in the water had been brief, but intense, especially when he had pushed back her hair with a large hand, pinned her with his fierce green stare and whispered, "Ah, wren, how I burn for you...."

The memory made her weak at the knees, and Marion had to hurry to catch up to him. The Wolf walked silently, with the grace of his namesake, prowling ahead, stopping and then listening before moving on, his caution apparent. Obviously, he did not think they were safe yet from her uncle's soldiers, and the thought made Marion nervous.

She said nothing, however, and in truth they had talked very little. All the questions that Marion had brought with her from Baddersly remained unasked and unanswered by their fevered lovemaking and in the rush to be off again.

Eventually, Marion knew they would have to settle things more prosaically between them. At the very least, she ought to prod Dunstan for their destination.

And yet she was not eager to do so. Although she longed to return to Campion, Marion knew that might not be wise, and she hesitated to examine the alternatives. Once, she had begged Dunstan to leave her in the nearest town. Would he? She cleared her throat, but words did not come. With a sinking feeling, Marion realized that she did not want this dream to end. She would rather wander through the wild, the Wolf at her side, indefinitely, than face a future without him.

When Marion's stomach began growling loudly, Dunstan called a halt, that smile that was not quite a smile gracing his wonderful mouth. They stopped under the shade of a great willow, and he handed her a chunk of bread from his pouch.

"By faith, I long for a real meal myself," he said gruffly, as if to take away any of her embarrassment, and her heart warmed at his unexpected thoughtfulness.

He ate quickly, then leaned back against the tree, his elbows upon his knees in a relaxed pose. "The river should take us up to Stile, where we can get horses, decent food and even a bed at an inn. That, I am thinking, will be a pleasure beyond price," he noted with a weary sigh.

His casual mention of a room for them filled Marion with yearning. Mercy, but she loved him! She let her gaze wander over his handsome features as he rested his head back against the rough bark. His eyes drifted shut, the small surrender softening his features. Suddenly, Marion felt a lump in her throat. "You came for me," she whispered.

Dunstan's response was a noncommittal grunt, so familiar and dear that Marion smiled, but she would not be deterred. "After dragging me forcibly, mile after wretched mile, to that horrible place, you turned around and rescued me from it."

Although his eyes remained closed, Dunstan answered her gruffly. "I followed your trail to Baddersly, but I had to see for myself if you had arrived safely." The brief explanation, devoid of any emotion, reminded Marion that she was his charge. A piece of baggage to be delivered. Faithful Dunstan, still trying to fulfill his father's mission, Marion thought, surprised at the bitter taste the knowledge left in her mouth.

"Your uncle denied that you were there." That comment, uttered in a rough voice, brought Marion up short. So, her uncle had planned to dispose of her quickly, claim that she was still missing . . . and blame Campion. Marion felt disappointment, hot and heavy, weigh upon her chest as her myriad questions were answered in one fell swoop.

Dunstan had come for her to protect his father's good name. He had not climbed the south tower because he cared for her or because he had lain with her. He had risked his life to retrieve a troublesome package for which he was responsible. Marion's throat went dry at the discovery, and the bread she had eaten sank like a stone in her belly.

Wiping her hands upon her skirt, over and over, she sought a composure that was difficult to find anymore. What had once come so easily now seemed out of reach. Slaughter, mayhem and the return of her memory had taken toll of her. Days of trudging through the wilderness, living hand to mouth, had strained her, as had the nights, especially the last one, spent in Dunstan's arms. Joining with the Wolf had been folly, for more than any of the mishaps that had plagued her, it had laid her bare and made her vulnerable to a pain more powerful than any other.

Marion drew in a ragged breath as she sought a calm demeanor. She was struck suddenly by the image of a vase she had once seen. Its surface was riddled with cracks, but it remained intact, and she realized that was the way she felt—as if she might break apart at the slightest touch.

"One of your women, an old lady with white hair, told me where to find you," Dunstan said, blithely unaware of the havoc his words had wrought, and Marion could only be grateful for that.

"Fenella," she noted, surprised and gratified that anyone at Baddersly had seen fit to help her. She sent up a fervent prayer that her uncle never discover the brave servant's complicity, for the woman had undoubtedly saved her life. But for what? What did her future hold now?

Her pleasant dream was over. It was time to face the cold, harsh truth. "I am grateful to her, and to you, for saving my life," Marion said, hating the way her voice wavered. "But I would know what to do with it. Where are you taking me, Dunstan?"

"We go to Wessex," he answered. A scowl descended, and he opened his eyes, revealing a haunted look at the mention of his holding.

He was probably angry, yet again, at the delays that had kept him from his lands, Marion thought. And although she appreciated his eagerness to return home, she had no wish to join him there. What would she do at Wessex, but long for a life she could never have? She shook her head sadly. "My uncle will surely look for me there and do you ill."

Dunstan smiled grimly. "Ah, but this time we shall make sure he has no right to you."

"How?"

"We shall wed," he said. Then, as if he had mentioned nothing of consequence, the Wolf tilted back his head and closed his eyes.

Chapter Fourteen

Wed the Wolf? Marion stared at him, her cheeks flaming. Was he mad? Surely he did not take his duty so seriously that he would sacrifice himself for it? She wanted to scream, to pummel him with her fists for being so cold about taking a wife—and so fiendishly devoted to his father's errand.

It was ridiculous, of course. He did not truly desire her hand, and she...Mercy, but the very thought of marrying him sent pain dancing through her so starkly that it robbed her of breath. How could she spend the rest of her life looking at the face she loved and knowing that he cared naught for her? How would she bear it when he looked right through her? Away from him, she might be able to remain intact, like that long-ago vase, but married to him, she would surely shatter irrevocably....

"No," she said softly.

"What?" Dunstan muttered, as though he had not heard her correctly.

"No," she repeated.

He was silent for so long that Marion wondered if he had fallen asleep, but then his eyes shot open and she saw the stunned look in them. The de Burghs were all full of themselves, as she well knew, and the Wolf more so than most. Undoubtedly, the thought of anyone refusing him was incomprehensible. He would want to know why.... Marion felt like squirming as his fierce green gaze sought her own, but she schooled herself to return his regard without flinching.

"'Tis too dangerous. I would not have you risk your life any further," she explained, staring directly at him. "With the jewels, I can buy a new life in some town along your route. It will be much simpler, Dunstan. You will have discharged your duty to Campion and you may see to your own business."

Marion finished, proud of her control, and even managed to conjure up some semblance of a smile. However, all of her efforts appeared to have been for naught, because Dunstan gave her a long-suffering glance that told her he dismissed every word as female foolishness.

"Stop your chattering, wren," he said, shutting his eyes again.

"Dunstan de Burgh! Listen to me," Marion cried, a bit desperately. "I will not wed you!"

Without lifting his lids, he smiled smugly in that exasperating way of his. "Save your shrieks for our marriage bed," he whispered.

Marion began to protest, but thought better of it. How quickly she had forgotten the uselessness of arguing with the Wolf. He would always have his own way, right or wrong, great bully that he was! How dare he force her to marry him when he acted only out of honor or pity—or some such emotion?

Marion's nails dug into her palms as she struggled with her own despair. She could not wed him! There had to be a way out of this.... She glanced over at him suddenly. He was breathing in a low, even rhythm, as if he dozed, and Marion knew that he caught snatches of sleep here and there when he could.

If he truly slumbered... Marion's agile mind grasped a plan, spinning out the possibilities. It would not be the first time she had fled from Dunstan's wardship, and now, since they no longer traveled to Baddersly, he would not expect her to try again. They were all alone out here. All she had to do was get up and go. She would head east to one of the coastal towns, and present herself as the widow of a soldier. It would not be easy, without protection, but perhaps she could hire a manservant....

Money! She would need her jewels, which were in a small pouch attached to Dunstan's belt. Marion had never asked for them back, and why should she, when they were safe where they were? Marion bit back one of Dunstan's foul curses at her own foolishness. Well, she would just have to get them now, before she left. The thought of retrieving them from where they lay, against the top of one of Dunstan's steely thighs, set her cheeks to burning, but she would have to do it, and without disturbing him, either.

Drawing in a deep breath, Marion inched closer. Dunstan's visage remained unchanged, his long lashes still and flush against his broad cheeks. The beauty of the man struck her to the bone, and she faltered, but then she bent over him, her fingers reaching toward it....

His hand flashed so quickly that Marion blinked, dazedly surprised to find him grasping her wrist in a tight hold. She looked up into his eyes, fierce and alert, glaring at her with obvious menace. "You desire something, Marion?"

He was angry, and so big and dangerous that Marion nearly quailed before him, but somehow she summoned the courage to respond. "I was but after my jewels," she whispered.

His lips curved in a wicked, feral smile. "You disappoint me, wren. I thought 'twas my jewels you were after."

When she eyed him blankly, he loosed her and swore, long and harshly. Absently, Marion rubbed her wrist, while she stared at him, wide-eyed and uncertain.

"Did I not warn you never to flee from me again, Marion?" he asked.

She nodded mutely before finding her voice. "But, Dunstan, it is different now. You rescued me from my uncle, and I am grateful, but you need do no more, truly." She backed away from the murderous scowl on his face and raised her palms in supplication.

"Do not glare at me so. I was but trying to save you from yourself! From the very beginning, you have complained that you wanted to be rid of me, a troublesome piece of baggage." To her horror, Marion felt her lips tremble and tears press at the back of her eyes. Not now...she could not break now. Silently, Marion willed herself to go on firmly, but she could not meet his gaze. "Surely, you do not want to bind yourself to me forever?"

She felt his huge palm against her cheek, gently turning her toward him, and she saw something pass across his features, easing the lines of strain there. Apparently, she had soothed the Wolf's sore temper, though she was not sure how.

"Do not fret so, wren. I am well satisfied with my decision," he said gruffly. He ran a thumb down her cheek, causing her to shiver, and then he smiled—a smug, infuriating, male gesture.

"Come along, before you tempt me to prove my satisfaction," he growled. Then he rose in one swift, graceful motion and pulled her with him. And Marion had no choice but to follow.

Dunstan strode along in the tall grass by the river's edge, intent upon any sign of danger, but the woman at his side intruded in his thoughts more often than not. Why would she refuse him? He was titled and landed and no pauper. He had saved her life more than once, and he had brought her pleasure such that she screamed out in ecstasy. By faith, she had given him her virginity, why not her hand in marriage?

He grunted in annoyance. Why must anything involving the wren be fraught with complications and complexities? He liked them not. And she was the most perverse of females! Why could she not tell him the truth? Instead, she gave him an explanation that he knew to be a lie.

Of course, her opinion mattered little. They would be wed, Dunstan thought grimly. It was the most sensible solution to the threat posed by her uncle. Legally, Peasely was still her guardian, and the swiftest, simplest way to remove him from that position would be to get her a husband. Since she had no suitors or otherwise eligible parties to choose from, he was the logical choice. And since she had given him her maidenhead, he was the *only* choice.

As far as Dunstan was concerned, she would do as well as any other for his wife. He had been thinking of setting up his household anyway. It was high time that he got himself an heir, and Marion was not too old to provide him with one. In some areas, most notably in the bedchamber, she would do even better than most. By faith, after sampling the passion that flared between them, Dunstan knew he would never be satisfied with anyone else.

She would suit him admirably, especially when she was installed at Wessex. Then he would no longer be bound to her day and night, but could go about his own business without her vexing interference, and return home to her heated embrace. Dunstan knew he would gladly look forward to such a routine, if he could only put up with the foolishness that she exhibited other times, such as now....

Dunstan clenched his jaw. Her reluctance to marry him made him feel oddly vulnerable, something distasteful in the extreme to a battle-hardened warrior. That left him bitter enough, but to make matters worse, she had tried to escape again! Dunstan's rage surged back at what seemed to him a betrayal, especially after the way she had come to him last night, all sweet and hot and eager.

By faith, he would never understand her! One minute she was staring at him, those huge eyes filled with adoration, and the next she had the look of a wounded fawn, her lip trembling as if he had beaten her! And in the interim, he had done nothing! Grunting, Dunstan rubbed the back of his neck, sorely aggrieved.

She was lagging behind, and he turned swiftly to flash a scowl at her. If she thought she was going to escape again, she was even more senseless than he imagined. Let her dare it, and he would tether her to himself, just like a mule. And when he reached Wessex, he would chain her to his bed!

While there was something tantalizing about that idea, Dunstan did not pursue it. Instead, frustration filled him. What was she about? Although she acted silly enough at times, he knew there was a clever brain in that pretty head of hers. What was going on in it?

With a low oath, Dunstan told himself it mattered not. They would reach Stile soon enough and there the business would be finished. Despite any protestations to the contrary, Marion Warenne was going to be his wife, and despite his own ill humor, Dunstan took a certain grim satisfaction in it.

He was in one of his moods again, grunting and growling at her like a baited bear, and Marion was too distraught herself to find it at all amusing or endearing. Although she hurried beside him, her thoughts were directed toward leaving Dunstan de Burgh, her plans for escape only momentarily thwarted by the tight grip of his hand upon her arm.

Stile was a town, not a village, and when she saw the crowded marketplace, Marion hoped to disappear among the stalls. Dunstan seemed to read her mind, however, for the minute they came to the busy streets, he took hold of her. Although she knew that he was being careful not to bruise her, his grasp was firm, and she could hardly fight the strength of the Wolf of Wessex.

He had asked after a horse market, and now here they were, Dunstan striding back and forth, dragging her with him, as he viewed the mares and foals, palfreys and chargers. He halted before the largest beast there, eyeing it up and down, and although it was not as huge as his old destrier, Dunstan seemed well pleased.

Marion was tugged along while he investigated the horse further, and then, apparently satisfied, haggled with the seller. Plotting her escape, she listened but absently to their conversation. Perhaps tonight, after he fell asleep... Even the Wolf of Wessex could not stay awake forever, and it would be so easy to vanish among all these buildings in the darkness.

When Dunstan lowered his voice, Marion turned her attention back to him. Tall and threatening-looking, the Wolf was asking the man where he got his stock and if he had seen any horses put up for sale in the past week. Surprised, Marion realized Dunstan was describing his destrier and the mounts that had served his men. A waste of time to look for them here, she thought dismally, when they were, no doubt, filling up her uncle's stables.

A saddle, which Dunstan claimed was a sad piece of workmanship, was found and the purchase completed. Then Dunstan mounted and lifted her up before him. Marion had barely settled in against his chest when he turned the beast away from the market to head down the street.

"Wait! Where is my horse?" Marion asked, straining to turn toward him.

"This is it, wren. Under the circumstances, I thought it best if we share," he said, giving her a tight, hard smile. His features were set in a scowl, his eyes narrowed and his jaw clenched. Marion whirled back around. Obviously, he was beginning to know her too well. He expected her to bolt, and he was not happy about it.

Well, let the Wolf grunt and growl. She cared not! His boorish behavior only made her more eager to be rid of him forever! Pressing a hand to her skirts, Marion smoothed the material and stared straight ahead.

She spoke not another word, so they traveled in silence until Dunstan reined the horse to a halt in front of a stone building. He deftly slid to the ground and then pulled her down beside him. Did she imagine it, or did his hands linger at her waist, his breath caressing her hair intimately?

Marion glanced up at him to see his face taut above hers, his eyes glittering and dark. Despite his foul temper, he wanted her, and she knew it. Her fingers dug into the huge muscles of his upper arms even as her heart swelled . . . and her stomach protested loudly.

He smiled, flashing his white teeth in a way that made her knees wobble. "Behave inside and I will feed you, wren," he promised.

Marion found her voice, with difficulty. "Where are we going now?"

"We have one more bit of business to take care of, and then we shall find an inn and fill your belly." Dunstan's mouth curled up at that, as if he saw some private amusement in the words, then he hurried her inside.

It took Marion's eyes a moment to adjust to the dim light, but all too soon, she realized where they were. A church! Rage sparked in her, surprising in its intensity, for she had never felt such anger before, even toward her uncle.

For a moment, she tried to check it, but it only flared higher, driven by weeks of ill usage. By faith, ever since she met him, Dunstan de Burgh had dragged her this way and that, according to his male whims, while ignoring her wishes and her feelings. It was going to stop now.

"No." Wrenching herself from his grasp, Marion turned and folded her arms in front of her, her legs spread in an echo of the Wolf's own unyielding stance. "You cannot force me to marry you, Dunstan."

Glaring at her, he swore a low string of foul curses, and then swung away, as if he would put a fist through one of the wooden settles.

"Watch your tongue! Have you no respect for the Lord's house?"

At her reprimand, Dunstan growled out his displeasure. In one swift, graceful movement, he whirled around, put his hands upon his hips, and stared down at her, his face implacable. Out of the corner of her eye, Marion saw a priest approach them, only to take one look at Dunstan, turn tail and scurry back into the shadows.

But Marion did not retreat. She simply stared right back at the man towering over her, and she realized, suddenly, how very silly she must appear, one tiny female standing up to this huge, dangerous knight. She realized, too, that neither one of them saw anything odd in their confrontation.

The Wolf, it seemed, had become used to her arguments. He did not use his great strength to subdue her, nor did he threaten her with it. He was furious, and yet he waited, determined to sway her by sheer force of his will. He was not tamed, by any means, but he had changed....

"Why, Marion?" he finally said, in an oddly strained voice. "Give me one good reason why you deny me. Give me one good reason, and perhaps I shall reconsider my course."

Marion looked up at the face that meant so much to her, and her anger dwindled away. Her refusal had stung his pride. The evidence was there in his green eyes, fierce and bright, as they sought her own. He was truly baffled, and yes, perhaps even hurt, by her rejection.

Suddenly, Marion wanted nothing more than to reassure him, to soothe his wounded dignity, to lift her hands to his face and kiss his wonderful mouth, proving to him just how much she would like to marry him—if only things were different. Instead, her gaze slid away from his piercing one. "Because you do not love me," she whispered.

Dunstan snorted loudly, and she saw him throw back his head as if he would laugh, but noting her horrified expression, he restrained himself. He frowned at her instead. "Of all the ridiculous notions!"

Marion reached down to smooth her gown, as though by that gentle motion, she might ease her aching heart. What use to tell him the truth, for he only scoffed, as she should have known he would? Obviously, the Wolf had not changed very much, after all. She looked down at her hands and then clasped them neatly together before her.

Although she said nothing, Marion could feel his eyes upon her, and when he spoke, his voice was softer, as if he sensed her distress. Still, his exasperation showed in his tone and in his question. "We are talking about life and death, here, Marion, of protecting you from your uncle, and you are worried about love?"

When she glanced up at him, Marion realized that he had on his long-suffering face, the one he wore whenever he thought her foolish. He stepped closer, his speech measured in an apparent attempt to appeal to her better sense. "Marion, love is naught but some silliness con-

cocted by the troubadours. 'Tis not something known to
real men and women, to husbands and wives.''

Marion felt a pang at his words, along with a deep sadness for him—and for herself. How could she convince
him? Arguing with the Wolf was a useless enterprise, and
yet she had to try. She held her fingers tightly before her,
drawing strength and composure from the familiar pose.
''Yes, it is, Dunstan, for I know my parents loved each
other,'' she said, her head bent, her throat thick. ''And do
not tell me that your father did not love his wives.''

Dunstan hesitated, obviously caught unawares by her
statement, and Marion felt emboldened as long as she did
not look at him. She went on, recklessly taking the final
step, baring her soul in one heedless moment. ''I know
love exists, Dunstan, because I feel it myself... for you.''

Marion heard his harsh hiss of surprise, and then he
was silent for so long that she yearned to take back her
confession. When she finally dared peek up at him, she
saw something pass across his face, as if he were involved
in some inner struggle with himself, before it was gone,
subdued by his supreme discipline. His handsome features revealed nothing as he took her hands gently. ''All
the more reason to marry me, then,'' he said, his lips
curving in the most pathetic excuse for a smile she had
ever seen.

Marion drew back at his attempt to humor her. She had
tried to pierce that thick hide of his and failed. Obviously, the Wolf felt nothing for her, and her wrenching
admission had won her naught but his contempt. It was
no more than she had expected, yet it pained her still. She
smoothed out her gown, ostensibly concerned only with
each rumple and crease.

''Marion...''

''No,'' she said softly.

''Wren...'' He whirled away, and in that moment,
Marion's fragile determination shattered. Had he argued

further, she would have remained steadfast; had he growled and cursed, she would have been unmoved. But whatever he felt, he did not want her to see it. Perhaps he did not want to see it himself.

Placing his hands upon the back of a settle, he leaned upon it, his great shoulders sagging and his dark head lowered in a pose of defeat she had never expected to see the Wolf assume.

Marion was lost.

Blinking back the tears that threatened, she knew then just how much she loved him—enough to concede her hard-won freedom for now. Perhaps forever.

"All right, Dunstan," she said.

True to his word, Dunstan fed her. They stopped at a tavern for hot stew cradled in loaves of bread and then left, taking it with them, for Dunstan had no wish to stay inside for the meal. As a lone knight and a lovely woman, they were conspicuous, and without his men, Dunstan felt too vulnerable to linger, especially when Peasely might still be looking for them.

The stealth did not sit well with Dunstan, a man used to open warfare and honest dealings. He felt naked without his knights, and frustrated, but he could do nothing more to protect Marion and he had no wish to spend his wedding night on the road. Still, he chose a room at a quiet inn near the edge of town, in case a quick departure became necessary. Although he was fairly certain that Peasely would not be searching this far east, he would not gamble his life upon it, or the life of his wife.

His *wife*. There was something strangely satisfying in the knowledge that he possessed the wren. She was his, now and forever, to warm his bed every night, to nurture him in that motherly way of hers, to bestow upon him the light of that smile, complete with dimples....

Dunstan scowled. There had been little enough smiling of late. Although the wren had capitulated, she bore no resemblance to a beaming bride. On the contrary, she had about her an indefinable air of sadness that made her seem even more fragile and small. It was like a mantle of grief, appropriate if he had killed her horse or some such despicable deed, but hardly justified by his noble gesture of marriage.

Her manner pricked at his pride and made him surly, and with each grimace and growl, Dunstan felt her slipping farther away. By faith! Where was the Marion who had pressed him down upon the bank of the stream, pleasuring him with her touch and her mouth? This doe-eyed creature was but a shadow of that woman, and if this was love, he could well live without it!

Dunstan snorted in disgust at the thought. Female foolishness! Courtly songs and poems celebrating this fanciful emotion did naught but make a married woman unhappy with her lot and set her to dreaming of some pasty-faced bard who dripped honeyed phrases over her hand, but could not hold a sword. What good were sweet words? A woman should be content with a decent home, a life free from want and toil and a strong man to protect her.

That was just what he could provide for Marion. Why then was she not happy? Why were women so wretchedly perverse?

Grunting in bafflement, Dunstan glanced toward her. After having eaten in silence and prepared for the night like a doomed woman receiving her last food and rest, Marion lay in the big bed, covers up to her chin, just as though she were a virgin looking forward to a night of ill usage.

Well, he knew better, and so did she, by faith! Dunstan let his mail fall to the floor loudly. She did not flinch, but remained still and silent, in her composed pose, which annoyed him further. He wanted her to smile at him, dimples and all, to beckon to him in her own innocently alluring way, to show some small measure of contentment in their marriage.

She did not. Blowing out the candle, Dunstan quickly shed his garments in the darkness and stepped to the bed. "Have you no welcome for your husband?" he asked. Although her manner sorely plagued him, his body was already responding to the thought of her naked beneath the sheets. *His wife.* He climbed in beside her and stretched out.

"Yes, I welcome you, Dunstan." Her voice was soft and sad, irritating him further. He moved atop her, bracing his arms at her sides and sliding his fingers into hers, as if by his own strength, he could bend her to his will.

"I have no honeyed words for you, wife," he ground out harshly.

"I know that, Dunstan." Her voice broke, and he thought she might be crying. Day of God, what a wedding night! He felt like rolling from her, but he was already painfully hard. Her soft breasts pressed up into his chest, and he could smell the earthy scent of her hair, like flowers and fresh fields. He wanted her. He had an insidious suspicion that he always would.

"I would give you my protection, and a home and children," he rasped, his breath coming faster.

"I know."

"Then what is it?" Dunstan growled, impatient with her mood.

"You will not give me love or respect or freedom of will."

Dunstan snorted. More female foolishness. Perhaps it was her flux time. He pressed her wrists into the mattress. "But I will give you pleasure, wren," he whispered before he took her mouth with his own and silenced all debate.

He was hungry for her. The morning's joining in the stream seemed years ago, and he had to have her, like a man possessed. He was grateful that she was, indeed, no virgin, for he did not have the restraint he had shown in the shepherd's hut. Not tonight. Not when she was well and truly his, and he must needs possess her.

His lips moved across her tender cheek to her throat and slid along the sweet slim column to the round curve of her shoulder. By faith, she felt so good. The passion that always sparked between them flared brightly, heating his blood and dazing his mind. What magic did this woman weave that made all his senses keener, all his feelings run deeper?

Moving lower, he tasted her breasts, full and firm and round, suckling them until she whimpered and writhed beneath him. Whatever else stood between them, here in bed there were no constraints—or complaints. Dunstan smiled smugly, using his knee to nudge apart her legs and positioning himself between her thighs.

Wife, he thought when he filled her in one eager motion. *My wife.* His fingers still entwined with hers as he thrust home, again and again, into the sweet, hot haven of her body. Day of God, nothing could ever be so good as this....

She was making the pleasure sounds that excited him beyond bearing, flinging her head from side to side as she rose to meet him eagerly. And when she cried out, Dunstan cut it off with his mouth, drawing in the frenzied joy of her climax and plunging himself over the edge into the violent, shuddering world of surcease.

Chapter Fifteen

From past experience, Marion guessed that Dunstan would sleep like the dead after performing so lustily. He was snoring again, a good sign that he would not wake easily, and Marion knew this was her chance. She slid out of bed.

She dressed quietly, without glancing toward him. She did not want to remember the rough, hot bliss of their mating, for then she might be tempted to stay with a man who did not love her—who did not even believe in such tender emotions.

Although Dunstan had promised her a home and family, Marion knew their marriage would be but a hollow mockery of the happy life at Campion. As innocent as she was, she could tell the difference between true caring and desire. Passion, she suspected, was all that she would ever get from her husband. And when it faded? She could never again bear to be shut away from life, shunted aside, locked away....

Swallowing a lump in her throat, Marion wasted precious minutes groping in the dark for his belt and the bag that held her jewels. When she found them right beside the bed, she realized that Dunstan did not expect her to flee him now that they were wed. The thought moved the thickness in her throat down into her chest, filled to bursting with yearning and grief.

Although she knew she must hurry, Marion found that her limbs were slow to move, as if her body, disputing her brain's plans, was reluctant to leave. But she knew that this night held her best chance for escape. He was asleep, unsuspecting and…vulnerable. Unwilling to think of the Wolf in such terms, Marion disregarded her own observations, but they continued nonetheless. And when he woke to find her gone?

He would feel betrayed.

Trying to ignore her sudden, fierce sympathy for the man who did not love her, Marion forced her rebellious legs to action and crept carefully to the window. She opened the shutters and looked out to total blackness. In town, the darkness seemed absolute, and it took her a while to see the ground below. From the high, narrow ledge, she would have quite a jump, but if she could climb out and swing herself down, she could manage it.

The sudden sound of voices below made Marion freeze where she was, for she had no desire to land among a group of ruffians, especially at this hour. Although she could not tell how many they were in the darkness, Marion heard one man speak, low yet clearly as they approached.

"They are here at the inn," he said.

"Are you certain?"

"Aye. The innkeeper said a huge, dark-haired knight and a tiny lady took all of one room from him. Although the fellow feared to betray Wessex, he was more than ready to accept my money. We shall have no trouble gaining entrance."

They passed right beneath her window as Marion stood stock-still above, frozen in shock. *Someone was after them.* Her uncle! Unsure of how much time they had before the knaves would burst into the room, Marion rushed to the bed. She put a finger to Dunstan's lips and her mouth to his ear.

"There are men in the alley coming for us!" she whispered frantically.

She did not have to speak again. The Wolf was up instantly, pulling on his clothes, while she grabbed their pouches. With astonishing speed, he swung his great, agile body out the narrow window and dropped to the ground. In another moment, she was in his arms and they were off, running around the back of the building to where the horse was stabled.

Mounting in tense silence, they galloped off into the darkness even as the disappointed shouts of their pursuers rose to meet their ears from the room they had left behind.

They did not take the road, but wound out into the darkness until Marion was hopelessly confused. Dunstan seemed to know where they going, so she made no argument, but slept against him, grateful now that they shared a mount.

He had purchased a bow and arrows in Stile, which he put to good use come morning, and they dared a small fire to dine on roast hare. Although Marion had a hand in cooking it, she swore nothing had ever tasted as good. When she said so, Dunstan rewarded her with one of his infrequent, flashing smiles, and, for the moment, she was content.

The night's near calamity had convinced her that, for now, they were both safer together. Although she still had no intention of living as wife to the Wolf of Wessex for the rest of their days, Marion would stay close by him at least until her uncle no longer posed a threat. *Then* she would decide what to do and where to go.

"You did well last night, Marion." Surprised at Dunstan's words, she glanced up to see his eyes upon her, grave and proud. Stunned, Marion could not stop the swell of love she felt for him. When he looked at her this way, as an equal instead of a mindless fool, she felt the power of him, right down to her bones.

Strength, dignity, loyalty, gentleness and a fierce pro-tectiveness—the Wolf had all these in abundance. Would that he showed her less growling and more of this side of him, and Marion might be tempted to stay with him for-ever. Swallowing the last of her rabbit with difficulty, Marion basked in the warm glow of his praise, so rarely given.

"Your attentiveness and quick thinking saved our lives," Dunstan added. His face was serious, his words simple and sincere. He did not rant about his own help-lessness, asleep in the bed, nor did he make light of her part, as some men might have done.

Words did not come easily to him, and knowing that, Marion was well pleased with his speech. She smiled at him, her love for the Wolf threatening to spill out of her, for he was, indeed, a different beast than he once had been. "Thank you," she said.

"Thank *you*, my wife," he said gruffly. Marion began to wonder if she had earned his respect at last. How ironic that she should prove herself in what had begun as an at-tempt to escape him. Praise God that Dunstan would never know that small truth! He cleared his throat, draw-ing her attention back to him, and she saw something in his face for a fleeting moment that stole her breath. "It seems that I am well served in our marriage," he said.

Then it was gone, and he rose to put out the fire, leav-ing Marion to gape after him, uncertain how to respond. Was he being sarcastic or serious? Did he make reference to her own discontent, which, she knew, tried him sorely? Or was he, truly, satisfied?

Too confused to reply, Marion said nothing, and when it became apparent that Dunstan was not going to elabo-rate, she rose and washed her hands in the nearby stream.

When she returned, Dunstan was seated, his back against a tree, his knees bent before him. His concentration was focused on an arrow that he held between his hands, and he turned it slowly while he studied it.

As she watched, Marion realized it was not any shaft, but the one he had taken from the sentry's body at their ill-fated camp. Having carried it south to Baddersly, he kept it still. Marion made some noise at the discovery, and he looked up at her, a question on his handsome features. Seeing her distress, he said simply, "We know not who came upon us last night."

"No," Marion agreed, after a brief hesitation. She had related the overheard conversation to him already, and though she assumed the men under their window to have been sent by her uncle, nothing in their speech had given away their identity. She sighed softly. "Mayhap everyone in the world is out to do us murder."

Dunstan smiled grimly. "It seems that way, does it not, wren?" He gazed down at the missile, running it through his fingers and examining the fletch. Then, as if suddenly seized by an idea, he leaned forward and sniffed it. His eyes narrowed, and his features grew taut and troubled at the scent, but before Marion could ask him what that meant, he put it to his mouth and tasted it. She stared, astonished, as Dunstan's jaw clenched and his handsome face became more hard and set than she had ever seen it.

"What is it?" she managed to squeak.

Glancing up at her, Dunstan appeared strangely distant for a moment, as though he did not know her. Then he hefted the weapon in his hand. "This arrow was made with hide glue, not a fish-based substance," he explained. At her blank look, he added, "'Tis more expensive and not widely employed, but I know someone who uses naught else."

"Who?" Marion asked, half fearful of the answer.

"My neighbor, Fitzhugh." He hissed the name like an obscenity, and Marion blanched. She had heard Dunstan speak of the man before, as an enemy of Wessex, but why would Fitzhugh slaughter their train? Dunstan had been on an errand for Campion, escorting a woman south to her home. What business would Fitzhugh have with them?

"But surely our camp was too far from your holdings to attract this man's attention," Marion protested. "Why would Fitzhugh follow you so far?"

Even she was startled by the black hatred that passed over the Wolf's face, reminding her what a ferocious warrior he would be when roused.

"Why?" he asked, in a tone heavy with bitterness. His eyes met hers over the tip of the arrow he now clutched in a death hold. "I would give you an answer in one word, Marion—murder."

Marion drew in a sharp breath at his reply. He had spoken of Fitzhugh as harrying his people and his lands, but cold-blooded murder? "Why?" she asked again.

Dunstan laughed, a harsh, sickening sound. "Because he covets Wessex. Because it meets his own property, he has thought of it as his own for many a year. I have heard that he was enraged when Edward awarded it to me. Yet he knows that he has no true claim to it, so he cannot obtain it through legal means."

Marion went still as his meaning dawned on her. "He thinks to gain it by killing you?"

"Greed drives a man to many things, wren," he said. His tone gentled when he added, "As your uncle has proved."

"Yes," Marion admitted. She frowned, a pale copy of Dunstan's own scowl. "'Tis the same thing, is it not? He would murder me for what I have, as Fitzhugh would you."

"Yes," Dunstan agreed, his mouth a grim line. "'Twould seem we have too many enemies, my wife, and too few friends."

Marion lifted her head, taking umbrage at that. "No. That is not true. We have your father, a powerful earl, and your six brothers, good men all, to aid us. Methinks they are worth more than any friends."

Dunstan's hard lips softened a bit. "Perhaps, wren, but we must reach them first."

"We go to Campion, then?" Although Marion could not contain her pleasure at the thought of seeing the earl and his sons again, she immediately regretted it, for Dunstan shot her a strange look, fraught with possessive fire.

"No. We go to Wessex." He spoke in a challenging tone, as if he expected her to argue, but Marion did not. She hid her disappointment smoothly, unwilling to rouse the Wolf further.

"To Wessex, then," she agreed, though she longed for familiar faces.

"Yes, let us go to Wessex," Dunstan said, his face suddenly pensive. "But let us go warily, wren. Warily."

Warily was the watchword, for they stayed away from the roads and wound their way through woods and countryside until Marion had no idea where they might be. The long days of travel were tiring, and when at night they fell asleep, they were often too weary even to join together on their haphazard beds.

Although some part of Marion missed that hot passion, another was glad for the respite. She could not think clearly when Dunstan touched her, setting ablaze whatever raged between them, and she refused to let lust rule her mind. She had temporarily set aside her discontent, and his temper seemed to have eased, but a constraint still existed in their marriage. Underneath the surface of their polite behavior were the same conflicts, untended and unresolved.

Marion was of a mind that these concerns could wait until they were safely somewhere—at Campion or Wessex or even Baddersly, if her uncle be routed. Then, she would address them and decide upon a course for her future. It was a determination she did not mind putting off for the moment.

As bittersweet as her time with Dunstan might be, Marion could not help clinging to it a little while longer. In truth, she found her resolve to leave her husband wavering as they continued on together. And yet, a life with the Wolf held out little promise. She might have won his respect, but she did not have his love, and he was still the most stubborn, foul-tempered, domineering man who ever lived.

She only let him push her so far, and then she would stand her ground until either he stomped off, cursing and muttering, or he gave way, with a rather surprised look of admiration on his face that made her want to kiss him.

Dangerous thoughts. Marion was trying very hard to keep her love for him firmly contained. When she let it swell and burst forth, she hurt with the tender ache of it. And besides, she told herself, they both needed their wits about them now simply to survive when they were nearing his home.

Taking in a deep, calming breath, Marion looked about her. The countryside reminded her of Campion, with its beech-covered heights and lush vales, and she held out a hope that they might stop there yet. "Surely we cannot be far from your father?"

"No. Campion is but three days' ride from here, almost due west, for it lies southwest of Wessex," Dunstan said, rather shortly, and she felt his body tense behind her. "But, look, these are my lands."

"Already? 'Tis beautiful, Dunstan, green and fine and rich," Marion said, honestly approving the world around her.

Dunstan did not relax, but remained stiff against her as if the sight of his holdings displeased him in some way. "'Tis not as vast as Campion, but it is mine, won by my own hand," he noted gruffly. "I would you not be disappointed with the castle, for it needs some repair yet. I warn you now, Marion, 'tis not as fine as my father's house nor your own Baddersly."

Marion felt the traitorous surge of love in her at his ill-disguised vulnerability and firmly quelled it. "Dunstan, I care not for riches. You must know that by now," she answered. "I am sure that your home will serve us well." A lump formed in her throat, for how could she promise him to cherish his holding when she still held out plans to leave him? With the bitter knowledge of hindsight, Marion knew she should have never come so far with him, for each moment spent with the Wolf only bound her more closely to him.

He grunted, as if unconvinced by her answer, but Marion felt him relax. "Methinks that Wessex will seem a palace after so much time spent on the road," he said finally.

"Yes," Marion agreed hurriedly. "I have no further taste for travel, but would be content with hot food and a soft bed." Too late, she realized her poor choice of words, for the mention of a bed made them both aware of their close proximity on the shared mount. As if called to attention, the length of him hardened against her buttocks, and Marion flushed at the bold evidence of his desire.

Dunstan grunted again, one of his unintelligible comments, and Marion struggled to change the subject. "Will we see Wessex soon?" she managed to squeak.

"I would not ride straight to the castle, but first to Seer's Hill."

"What is that, some magical spot?" Marion asked, twisting to look up at him with a smile.

"No," he said, his lips curving upward in answer. "'Tis a promontory where you can see much of the countryside, the valley and the rise where my castle lies. I wish to have a look and judge the state of my holdings from there."

"Do you fear trouble from Fitzhugh?" Marion asked, uneasiness settling over her at the thought.

"No, but I would know what he has been about in my absence. I left soldiers here to guard what is mine while I was gone, and I would see how well they stood against any threat from my neighbor. Unfortunately, we must consider all possibilities, including the worst. And, if so, I wish not to walk into a trap."

Marion stilled as dismay filled her. "But if Fitzhugh truly did murder the train, then he must think you are dead," she protested. "He cannot be expecting you to return home."

"Perhaps," Dunstan said a bit ominously. His eyes narrowed and his mouth tightened, making Marion realize that there was something he was not telling her. Apparently, he had not lost his penchant for keeping his own counsel, even though he had taken her to wife. However, Marion felt she ought to know all that might affect them, especially since they were alone, without soldiers, servant or attendants to aid them in their search for a safe haven.

She opened her mouth to protest, but a glance at his face silenced her. Mercy, but what else could plague them? She turned back around stiffly, uncertain if she had enough courage to bear the answer, should she seek it.

Her fear escalated when Dunstan slowed the horse, hushed her with a word and dismounted stealthily. He lifted her down beside him in one smooth, silent movement, and told her he planned to go up Seer's Hill alone.

"But Dunstan—"

"Do not argue with me, wren," he growled, his attention already ahead of him. "Stay here with the horse and wait for me. I but want a look around." As if as an afterthought, he turned toward her and put a hand to her cheek. "I will be back."

Marion was not reassured, but she knew better than to argue when he was in one of his moods. Although she wanted to fling herself into his arms and kiss him with a wolf's own fierceness, his mind was elsewhere, and she sensed he would not appreciate her distraction. With a reluctant nod, Marion let him go, sighing softly as she watched him disappear into the thick underbrush.

She watered the horse at a spring and then sat down under a tree, methodically smoothing out her sad-looking gown. She told herself that Dunstan would call her any moment to come up and join him, to get her first view of his home. But he did not, and Marion found that she could not sit idly while the minutes dragged by.

The stillness that had given her strength before her uncle's tempers seemed to have deserted her, and she stood up to prowl about the small clearing like the Wolf himself. She bent and splashed some water on her face, letting it dribble down her heated neck before she realized that the horse had wandered after its new master.

Mercy! She leaped to her feet, certain that Dunstan would roar his displeasure if the animal burst in upon his reverie. Scrambling through the bushes, Marion caught up with the horse before it reached the top of the hill. There, she tied it securely to a tree, and then stood, silently, for a moment, stroking the beast in a gesture designed to calm them both.

And, tilting her head upward, she listened.

Ahead, Marion could see nothing through the trees, and she could hardly believe that a great view lay just at the top of the rise. Did no one ever venture up Seer's Hill, or had Dunstan taken a roundabout way to the top? His furtive behavior fed her anxiety, and suddenly she felt a sharp stab of fear for him. Without pausing to consider her actions, Marion moved, climbing higher to stop and listen—until finally she heard something.

Voices? Marion stopped dead. Was Dunstan meeting someone here without her knowledge? Against her will, Marion found herself picturing a clandestine rendezvous with a woman, and she realized that she knew naught of the Wolf's private life. Perhaps he had a leman or a lover, who would be ill-pleased to discover him married.

Marion froze, hardly able to draw in breath at the dreadful implications. Perhaps she should fly now.... She could go back down the hill, take the horse and leave Dunstan to his Wessex and whatever awaited him there. *Go,* she told herself, *before the pain of loving him destroys you!*

The old Marion would have fled, unable to face her demons. But the new Marion could not. Whatever the Wolf's failings, she knew that he did not deserve to be abandoned alone in the wilds, without a horse, especially after all he had done for her. And, the sense of danger that had driven Marion upward still lingered in the air. She could not leave him when he might be in peril.

Drawing her strength together, Marion forced herself to creep forward, until a loud laugh startled her to stillness again. With dizzying relief, she recognized the voice and realized that it was no woman who spoke, but Walter, Dunstan's vassal. Only he sounded different. Decidedly different.

"I thought you might come crawling back here," Walter crowed. "You are hard to kill, Dunstan, but then, I have known that for a long time. 'Twas one of the reasons I stayed by your side so long, so that you might keep me alive, too. But now 'tis I who wields the power of life and death, and you are long past your due, old friend."

Walter's normally low and even tones were loud and harsh with bitterness. "If not for that stupid wench, who kept leading you such a merry chase, you would have been killed with the rest of them. But 'twas too late to change the plans, Dunstan, and you escaped yet again, with your bastard luck and your little heiress. Dutiful Dunstan who must not disappoint his father, who must needs always do what is *right*." Walter coughed up some spittle, and Marion cringed at the sound of him releasing it contemptuously.

"Always alert, always watching, always cursed with the bastard luck of the de Burghs! If you would have but left the wench at the end of the train with me and had not stopped early, by the rood, I would have saved her myself—for myself. Not my usual style, but I would have enjoyed taking her, simply because you were so besotted with her!" Walter laughed cruelly.

Marion trembled as she heard Dunstan's angry grunt. At least he was alive, but in what condition? Had Walter hurt him? Desperate to see, Marion could not force herself to look, for after what Walter had said about her, she had no wish to be discovered by the vassal.

"Ah, have I touched a sore spot, Dunstan?" Walter asked, goading his former lord. "Did you never get to touch her? You must be the only one, for I had it from the men that your brothers, yea, even your father, passed her around until she was well used!"

There was a pause, and Marion sensed that Dunstan's lack of reaction was frustrating his tormentor, for when Walter spoke again, it was in an impatient snarl. "But good son that he is, Dunstan would nay e'er touch his charge. And care he not that his men lay dead, he must deliver her safely," Walter mocked.

"I looked for your body among the slain, but did not find it," Dunstan said. Marion shook with relief to know that he was well enough for speech. And the Wolf's simple statement told her what had driven his secret approach to Wessex. Not knowing whether his vassal lived or died, fled or hid or consorted with his enemies, Dunstan had come warily. But not warily enough.

"Why, Walter? Why turn against me after all these years?" Although the Wolf's voice was calm and clear, Marion felt the pain of his vassal's betrayal down to her bones.

"Why, for coin, of course. Money and lands and power—what every man wants, Dunstan. You see, not all of us are born to the rich, pampered life of a de Burgh, and we must struggle for all we can get. No more for this knight. I have taken enough orders."

"And who would give you this great wealth, Walter?"

"Fitzhugh, as you should know! I shall marry his daughter and have all that I have so long desired."

"You would wed the shrew?" Dunstan's tone relayed disbelief.

"I will tie her to the bed and ride her till she knows her master," Walter snapped. "And what care I for her temperament? All this will be mine!"

"Wessex?" Marion heard the small thread in Dunstan's voice that betrayed his pain, and she wanted to weep, but Walter went on, obviously unknowing.

"Aye, Wessex. Your minion Collins was easy enough to dispatch, and now I'm in control. And when Fitzhugh is gone, I will have it all. All of it, Dunstan! Perhaps I will get some heirs on the Fitzhugh witch's body and start my own line, to rival the dying blood of Campion!"

Dunstan snorted. "Promises aplenty! Only a fool would put his trust in Fitzhugh. He will share naught, as you well know. Before you finish bedding his daughter, he will have a knife in your back, and then he will take it all, Walter. All of it, for himself."

"Shut up!"

"Think, Walter. Think of how Fitzhugh works," Dunstan said. "Think of his lust for this land. He will use you to get what he wants, Walter, and then—"

"Shut up!" Marion flinched as she heard a striking sound. *Dear God, what has he done to the Wolf?* She put a fist to her mouth to keep from crying out and revealing herself, for what could she do against a seasoned knight?

"Shut up, and get up, Dunstan," Walter said. "I had planned to kill you here, swiftly, in memory of our long friendship, but your speech has earned you a more interesting fate. I shall take you back to Fitzhugh and let him have at you! Perhaps a few weeks in your own dungeon will take some of the de Burgh braggart out of you."

Walter laughed again, and the sound made Marion's blood run cold. She heard horses, and peeking through the leaves, she saw Walter and two other men mount. At first, she could not find Dunstan. For one terrifying moment, she thought that his vassal had slain him, after all. But then she saw him, tied behind the horses, a huge, proud figure, who took away her very breath.

As she watched, horrified by the sight, Walter rode on, jerking Dunstan forward, and they left the top of the hill, half dragging the Wolf behind them.

Marion sank to her knees, a low sob escaping. Dear God, what was she to do now? The answer came all too quickly. *You must ride to Campion, Marion.*

She shook her head, fear and desperation making her tremble from head to toe. Although she knew the general direction of the earl's lands, she could become lost all too easily. It was several days' ride way, and by now, Marion knew very well the dangers that menaced lone riders, not to mention the danger of meeting Walter or his men. She had little food and no weapons, but for a paltry dagger. How would she ever make it to Campion?

Kneeling there in shocked despair, Marion reminded herself that not too long ago she had made several attempts to flee into the wilderness alone, although ill-equipped and afraid. She told herself that this journey would be no different. But she knew that it was—for the Wolf's life hung in the balance.

How ironic that she, Dunstan's tiny, foolish female, was the only person in the world who could help him now. She, frail, fearful Marion Warenne. Wessex stood between him and certain death.

Lifting her head slowly, Marion rose gracefully to her feet—and to the challenge of being the Wolf's wife.

The first night was the worst. Mortally afraid of predators, but unwilling to risk a fire, Marion climbed a tree. She huddled there, uncomfortable, remembering the time she had shared such a nest with Dunstan, and though she thought never to close her eyes, she fell into an exhausted sleep.

She rode all the next day, grateful for the sun, from which she took her bearings. Her provisions gone, she dined on whatever nuts and berries she could find and prayed for the strength to carry on. And when she felt it wavering, she thought of her husband locked in some dark, dank, unwholesome place, with little food and water, and she continued.

The third day dawned cloudy, and although Marion hesitated to go in the wrong direction, she could not stay still, so she rode on. When she could, she took a sighting from the sun in the way Dunstan had, while she tried to rouse her fading hopes. Once, she came upon a road and a group of travelers, but fearful that they would do her harm, she went around them, out of her way.

When the sky grew dark with the threat of rain, Marion began to court despair. She had no idea where she might be, and the thought of an impending storm preyed upon her last reserves of strength. Topping a rise, she saw a field below and the dark figures of people working there, but this time, she did not turn back. Weary and hungry and frightened, she sent her mount toward the tallest of the men, intent upon begging him for direction, food and shelter.

She still had her jewels, and if these fellows were not ruffians, she could pay them handsomely. And if they were...it could not be helped, for she was running out of time and alternatives. Eyeing the brewing clouds, and laying one hand upon her dagger, Marion approached.

The tall man noticed her, stopping his work to stare, and Marion was heartened to see him draw no weapon. Then a glint of errant sunshine pierced the clouds to light his face, dancing over his mane of thick, dark hair, and Marion cried out, trembling with the force of her relief.

"Geoffrey!"

Hearing his name, he looked at her more intently and opened his mouth in astonishment when recognition came.

"Geoffrey!" With a last surge of strength, Marion urged the horse forward until, weeping uncontrollably, she tumbled into the waiting arms of her husband's brother.

Chapter Sixteen

When Marion saw the golden towers rising into the darkening sky, she felt the hope that had dwindled down to nothing resurge, for to her, at least, Campion was invincible. Beauty, majesty and power were reflected in its warm stone, while supreme male confidence radiated from all who dwelled within.

They gathered the other brothers to them along the way, Nicholas from another field, Reynold from the forest, the rest swarming about her in the yard, rushing through the great doors of the hall to meet her just as the heavens opened, drenching them all. And once inside, Marion trembled—not from the soaking wet state of her clothing, but from the knowledge that she was safe at last. And yet her mission had just begun, and in the warm, throbbing emotion of her homecoming, she had not forgotten it.

She had tried to tell her story to Geoffrey in between her tears of relief, but he had been too sensible to listen. "Save your strength," he had told her. "To tell Campion."

Geoffrey fended off the pounding questions of his siblings, too, wrapping her in his protective embrace, and half-carrying her through the massive doors of the hall as the noisy tumult of the de Burgh brothers and their dogs surrounded them.

Mercy, but Marion had forgotten what a welcome was here! Once, she had longed for nothing more than to be a part of this family, and now they greeted her just as if she were—without even knowing that, in truth, she was a de Burgh. New tears arose at the thought. What would they say to know she had married their brother, the Wolf?

Looking up through a haze of sentiment, Marion saw the earl of Campion, her father by marriage, coming down the steps in stately elegance. His wise eyes were bright with concern as they lit upon her, and seized by a sudden heedless urge, she ran across the tiles to throw herself into his arms.

"Marion, Marion, my child." He murmured soft, comforting words as he led her to a chair and settled her in, just as if she were a child. Indeed, she felt like one again, enveloped in warmth and strength. "Wilda! Fetch some wine and food for the lady, and a dry cloak."

Like a drowned rat, Marion sat shivering with the intensity of the emotions whirling through her, but when she tried to speak, a look from the earl silenced her. "Wait, my dear, until you have had a bite. And then, you must begin at the beginning, when you left us."

Nodding her agreement, Marion waited, letting herself absorb the sights and sounds of the beloved hall around her—and the faces! Although she spoke not, her companions did, and she welcomed the babble of familiar voices and the dear features, all topped by that thick, dark hair that named every one of them Campion's son.

The earl signaled his readiness without a word, and Marion managed a slight smile. She had forgotten his great dignity, his easy command. How different he was from his firstborn! Marion's mouth dipped precariously at the thought of Campion's eldest son, and she folded her hands neatly in her lap in an effort to keep herself calm. Although she wanted nothing more than to drag the boys off to Wessex at once, she knew she needed to tell her tale slowly and coherently. Taking a deep breath, she began to speak.

Although ashamed to admit that she had not completely complied with the earl's wishes when Dunstan tried to take her home, Marion dutifully related the truth. "I am sorry, my lord, for repaying you in such a fashion, but I was afraid to go to Baddersly, so I fled the train you so kindly provided as my escort."

Seven pairs of eyes met over her bent head before Geoffrey cleared his throat. "You...escaped from... Dunstan?" At Marion's nod, there were several groans, a laugh from Stephen, and one whoop, as Nicholas relayed his astonishment.

"Yes. He always found me, but he was not very pleased," Marion admitted. The seven pairs of eyes met again, in silent accord, at what had to be an understatement. "The third time—"

"What?" A flurry of voices erupted around her as the de Burgh brothers protested that she could not have thrice managed to leave their oldest sibling, the largest, most skilled and most ferocious knight among them.

Marion waited until the denials died away before continuing. "The third time, we were forced to spend the night in the woods, and the next morning, when we returned to camp," she said, her voice breaking, "we found everyone slain."

"Where was this?"

"Everyone?"

"By faith, we shall be avenged!"

Marion ignored the outburst as each de Burgh brother spoke at once until a gesture from their father silenced them. With a flick of his gaze, Campion motioned for her to proceed. "When I saw the...bodies, my memory returned...because 'twas so much like what happened to me. Remember, when you found me, Simon, Geoffrey?" She glanced at each of them, touched by the gentle compassion on Geoffrey's face, and the fierce outrage that twisted Simon's features.

"When I remembered, I knew not only who I was, but that 'twas my uncle's men who had attacked my train. And so I thought this new massacre was his doing, too, to kill me." Although Marion tried to speak slowly, she could not dam the pulsing tide of agitation that grew within her. Every moment signified a delay that might cost the Wolf his life, and she rushed to finish.

"But Dunstan recognized something about one of the arrows and knew it to be from his neighbor, Fitzhugh. And now Fitzhugh has him, imprisoned in his own castle. Oh, you must go, at once!"

Around her, the babble of voices exploded again, but Campion stopped it swiftly. "Marion," he said softly, his brow furrowed. "What of your uncle?"

"He would still kill me! He locked me up in the tower, but Dunstan rescued me."

"Now, wait a moment," Campion said, even his gentle demeanor showing a strain. "You are telling me that after taking you all the way home, Dunstan turned around and freed you?"

"Yes, my uncle tried to have him killed, too! We were pursued at every turn, and ofttimes knew not who was after us."

"Just you and Dunstan?"

Marion nodded. She opened her mouth to speak, but Campion held up his hand to halt the flood he obviously knew was waiting to issue forth. "So you came back here."

She faltered for a moment at that, wishing that for once the Wolf had considered her opinion, but he had not, and now he was held. "We went to Wessex, but Walter, one of Dunstan's most trusted men, was waiting. He betrayed Dunstan. And he and his men took him, my lord! They tied him to the back of a horse and dragged him away!"

Marion lifted her hands to her face, a sob escaping into the deadly silence of the hall. Either the de Burgh brothers had been struck speechless or Campion was keeping his sons quiet. "They did not see you?" the earl asked gently.

She shook her head and dropped her palms. "No. Dunstan told me to stay back, so I waited. And then I came here to you."

For a long moment all was still, and then she heard Nicholas's hushed voice. "You rode all the way from Wessex by yourself?"

Marion looked at him. She wanted to smile at his wide-eyed wonder, but she could not, so she simply nodded. Six pairs of de Burgh eyes looked upon her with a stunned admiration that would once have been the height of her existence. Now, their respect was bittersweet because of the cost. "I had to," she said. "He was taken three days ago, and Walter said that Fitzhugh would have at him. They will try to break him, I know it."

Simon leaped to his feet. "Then let us go! By faith, this Fitzhugh will know the might of Campion! Why do we dally?"

"Hold, Simon," Geoffrey warned. "If we march on Wessex, the man could kill Dunstan, or we might end up in a long siege, destroying our brother's castle in the process."

"Geoffrey is right," Reynold said, and Marion paused a minute to marvel at the sight of two brothers in accord.

"Mayhap he could ransom Dunstan," Robin said, his normally light tone startling in his seriousness.

Marion spoke up. "No. According to Dunstan, Fitzhugh has coveted Wessex for a long time, and he will be satisfied with nothing else. He wants Dunstan dead."

"Perhaps if we took just a few men and tried to find a way in," Geoffrey said. The brothers were all quiet, pondering that suggestion, until the youngest of them spoke.

"I know a way in," Nicholas piped up. "Dunstan showed me once. There is a passage."

Eight pairs of eyes met in stunned silence.

"Let us all go," said Robin.

"Aye!" They spoke as one, the de Burghs, for once, all in agreement. Marion shuddered in relief.

"Simon, you shall lead," Campion said. "But I wish you to heed Geoffrey's opinions. Take a small force with you, little enough to escape attention, but strong enough to retake the castle. Unfortunately, we know not what the situation is inside. Nicholas must go to point out the passage. The rest of you make your own choice."

Hearing each brother voice his assent, Marion nearly wept. They would all go to Dunstan's aid, just as she had known they would, and she fought the urge to hug each one of them gratefully. But what of herself? "I would go, too," she said softly.

"You!" snapped Simon, in a growl so reminiscent of his elder brother that Marion nearly smiled.

"You shall stay here where you are safe," Geoffrey said.

"This is not woman's work," argued Robin.

"Hmm." Everyone quieted at the sound of Campion's low murmur, and they all turned to look him as he rubbed his chin and regarded Marion thoughtfully. "Perhaps there is something Marion has neglected to tell us."

Marion glanced away from that all-knowing gaze, uncertain just how they would take the news that she was not eager to impart. Somehow, she had hoped that if she told no one, the marriage between Dunstan and herself could be forgotten, as well it should be. However, Campion obviously guessed at something, and there was no point in trying to dissemble before the de Burghs. With bent head, Marion drew a deep breath and admitted the truth.

"Dunstan is my husband," she whispered.

When she dared look up, Marion saw that they all gaped, mouths hanging open in their handsome faces until the earl spoke again. "Congratulations, my dear."

Overcome with sudden shyness, Marion looked down at her lap. "I did not want to wed him, but he thought it best, to save me from my uncle."

"But it was a true wedding, before a priest?" Campion asked.

Marion nodded.

"And it was consummated?"

Lifting her startled wide eyes to the earl's, Marion blushed scarlet and nodded painfully. If he only knew of the beddings that took place *before* the ceremony...

The smile that slowly eased across Campion's face made her realize just how attractive the earl was, despite his years, and where his sons had come by their own rough charm. He looked positively wicked as he rose and clapped her on the back. "Well, then, welcome to the family!"

Dunstan stared into the darkness, concentrating intently, and identified the sound with a groan. Dripping. Dripping water. It must be raining, and when it rained heavily, the dungeons flooded. Tilting his head back, he prayed for sunshine, though he would not see it where he sat, trapped in a bare stone cage little better than a hole.

Of course, he had planned to completely dig out the lower levels and rid himself of the flooding problem when he had the funds, but, like so much at Wessex, it had gone wanting for lack of monies. And now he was reaping the harvest of his delay, for he was locked in his own dungeon, a place so cold and dark and dank and fetid that he would loath use it for animals, let alone a human being.

The dripping grew louder now that Dunstan was aware of it, and he shut out the noise the only way he knew how: he closed his eyes and thought of Marion. His wife. Of kissing her, touching her and claiming her as his own. And he cursed himself for being so driven to return to Wessex that he had reined in his passion those last few days with her, instead of riding her often and well.

Now, he had only the imaginings. But Dunstan took what he could from them, dreaming of how he would pleasure her until she screamed in that high, breathless way of hers, and how she would wring him dry, as no woman ever had before. And then he thought of simply holding her, warm and soft against him, and her fragrance, like wildflowers, weaving round him. Her smile. Those dimples.

He slept.

Dunstan had lost all track of time. After Walter had tossed him in the dungeon, he had remained there, forgotten, for what seemed like a day or two, growing lightheaded from the lack of food or drink. Then, finally they had come for him, dragging him before Fitzhugh—in chains, no less. He had felt like an animal, but remembering his blood, he stood tall, in his father's image.

A small, thin man of indeterminate years, Fitzhugh preened like a peacock, trying to look distinguished in his elegant finery. He was not pleased by Dunstan's show of dignity, and ordered Walter to beat the "de Burgh arrogance" from his hide. And so Dunstan had been clubbed, right there in his own hall, the frightened eyes of his former people peering from the shadows to watch.

When Walter struck him with a gauntleted fist, Dunstan held firm against the taste of his own blood on his lips—and the frustrated need to fight back. He took the blows to his arms and legs without flinching, too, though he wondered just how far Walter would go. A broken bone or misplaced joint could mean a long, painful death.... And then Dunstan was hit in the gut, and he doubled over, sucking air desperately into his starved lungs, unable to rise.

Finally satisfied, Fitzhugh had laughed and clapped his bony hands—and had sent Dunstan back to his black hole. That had been yesterday or the day before, Dunstan was not sure exactly, and now he lay in the dark again, his body screaming its protest. He marked the time, waiting to be dragged above for his next performance, eating the scraps of food that were tossed his way, and listening to the water creep up below.

Except right now there was another noise, a clanging that signaled the arrival of someone from above. Dunstan opened his eyes, poised, as always, to take whatever opportunity might present itself. Although chained to the wall and drained of his strength, he still had his wits about him.

"Dunstan?"

The furtive whisper brought his head up swiftly. Who was there, one of his men? Dunstan had thought them all killed, captured or sworn to Fitzhugh. A light bobbed in the darkness, and he called out softly.

"Here."

"Dunstan! Thank God!" At the sound of that voice, Dunstan jerked away from the wall, clanking his bindings in strained disbelief. Surely, it could not be...and yet the figure that appeared before him was his brother Geoffrey. Or was it? Ever wary, Dunstan wondered if he were lost in some hazy vision brought on by pain and deprivation, or worse, some trickery of Fitzhugh's. But, if so, why Geoffrey?

"Geoff?"

"Dunstan! Mother of God!" Upon seeing him, Geoffrey's face washed white in the torch's flame, and Dunstan realized that he must look like death, lying there locked to the wall, bruised and bloody and stained with filth. Geoffrey's shocked gasp rang out in the stony space, and then he fumbled for a key. "Hang on, brother, I have the key."

"Geoff?"

"Aye. 'Tis me, Dunstan," he murmured, his features strained as he removed the shackles. Groaning with relief, Dunstan rubbed his wrists and let his brother help him to his feet, but he found standing nearly more than he could manage and swayed precariously.

"Hang on to me," Geoffrey urged. And Dunstan did, slinging an arm around his younger brother's wide shoulders. When had scholarly Geoffrey filled out to become strong and broad enough to carry his weight? Dunstan shook his head, as if to clear it, still uncertain whether he moved in a dream or reality.

In the low, dank corridor, they were met by others, and a whispered conference ensued. Although he did not hear all of it, Dunstan's ears pricked up when Geoffrey said, "Let me take him back out the passage. He is in no condition—"

"Halt there, Geoff," Dunstan broke in. Just because he was not up to his usual self, he was not about to let his intellectual brother coddle him like a babe. "This is my castle."

"Give him a sword," Stephen said tersely. Stephen? Surely, Dunstan was lost in some fevered vision to imagine his wastrel brother Stephen crawling about underneath Wessex! Perhaps Fitzhugh had put some herb into his food, and even now he lay still in the hole, locked in vivid imaginings, rather than standing here arguing with his young siblings....

Before Dunstan could marvel further, a weapon was thrust into his hands and he was dragged along, stumbling up the stairs into blinding light. He flinched against the brightness after long days spent in the dark, and he fell back against the wall of the buttery, blinking, until his eyes could focus. Then Geoffrey pulled him along as they rushed into the great hall.

"Fitzhugh cannot be found!" someone shouted from across the room, and several figures separated themselves from the group to run up to the solar to search. Before him, the vast space stood empty, but a few over-turned tables gave testimony of some upheaval, and through the open doors, Dunstan could see the signs of battle in the bailey. Who? And why? Shaking off Geoffrey's help, he took a step forward. By faith, Fitzhugh's men were surrendering!

"Nicholas, you stay here with Dunstan, while I help them look for Fitzhugh," Geoffrey said. Without waiting for reply, he took off, disappearing into the kitchens.

Nicholas? *Nicholas?* Was that his baby brother beside him, taking his weight? Dunstan cursed his foggy head as he stepped back to look. "Nicholas?"

"Yes, it is me, Dunstan. I remembered the passage you showed me, so we came in to retake your castle." The boy looked up at him, young, smooth-faced and proud.

"You did well, Nicholas," Dunstan said, his voice breaking oddly. "I fear I am a bit slow yet."

"Simon has the opposing force well in hand," Nicholas explained with a nod toward the doors, "but your enemy has not been found." Nicholas's dark eyes brightened with excitement. "Is there some place where he could hide?"

Fitzhugh, somewhere inside the castle...Dunstan stopped to think. There was an odd sort of hidey-hole in the great chamber that he had always thought of as a place to secret a lover, but the small space, more confining even than his cell, gave Dunstan the chills.

Still, a man could sneak in there during a battle and walk out later, unscathed. Dunstan lifted his head, gesturing toward the stair with a tilt of his jaw. "Up there," he said to Nicholas. Then he moved over the rushes faster than he would ever have thought himself able, his baby brother hurrying to keep up.

Perhaps it was the hope for revenge that finally cleared his benumbed brain, pulsed renewed strength through his weakened body, or maybe it was the scent of victory. Whatever the cause, Dunstan found himself taking the stairs swiftly, hell-bent upon the great chamber.

They passed Robin in the hall, and Dunstan barely blinked, having grown accustomed to the sight of his siblings. Without a word, Robin joined them, and the three burst into the room to find it silent and still—and empty.

Dunstan did not hesitate, but walked to a large tapestry that draped one wall and, reaching up, pulled down the material with one fierce yank. Nicholas's soft hiss of surprise sounded behind him as a wooden door, flush to the wall, was revealed.

"Come out, you bastard!" Dunstan shouted.

No noise emerged from within, so Dunstan tugged at the ring, but it held fast. Someone was inside.

"Burn him out," Dunstan said, and Robin rushed from the room, shouting for fire. The threat must have penetrated the door, for just as Robin left, it swung open and Fitzhugh stepped out, looking positively regal in his colorful finery—and totally untouched by the events around him.

"Well, well, Wessex," he said smoothly. Although he held his head high, Fitzhugh's eyes darted around the room like a cornered hare's as he took in his situation. "So, you are still standing, are you? Amazing. But for how long?" His gaze finally settled on Nicholas. "You, boy. See my way out of here and you will be well rewarded."

While Nicholas stared at him in awed surprise, Fitzhugh moved slowly around the perimeter of the room, giving Dunstan a wide berth. "Quick, boy, take the hulking brute, so that I might make my leave," he ordered.

When Nicholas did not respond, Fitzhugh smiled slyly. "Well, obviously, you are not a threat to anyone, boy, and as for you, Wessex, I am surprised you can even keep your feet—"

With a deceptively swift movement, Fitzhugh made it to the door just as Robin filled it.

"You! Out of my way," he snapped in frustrated anger. "Know you who I am?"

"Although we have never met, I suspect you are Fitzhugh," Robin said, his normally bright countenance dark and somber.

"Yes. I am Fitzhugh, and I would go below. Give me an escort, good fellow, and I shall see you are well rewarded."

"I care not for the kind of rewards you would dispense," Robin said. Although more accustomed to merry japes than making war, he assumed a fighting stance, his feet apart, and put his hand to the hilt of his sword.

Fitzhugh's voice rose, high and harsh. "Listen to me, fool! I am wealthier than you would ever dream. Serve me, and I shall gift you with all you could desire—gold, jewels, manors, land—whatever you will." He was babbling now, while his eyes flew to each of them in turn. "My daughter's hand!"

Robin snorted. "I want no part of that shrew—I have heard of her temperament."

Fitzhugh did not even flinch at the insult, but glanced behind Robin toward freedom and licked his lips nervously. "'Tis well-known that Wessex has nothing. Hurry, man, and let us go."

Robin made a low noise of disagreement. "You are wrong, Fitzhugh. Dunstan has more than you ever will. You see, he has us." Robin sent his hand in a sweeping gesture that took in Nicholas and himself.

"Us? You need feel no loyalty to Wessex, fellow. His own vassal, Walter Avery, has joined with me, as should you," Fitzhugh argued, desperation now evident in his tone.

"Pah! I spit upon Avery. He is nothing but a boughten whore," Robin said, in a voice more grim than Dunstan could ever have imagined from the carefree youth. "Save your breath, Fitzhugh, for you cannot purchase me. I am Robin de Burgh, and Wessex is my brother."

Dunstan's chest tightened as a mixture of amazement and pride swept through him, touching him more deeply than he would ever have thought possible. Fitzhugh blanched. The hand that had reached out to Robin trembled and faltered, and he looked sharply to Nicholas, as if finally seeing the resemblance between them all.

"He is my brother, too," the boy added. "I am Nicholas de Burgh."

With a vicious oath, Fitzhugh drew his sword and leaped at Robin, but the younger man sidestepped him easily and swung his own weapon in a fatal arc.

"No, Robin! He is mine!" Dunstan shouted, and Robin stayed his hand, while the Wolf gave chase to the fleeing villain.

Down the darkened hallway they ran before Fitzhugh turned to fight upon the stairs. "How is your head, Wessex?" he taunted. "Can you keep your balance? 'Tis steep and slippery here."

Once, Dunstan would have overpowered the older man in a single blow, but now, bruised and weakened, he struggled to parry and make his way down the steps at the same time. Below, hushed voices greeted the sight of the dueling enemies, Fitzhugh richly and immaculately garbed and Dunstan dressed in a torn tunic, stained with filth and blood.

While Fitzhugh danced about, agile for his years, Dunstan stood his ground and advanced, slowly but surely. Impatient, the older man finally jumped to the floor below and ran across the tiles, but his flight was blocked by three tall, dark men, who looked suspiciously like de Burghs. Cursing, he swung back to Dunstan, fighting with renewed energy to what he knew must be his death.

He was frenzied, his blade sliding under Dunstan's guard to slice a bloody line across the huge chest. Fitzhugh's glee was short-lived, however, as Dunstan did not falter at the wound, but brought his sword down like a hammer. Fitzhugh fell back, his eyes wide with stunned surprise when Dunstan's blade buried itself deep.

Drawing in great gulps of air, Dunstan stood over the body of his neighbor and felt not the sweetness of revenge—only a cold sense of justice done. Wessex was now his, and let no man dispute it. With an overwhelming yearning, he hoped that perhaps he and his people could know peace.

Vaguely, he heard Nicholas's cheers and the shouts of admiration from his other brothers as he removed his weapon from Fitzhugh's corpse, but the sounds dimmed to a dull roar. Lifting a hand to his bloody chest, Dunstan watched his sword fall to the tiles. Then he swayed upon his feet, suddenly too weak to stand, and crumpled to the floor after it.

Chapter Seventeen

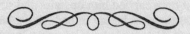

When Dunstan awoke, it was to sharp pain. He opened his eyes to see an old servant cleansing a wound upon his chest. He was in his bed at Wessex and, for a moment, wondered groggily what had happened. Every muscle in his body ached, his face throbbed, and his throat was dry and sore. Had he been in some battle?

Glancing blearily around the room, Dunstan saw his brothers Geoffrey and Simon... at Wessex? He shut his eyes in an effort to concentrate, and suddenly the past day came rushing back to him, along with a sense of peace. Fitzhugh was dead, his castle was his own, and he could now turn his attention to putting it to rights. All was well again, and yet... something was missing.

Marion. Day of God, where was his wife? Dunstan's mouth seemed inordinately dry and his lips slow to work, but he finally croaked out her name. "Marion."

"What?" Geoffrey stepped closer, his voice heavy with concern.

"Marion," Dunstan whispered.

"Marion? Oh, Marion! She is well. We left her at Campion," Geoffrey said.

Relief spilled through him like sunlight. The wren was all right! But why was she at his father's house? Dunstan frowned. "Have someone fetch her here." He wanted her with him. She was his wife, whether she would or no, and her place was at his side. He scowled more deeply as the old woman probed his injuries, and then he grunted aloud, his eyes flying open to glare at her.

"Is that rib broken, my lord?" she asked him, a pensive look on her aged face.

"No," Dunstan barked, rising onto his elbows. His brothers must have carried him upstairs and stripped him of his clothes, for now he lay in bed, like a babe, and it pleased him not. He growled out a protest, but it came out more like a cat's mew than the angry cry of a wolf. "Cease your poking, woman. I am fit," he managed to snarl.

"You were beaten most severely, my lord," she argued. "'Twas terrible. I saw it all." She opened her mouth as if to expound upon the episode to his brothers, but Dunstan grabbed her wrist, proving he still had strength enough to quiet her, should the need arise. Catching his warning glance, she paused before speaking again in a more positive tone. "Food and water, that is what he needs most. Here, my lord, have a drink."

The water revived him, and Dunstan sat up, surveying the room while he sipped some obnoxious gruel obviously meant for someone frail and weak. Nicholas was watching him with wide-eyed admiration, Geoffrey's brows were drawn together in worry, and Simon paced the floor impatiently, unhappy to be in the sickroom. Dunstan's lips curved into a reluctant smile. How long had it been since he had spent time with his brothers? In his single-minded quest to prove himself, he had missed something important—getting to know the men they had become.

"I believe I owe you my thanks, brothers," he said.

Nicholas beamed happily at his words, while Geoffrey seemed to relax, and Simon swung around with a stiff nod of acknowledgment. By faith, they were dear to him,

Dunstan realized with some surprise. What had kept him from sharing his life with them?

"We were happy to help you," Geoffrey said. "Now, you must rest. You gave me some gray hairs, Dunstan, when I saw you take on Fitzhugh, alone and in your condition."

Dunstan snorted, but in an affectionate way. "'Twas but little, compared to my brothers' contributions to my cause," he said. "And I am well enough to hear the state of my castle, if you please, Simon."

Simon smiled grimly, eager to impart the details of the battle, the casualties, the number of Dunstan's men who had been freed, and how many of Fitzhugh's soldiers were willing to pledge their lives to Wessex.

"And what of my former vassal, Walter Avery?" Dunstan asked roughly. The pain of that betrayal still stung, making the meat he swallowed go down hard. Perhaps a man was wise to trust none but his own brothers....

"Escaped," Simon said tersely. "He and a few went out the gates before we could close them, and I could not spare the men to give chase. He is probably halfway to Fitzhugh's manor by now." Simon's face was taut with anger and disgust.

Dunstan recognized the frustration Simon was feeling, for he had wasted plenty of his own energies in the futile exercise of hindsight. "You did well, Simon," he said. "None would fault you."

The sharp, quick glance Simon sent him showed surprise, disbelief and, finally, greedy acceptance of his praise. It stunned Dunstan to realize just how much worth his brothers placed upon his words.

"Perhaps," Simon said with a brief nod, "but now we are in a precarious position, with only a small force to protect Wessex. Although I would gladly go after this Avery, I have no idea what might await at Fitzhugh's holding. Frankly, I think we have too few men to make any showing of ourselves.'' Simon paced the room in front of the bed. ''With your permission, I would return to Campion and hand-pick some others to fill the ranks. I know Father will insist upon giving you men.''

Dunstan was dubious. ''Are you sure?''

Whipping around swiftly, Simon shot him a look that questioned his sense. ''Of course! Campion has men to spare, as you should remember.''

Of course. Dunstan smiled grimly. Perhaps Marion had been right and if he had swallowed his pride and simply asked, he would have had help long before now. He nodded and put his trencher aside. ''You take care of it, Simon,'' he said. Suddenly weary, Dunstan closed his eyes and missed his brother's startled look of pleasure at the charge.

Eager for the blessed comfort of sleep in his own bed, Dunstan relaxed against the pillows. He heard the movements of his brothers as they headed toward the door, then suddenly he opened his eyes wide, shocked to have momentarily forgotten something so vital.

''And bring Marion back with you,'' he said tersely.

In a few days, Dunstan was back to his old self, the healing wound on his chest the only reminder of his ordeal. His aches were gone, his belly full of food and drink, and he was whole again but for one minor thing. His wife was still gone.

Dunstan did not feel quite…complete without her. He swung between irritation at the odd sensation of need and exaltation at the thought of her return. It was ridiculous, but he wanted her here beside him. Now.

During their long, forced time together, Dunstan had grown accustomed to her presence, and he would have it back. It was as simple as that. He missed that smile of hers with its dimples peeping out brazenly. He missed her

graceful movements, her silly patter and the air of innocence that clung to her, despite her hot passions. He
missed the way she argued with him, poking her tiny finger into his great chest when she was particularly riled.

And he missed the way she fussed over him, full of
worry for him. Dunstan paused to savor that memory. He
liked being the subject of her concern. He especially liked
it when she turned those huge eyes on him and they shone
with an inner brilliance, just as if she adored him....

Of course, she did not. All that nonsense about loving
him Dunstan knew as so much fiddle-faddle, and yet if
she wanted to believe herself enamored of him, who was
he to argue? He enjoyed being the object of her affections—the *only* object of her affections.

Dunstan scowled. He found he did not like the thought
of Marion surrounded by his brothers here at Wessex.
Would her doe eyes look upon them with the same sweetness? Dunstan resisted an urge to slam his fist into the table in front of him. He would not care for that at all.

Marion was *his*, by law, by right and by possession. He
tried not to think of her back at Campion, greeting Simon, the returning hero. He tried not to think of her giving his brothers the gift of her smile and receiving their
proprietary glances. He tried not to think of her at all.

He cursed loudly.

"What is it, Dunstan?" Geoffrey asked, looking up
from the papers spread before him. They sat at the table
in the great hall, while Geoffrey went over Dunstan's accounts with an eye both to reduce expenses and increase
income.

"Nothing," Dunstan muttered. "I look for Simon's
return, 'tis all."

Geoffrey smiled. It was not the first time Dunstan had
suddenly burst out with an oath for no good reason.
Something, or rather someone, was preying on the Wolf's
mind. Geoffrey leaned back, twirled the quill in his hand

and wondered if Dunstan would bring up the topic of Marion again.

Although Dunstan had mentioned his wife several times, as if he could not help himself, he had been hesitant to discuss her, leaving Geoffrey mightily curious. Geoff never would have thought Dunstan, the toughest loner of all the de Burghs, would be struck by Cupid's arrow, and yet the Wolf showed indisputable signs of being smitten by dear little Marion.

Having heard Marion claim the marriage was not her idea, Geoffrey was interested to see how the couple would deal together. Although she had pleaded Dunstan's case to his family in a heart-wrenching manner, that did not mean Marion loved him. Yet Geoffrey suspected that Dunstan was very much in love with her. It was an intriguing puzzle, and Geoffrey had seen enough of his eldest brother's stubborn arrogance over the years to admit he was going to enjoy watching Dunstan squirm.

"What is it like, being married?" Geoffrey asked, tongue firmly in cheek.

"'Tis sorely aggrieving!" Dunstan answered, rubbing the back of his neck.

Geoffrey smiled. "That bad?"

As if suddenly aware of what he had said, Dunstan scowled. "I would have her here, that is all. 'Tis where she belongs. She is mine," Dunstan said, adding a threatening look to cap off his words.

"Ho, brother. No need to take that fierce tone with me," Geoffrey said. "We all came to care for Marion as a sister, but none of us desired to marry her. Remember?"

Dunstan's eyes narrowed, and Geoffrey realized that now might not have been the time to remind Dunstan that his siblings had rejected the hand of his wife. "Yes, I remember," Dunstan growled. "Why? Why would no one have her?"

Oh-oh. Now the Wolf was insulted. Although Dunstan had warmed considerably toward his brothers, he was still not a man to rile. Geoffrey paused to choose his words very carefully, then he simply shrugged and stated the obvious. "None of us were in love with her."

Dunstan snorted. "Love! You spout the same prattle as Marion. 'Tis all foolishness."

Oh. Geoffrey drew in a deep breath. Not only was the Wolf in love, but he refused to believe it. And, obviously, he and Marion had already had words on the subject. Unwilling to be drawn into an endless argument, Geoffrey asked his brother baldly, "Why did *you* marry her?"

Dunstan leaned back in his chair with a smug look, as if the answer was obvious. "'Twas for the best, to protect her from her uncle."

"I see," Geoffrey said softly. He laid down his quill and tented his fingers together, eyeing Dunstan carefully. "So you feel nothing for her but a sense of responsibility?"

Dunstan scowled blackly. "Of course, I feel something for her. She is my wife. She will serve me well and give me an heir...."

Suddenly Dunstan went quiet, then he rose from his chair as if his hose were alight. Geoffrey bit his cheeks to keep from howling with laughter. So the Wolf was hot for his wife, was he?

"Enough of her! I have work to do," Dunstan growled, stalking off with an odd gait.

Clearing his throat, Geoffrey turned his attention back to the columns of figures in front of him. This was too entertaining. By faith, he could not wait to see what happened when Marion returned!

Marion's heart pounded so loudly that she was sure Simon would turn around and tell her to quiet it. Well pleased with his new role as Dunstan's military arm, he was less than thrilled with the duty of escorting her back to Wessex. He had been tense and short with her, but she was used to adapting to the de Burghs and their moods, and, in truth, Simon concerned her little. It was Dunstan who had her in a turmoil.

When Simon had returned and told her in that stony way of his that "of course" Dunstan was all right, Marion had wept with relief. Now, as they approached Wessex, she was unsure of her feelings. Part of her worried still, and she was anxious to see for herself that Dunstan was well. From what Simon said, he had been imprisoned and wounded. Marion knew a desperate need to reassure herself that he was as he should be.

Beyond that, she did not know what lay ahead. If not for Dunstan's condition, Marion would have balked at joining him at Wessex. She would rather have stayed at Campion, surrounded by a family that loved her, than go to a man who did not to face an uncertain future. Despite her eagerness to see Dunstan, all her doubts about their marriage came rushing back.

By the time they entered the gates, Marion was still and silent with strain. Having soon forgotten her, Simon went off with the new soldiers to see to quartering them, and Marion was left to stand alone before the doors of the old, square keep. She eyed it critically before deciding that she rather liked it. Actually, after the rambling Baddersly and the awe-inspiring Campion, Wessex was rather cozy. Marion smiled. It would be easy to fill this small hall with laughing children....

She stepped inside just in time to hear the Wolf growl angrily. "Where is she?" Dunstan shouted, striding across the rushes with his usual grace and in all his great, handsome glory. Marion blinked rapidly as her love rose and burst forth, sweet and aching in its intensity.

"Marion."

He saw her. For a moment, she thought he would run to her, but then he seemed to catch himself. Hesitating briefly, he took long, easy steps to stand before her, a huge, dear, looming presence. Tall and broad as an oak, he looked hale and hearty, and Marion knew a swift, sharp relief. She studied his face, but he was difficult to read, and she was unsure whether he was even pleased to see her.

"Marion?" Dunstan seemed to invest the single word with a million questions, but Marion did not know how to answer. Finally, unable to help herself, she lifted a palm to his cheek, to touch him, to prove to herself that he was alive and well. He was warm and firm, the stubble of his beard rough beneath her fingers. "Thank God you are well," she said softly.

Dunstan crushed her to him so tightly that all her breath escaped. He was not wearing his mail, so she could feel the hard muscles of his chest through her clothing, a delightful warm pressure. As she struggled for breath, he whispered her name over and over in a low voice that awakened all her bodily humors and sent them catapulting through her with dizzying heat.

The bustling hall was forgotten as the magic between them sparked and flamed, and Marion gasped as he swept her off her feet and into his arms. He carried her lightly across the rushes, past servants awaiting an introduction to their new lady, past a startled Geoffrey and up the stairs.

"Dunstan!" she scolded. Paying her no heed, he swung through the doors of his chamber as if the hounds of hell pursued him.

As soon as he closed the door behind him, he was upon her, devouring her with his mouth and ravishing her with his hands. His kiss was hot and rough, a mark of possession, but Marion reveled in it and met his tongue with her own, her body burning where he touched her.

He walked to the bed, groaning as he laid her down upon it and spread her hair out about her. His fingers thrust into her bodice, baring her breasts, and then he just stood over her, drinking in the sight of her with green eyes dark and glazed.

Marion licked her swollen lips as she gazed up at him. His great chest was rising and falling rapidly, his breath quick and harsh, and his hands fallen to his sides. . . . The Wolf's hands were trembling. She felt dizzy with the force of that knowledge.

"Day of God, Marion, I have to have you now," he growled. Giving a weak nod of permission, Marion watched as he fumbled with his clothes, freeing his thick, hard length. Then he pushed up her skirts and pulled her to the edge of the bed, burying himself to the root in a primitive claiming that made her cry out her pleasure.

A smug smile appeared briefly on his handsome face, tense with strain, as he muttered, "These walls are thick, Marion. Yell as loud as you are wont." And she did.

Dunstan stared down the table with a scowl, his mood black as he contemplated the brothers he had but recently clasped to his bosom. Now, he eyed them with the same suspicious distaste he would feel upon viewing a nest of vipers.

It was all *her* fault.

He had been of a mind to keep Marion abed in their chamber for the rest of the day—and night—but she had insisted upon coming down to meet his people and greet his brothers. He should have kept her locked in the room forever, chained to his bed, as he had once imagined.

Instead, she was presiding over the table, conversing sweetly with all of them, giving them her smiles and her concern, and he would be damned but that jealousy burned hot within his chest. He had never been the sort to covet a female, having seen them as fairly interchange-able, until now. And Dunstan liked not the feeling.

He knew that she had not lain with any of his brothers. He knew that they had all refused to marry her and that they all supposedly saw her as a sister. And yet he knew that the first man who looked upon her with the slightest interest would suffer his wrath.

Seeing her reach over to touch Geoffrey's sleeve, Dunstan felt as if his very blood boiled. He pushed aside his trencher, knowing full well that he acted the part of a spoiled child, but unable to help himself. She was *his*, by faith, and he liked not sharing her with anyone—even his siblings.

Replete with food and drink and flush with victory and the coming of new soldiers, his brothers seemed oblivi-ous to his foul humor. Fighting for Marion's attention like a pack of favored dogs, they began boasting of their parts in the recapture of Wessex. Watching silently, Dunstan was prepared to brood, but he was soon brought out of his mood by his astonishment at Marion's skillful handling of the de Burghs.

Even master politician Geoffrey's abilities paled be-fore her deft maneuvering. When fights broke out, she knew just what to say to ease the tensions. If someone became too full of himself, she burst his bubble with a teasing gibe. If Stephen's tongue grew too sharp, she re-proved him gently, and the black sheep of the family ac-tually acceded to her wishes! Dunstan was stunned.

And, most astonishing of all, she managed to draw out silent Reynold. Everyone was singled out for her praise, even Nicholas, who, she pointed out, was the only one who had known of the secret passage into Wessex. With-out him, there would have been no rescue.

Nicholas, beaming with satisfaction, made Dunstan proud when he mentioned that none of them would even be here were it not for Marion. Six pairs of eyes turned toward her then, bright with admiration and affection, and Dunstan felt something inside himself give way grudgingly. They all cared for her, their faces said as much, but Geoffrey was right. They did not lust after her.

The fiery pain of jealousy dwindled to a manageable ache as he watched his brothers all stand and cheer his wife. To his surprise, Dunstan felt a kinship with them that not all the battles in the world could have created. It was born of caring for the same woman—in different ways.

Dunstan rose, too, then, though he said nothing. He simply stared at Marion, his own feelings for her growing within him. Looking at her seated there, small and dainty and dimpling prettily, one would never have guessed that this woman had ridden for days, alone and unarmed, through unfamiliar countryside in order to save his life.

She was truly amazing. All those times she had sought to escape him, Dunstan had thought her foolish and doomed, and yet, she had done it. She had managed. She had gone off all by herself. With a sudden jolt, Dunstan realized that she did not need him.

The knowledge was rather frightening, for if Marion did not want protection, why should she stay with him? Dunstan sat down again with his brothers, in response to Marion's modest disclaimers, but his attention was no longer on the present.

How would he hold her to him? The lovemaking was one way, for Marion definitely enjoyed her pleasures, and quick on the heels of that thought was the notion of an heir. Yes! He would get her with child quickly, and that would bind her to him more strongly.

Dunstan tamped down the fluttering edges of panic that had him nearly trembling and told himself that she was his, now and always, and yet...Deep inside, he wondered if anything could ever tie to him enough to satisfy him.

"Our sister, Marion!" The de Burghs were calling out endearments to her, along with demands for more ale, Dunstan realized. His own mouth felt dry, but he wanted no more drink. He wanted to take his wife to bed and claim her as his own. Now. He moved closer and tried to catch her eye.

When he did, she leaned close, but instead of whispering something provocative, Marion nodded toward one of his brothers. "See how Simon is whirling his cup between his hands."

With a lift of his brows, Dunstan showed her just how little Simon's habits interested him, and she frowned reprovingly. "It means he has something on his mind," she explained. Dunstan's next glance expressed his opinion of that notion, and Marion's frown grew, her expressive mouth curving downward in a lovely imitation of his own scowl. "Ask him," she said, nudging his side with her elbow.

Suspecting that he would have no peace until he did her bidding, Dunstan sat back and fixed his eyes on his brother, who was, indeed, playing absently with his cup. "So, Simon, what is on your mind?"

"What?" Simon's face lost its intent cast to startlement. "Oh, I was thinking of... that is, with your permission..." He straightened, his features closed and somber once more. "I would like to take a force to Fitzhugh's holding and see the state of things there."

Dunstan stared, stunned by his wife's perception. By faith, did she truly know his brothers better than he did himself? It would appear so, for she was smiling happily at his surprise. "'Tis sound thinking. What say you, Dunstan?" she prompted.

Dunstan grimaced. With Fitzhugh dead, he did not think there would be any more trouble from that quarter, but Walter might pose a problem. He could be long gone from the area, or he could be holed up somewhere, preparing to harry the outlying lands just as his master had done.

"It would leave the castle poorly defended, even taking into account the new men our father sent," Geoffrey pointed out.

Simon glared across the table at his brother. "But what if this Walter should raise a force of his own? And what of Fitzhugh's daughter? She is well-known for her foul temperament. Will she continue her sire's war upon us? I would know what goes on outside our borders." Simon's hand closed into a fist, and Dunstan realized his younger brother was eager for battle.

"But while you are away, Wessex lies open to attack. Even discounting the threat from Fitzhugh's brat or his allies, what of Harold Peasely?" Geoffrey asked.

"Peasely?" Dunstan snorted at that. "He has no claim to Marion now."

"No, but he has known her riches too long to give them up easily. And did he not try to have you murdered? I would not discount him," Geoffrey argued.

Dunstan weighed his brother's words carefully. Of them all, Geoffrey was most like their father, strong, but gentle and wise. With rueful candor, Dunstan had to admit that Geoff definitely had received the lion's share of the de Burgh intelligence, and it would behoove him to listen when sound advice was tendered. Although he did not really think Peasely would attack, he had also been unprepared for Fitzhugh's cunning. Better to send out a few men than leave the castle unattended.

"Perhaps only a small force should go, enough to scout out the situation," Dunstan mused. "Even with all the men, we would not have enough to take Fitzhugh's home, so the size of any group going there would matter little. We will go in peace, in the guise of giving word to the daughter of her father's death."

Several brave men flinched at the mention of the Fitz-hugh witch, and Dunstan hid his amusement. "I will leave on the morrow," he concluded.

"But, I—" Simon sputtered, looking both stunned and angry, and Dunstan glanced across the table in surprise, before Marion's hand closed in soft restraint upon his arm.

"Simon is bored here, Dunstan," she said. "He has proved that he is a more than capable leader. And did you not say that you were heartily sick of traveling?"

Dunstan scowled. For as long as he could remember, he had done for himself, by himself. It was not easy to relinquish his authority and his responsibility. What if something should go wrong? It went against his nature to let someone else do his job.

He opened his mouth to speak, but he felt the gentle pressure of Marion's fingers on his arm and closed it. What of his wife? Dunstan thought of leaving her here, surrounded by his brothers, and his chest ached anew. He thought of nights spent without her, on the road again with the fields for a bed, and his will wavered.

"Simon does seem the logical choice, Dunstan," Geoffrey noted. "Your place is here at Wessex."

Perhaps Geoffrey was right, Dunstan thought. How much time had he actually spent in residence at his own holding? Too little. He glanced at Marion's great doe eyes, pleading his brother's cause, and he grunted.

"Very well. Simon, I like not letting another man take on a task for me, but you are far more eager for this one than I am. I give you the charge."

Simon's head came up, and his eyes lit with a fierce glow that seemed to burn right out of his soul. He smiled, a rare and heartfelt gesture, and Dunstan felt himself grinning in response as he realized the pleasure to be had in giving to one of his own.

Dunstan was doubly rewarded when he glanced at Marion and saw, for the first time since her arrival, that soft, shining look of adoration in her eyes. He felt the warmth of that approving gaze down to his bones. Then she smiled, her dimples peeping out happily, and Dunstan relaxed back against his chair, feeling very well satisfied with himself.

Let poor Simon tramp the countryside mailed and armed and eager for a fight! He would much rather stay right here in the comfort of his own hall and get his wife with child.

Chapter Eighteen

"Geoffrey?" The sound of Marion's voice brought Geoffrey's head out of the accounts, and he saw her standing near the doors with Nicholas, who was awkwardly clutching a huge, empty basket. Dressed in a rose gown that complemented her dark hair, Marion looked even prettier than usual, and Geoffrey had to admit that marriage to the Wolf had certainly added color in her cheeks.

"Would you like to walk with us?" she asked. "I need to gather a supply of healing plants, and Nicholas is kind enough to come along," she explained, with one of those sunny smiles of hers that encouraged a like response.

"Where is Dunstan?" Geoffrey asked, aware that the Wolf rarely let Marion out of his sight.

"With Reynold and Stephen in the yard, training," Nicholas said, his wistful expression telling Geoffrey that he would much rather be with his brothers.

Geoffrey hid his amusement and stood. "I see. Well, I think I will join you. I have not walked beyond Wessex's walls since we arrived." Stopping only to put on his scabbard, he followed them through the doors of the hall into a day blazing with summer sunshine.

Although he was not especially anxious to watch Marion pick flowers, Geoffrey thought it best to accompany the two on their trek. The Wolf was a bit possessive of his bride, to put it mildly, and might growl and howl if he thought her off alone with one of his brothers, even the youngest of them.

Geoffrey smiled to himself at the change in Dunstan. Once, he could have sworn that his oldest brother had little interest in females, but for the occasional toss. Now, he was rarely separated from his bride, and when he was, he seemed distracted, as if his mind were with her, rather than on his surroundings.

It was vastly entertaining to the de Burghs, who whispered about it among themselves, but dared not tease the object of their amusement. Blood was thick among them, but none had a death wish. And Geoffrey had an idea that taunts to the Wolf about his newfound domesticity would be met with snarling violence.

At the very least, they could put to rest any questions Campion might have about the validity of the wedding; it was obvious that Dunstan's marriage was a true one. By faith, even Geoffrey had been shocked at the way Dunstan had whisked his bride off to their chamber as soon as she arrived.

They had returned several hours later, looking flushed and sated, only to excuse themselves again not long after the evening meal. Although Dunstan's claim that his wife must rest after her travels was transparent to everyone present, Marion acquiesced, and if she was embarrassed by her husband's eagerness, she did not show it.

Since then, the two of them had been going at it like rabbits. From what Geoffrey could gather, the Wolf seemed determined to swive his wife to death. Privately, Geoffrey wondered if that was the only way Dunstan knew to show his affection. The thought worried Geoffrey, for he wanted Marion to be happy, and despite all that lovemaking, she did not seem totally at ease at Wessex.

Obviously, she loved Dunstan. It shone in those huge, soulful eyes of hers, filled to brimming with emotion. Yet Geoffrey sensed that something was not right. There was a constraint between the two, and at times Geoffrey would catch Marion's face reflecting a sadness that she had never shown at Campion. And Dunstan looked far too frustrated and surly for a man who was spending so much time in bed.

It was puzzling. Geoffrey was struck by the difficulties inherent even in the most caring relationships. When he saw the way Marion looked at Dunstan, he felt a pang, a foolish yearning to know such emotion himself, and yet it seemed that even the best of marriages faced problems that he could not even begin to comprehend.

With a sigh for the vagaries of the human heart, Geoffrey lengthened his stride and followed the others up one of the gentle slopes not far from Wessex's walls.

The afternoon passed quickly, the three of them talking amiably while Marion searched for plants. Sometimes, she cajoled Geoffrey and Nicholas into helping, often she let them lie in the tall grass along the hills to soak up the heat of the day. The countryside had a wilder look than at Campion, where so much land had been cleared for farming, but Geoffrey liked it. All was quiet, but for the buzzing of bees and the wind in the trees. It was infinitely peaceful.

Until Dunstan arrived.

"Oh—oh," Nicholas said suddenly, and the tone in his voice made Geoffrey rise on one elbow to look below. He had been chewing on a stalk of grass, and it fell abruptly from his lips when he saw just what had prompted Nicholas's words.

Dunstan was striding up the hill, his hands fisted at his sides, his face black with fury and his jaw clenched so hard it looked as though it might pop. In an instant, Geoffrey leaped to his feet and the years fell away, making him feel like a boy once more caught in some mischief by his older brother.

"What the devil is the meaning of this?" Dunstan growled, just as if they were guilty of some vile transgression. Geoffrey was at a loss to answer, however, for as far as he knew, they had done nothing to rouse Dunstan's rage. He and Nicholas simply remained stiffly at attention, staring at their brother.

"Dunstan, what a surprise! Have you come to help us?" Marion asked sweetly, and Geoffrey shot a quick glance at her. She was still blithely collecting plants, just as if the Wolf of Wessex were not breathing down their throats with murder in his eyes.

"No," Dunstan answered, his voice low and menacing. He stood with his feet apart, his hands on his hips, his eyes narrowed and a ferocious scowl upon his features. "What do you think you are doing?"

Something in his tone stopped her, and Marion turned toward him, as if finally noticing his mood—a mood that kept Geoffrey and Nicholas warily silent. "Whatever is the matter?"

"The matter! You leave the safety of my walls to dally over the countryside with naught but these two as protection?" Although Geoffrey took umbrage at the implied insult in Dunstan's words, he said nothing. Past experience had taught him that it was useless to argue with the Wolf.

Dunstan stepped forward, gripping Marion's arms tightly. "Have you no sense at all? You could have been killed, you little fool! Walter, Peasely and God knows who else would love to catch you out here alone. Have you not seen enough bloodshed to have a care for yourself?"

Geoffrey liked not the way Dunstan grasped Marion, as if ready to shake her forcibly, and, despite his apprehension, he stepped forward. No matter what, he would not let Marion be hurt—even by her husband.

He need not have worried. With a jerk, Marion threw off Dunstan's hold, proving to Geoffrey that it could not have been as fierce as it looked. Then she pointed a tiny finger at the Wolf's massive chest. "Do not speak to me in that fashion, Dunstan de Burgh! I will not tolerate it!" she snapped, her face flushed.

"I needed to gather a stock of plants for cooking and healing, since you have none, and your brothers were kind enough to come with me." She poked her digit more firmly into his tunic. "If I am to be a prisoner here, as I was at Baddersly, you will have to tell me. My uncle, you see, made his rules very plain." Her voice broke then, but with a dignity that awed Geoffrey, she stalked past the Wolf without a backward glance.

"Nicholas, assist me, please," she called over her shoulder. For a moment, all three de Burghs stood gaping after her, then Nicholas took off, racing to catch up with her.

Uneasy with the volatile situation, Geoffrey was glad that Marion had taken Nicholas with her, but none too pleased to be stuck there himself—alone with a ferocious Wolf. Geoffrey was no coward, however, and he stood where he was, watching Dunstan's reaction. It was not pretty. Rage contorted the Wolf's face, drawing his mouth into a dreadful grimace, but it was soon followed by something else, something far more painful to see.

Was it regret or despair? Geoffrey eyed his brother in stunned surprise at the depth of the emotion passing across those familiar features. Marion must truly have changed him, for Geoffrey had never seen Dunstan so affected by anything or anyone. If he had not witnessed it himself, Geoffrey never would have believed that the Wolf had backed down from an argument. And not only that, he had acceded to a woman—and looked positively wretched over the entire dispute.

As if suddenly aware of his brother's presence, Dunstan turned, his face quickly becoming guarded once more. He glanced at the ground, seeming reluctant to look at Geoffrey, and rubbed the back of his neck.

"I was so worried about her," he admitted ruefully. "When I could not find her, and someone said she had gone outside the walls, I just... Jesu, Geoff, if you only knew how many times she has been in danger, how many times I thought I had lost her..."

At the sound of Dunstan's mournful words, Geoffrey felt a rush of sympathy for this great, fearless sibling, who had never bowed to anyone, but was now brought low by his affection for his wife. The Wolf loved Marion, that was obvious, but he had a poor way of showing it.

"You did not handle it well," Geoffrey commented.

"No. I..." Dunstan whirled away to look out over his lands. "It is difficult. I am consumed by her, Geoffrey," he said, laughing weakly in an effort to make light of his admission. "It is a strange feeling. It makes me vulnerable. I am not sure that I like it."

Geoffrey said nothing, his own opinion of the joys of married life plummeting swiftly.

"I want her to be happy, but she wants..." Dunstan shook his head. "She wants me to love her. And, Geoff, I do not think I have it in me. I do not think I can."

"Nonsense," Geoff said. "It is obvious that you love her."

Dunstan snorted and turned back around, his face a study in skepticism. "I have never even believed in that sort of thing."

"I know," Geoff said. "But whether you will it or not, you *are* in love, and you must tell her so."

Dunstan looked doubtful, but there was a hint of determination in his eyes.

"And, if I were you, I would go after her and apologize for growling at her in front of her brothers. Profusely. You may have to grovel, even," Geoffrey said with a smile.

Dunstan's lips curved at that, and they both chuckled at the thought of the great knight prostrate before his tiny wife. From the Wolf's smug smile, Geoffrey got the impression that whatever apology Dunstan planned would be tendered with his prick. Geoffrey shook his head, but said nothing. Sometime soon the Wolf would have to come to terms with his feelings—the ones that came from his heart and not farther down.

They walked back toward the castle walls in companionable silence, stopping only when a sentry from the battlements shouted for attention. Putting his hand over his eyes, Geoffrey looked off into the distance to see a large group of riders approaching, sporting colors he did not recognize.

"Who is it?" he asked, slanting a glance at his brother. Dunstan's face was once again taut with fury, his jaw clenched so tightly that when he ground out his answer, Geoffrey could barely understand it.

"'Tis Peasely, come to collect his niece," he snapped. And then the Wolf whirled toward the gate to prepare for the arrivals.

After making sure Marion was safely tucked away with Geoffrey to guard her, Dunstan called for Stephen. After a brief search, he found his brother in the buttery, trying determinedly to get under the skirts of a comely kitchen maid.

"Stephen!" Dunstan roared, scaring the girl so that she jumped visibly and fled the room. Obviously displeased at the interruption, Stephen leaned back against the wall and crossed his arms across his chest in a recalcitrant pose.

Dunstan tried again. "Stephen," he said more evenly. "I need you." The words made them both pause, probably because Dunstan had never uttered them before in his life.

Stephen paled and pushed off the wall. "Me?"

With a swift glance, Dunstan assessed his black-sheep brother. At least Stephen was sober, and he had proved that when called upon he could do a job and do it well. Perhaps he was not called upon often enough. "Yes, you. I need you to man the castle defenses while I go out and meet with Peasely."

"Me?" Stephen repeated, frankly appalled. "What of Geoffrey?"

"Geoffrey is guarding Marion," Dunstan said. Neither of them needed to go over Dunstan's reasons for not giving Stephen *that* job, although, to his credit, Stephen appeared chagrined. "Reynold can help you, of course," Dunstan said, not giving his brother a chance to refuse. "But you shall be in charge."

Turning his back, Dunstan strode halfway across the hall before Stephen finally caught up, his reluctance obvious. "But what if something should happen to you?"

Dunstan stopped dead and faced his brother. "If anything happens to me, your job is to defend my holding and my wife." Then he whirled on his heel, leaving the glib-tongued Stephen looking positively stricken.

After choosing a few good men to accompany him, Dunstan rode out to greet the approaching party, now clearly within view. He listened, with some measure of relief, to the gates closing behind him, for he had no intention of inviting the group from Baddersly inside his walls. With his own depleted forces, he would be lucky to hold them off, if Peasely decided to attack; he was definitely not going to give them any advantage.

A soldier came forward to meet Dunstan, and he recognized Goodson, the head of Peasely's guard and the man who had ordered him murdered. Tamping down the urge to kill the bastard right where he was, Dunstan re-

membered the large contingent that lurked behind. There
was strength in numbers, he knew, and he did not have
them at present.

With bitter insight, Dunstan knew this was a job for
Geoffrey, for the skills of a diplomat would be needed to
keep Peasely and his men from slaying them all and over-
running Wessex as surely as Fitzhugh had once done. The
violent emotions churning in his gut in regard to Marion's uncle did not help, and Dunstan struggled mightily
to keep a clear head. He could not afford any mistakes.

"I look for Baron Wessex," Goodson said in a tone so
arrogant that Dunstan had to grit his teeth.

"You have found him," Dunstan said, thinking *as you
know full well*.

"You are he?"

"Yes, I am he, but if you believe me not, *yet again*,
then feel free to turn around and get yourself gone."

The words made Goodson jerk to attention. He said
nothing more, but giving Dunstan an undisguised look of
loathing, he whirled his warhorse around and rode back
into the ranks—to report to his master, no doubt, Dunstan thought with contempt. Was Peasely sober enough to
ride a horse, or did they cart him around on a litter?

Apparently, Peasely was sober enough, for he came
forward, hailing Dunstan just as though nothing ill had
ever occurred between them. *Just as if he had not mocked
and threatened and tossed the Wolf from Baddersly. Just
as if he had not given his captain orders to murder the
visitor on the road.* Dunstan gripped the hilt of his sword
fiercely and clenched his jaw. He would like to kill Peasely
for that and more, for this was the man who had taken so
much from his precious Marion, who had even tried to
take her life.

"You are Wessex?" Peasely was not as haughty as he
had been in his own hall. Dunstan suspected it had been
far easier for Marion's uncle to taunt him when he was

alone and armed only with a sword. Now they were on his property, with his castle rising behind him, and Peasely had no way of knowing whether or not it was well defended.

"I am Wessex, as I told you before," Dunstan said evenly. "You seem to have a difficult time recognizing me. But as I told your lackey, if you care not to believe me this time, then get yourself gone from my lands."

Peasely looked a bit taken aback. "Recognize you?" he asked, appearing momentarily baffled. "Have we met?"

Dunstan snorted loudly, for Peasely had not the skills to pretend innocence. "Yes, we met—not long ago when you threw me from your hall and ordered your man to murder me upon the road."

Peasely blinked. "Surely you are not the man who came to Baddersly claiming to be Wessex? You must forgive me, my lord, for you looked not as you do now. And as for a plot to kill you, why, I know nothing! You must be mistaken."

Dunstan nodded toward Goodson, who was not far away. "'Twas no mistake. I heard your guard there telling his men to do me in."

Peasely blinked again, and then, as if coming to a decision, he turned in the saddle. "Goodson!" he barked. "What know you of these accusations? Speak now or I shall cut out your tongue!"

Under that kind of persuasion, Goodson gave up himself, but, wisely, not his master. "I thought the man was a ruffian, an assassin sent to gain entrance to your hall and do you harm. Forgive me, sir!" he begged. Although Goodson bent his head in apology, his eyes burned bright with hatred for Dunstan, easily exposing his sham confession.

The man's enmity mattered little to Dunstan. What interested him was Peasely's game. Why throw Goodson to the Wolf? And what was Marion's uncle about with his sudden friendliness?

"You there!" Peasely called to those behind him. "Relieve Goodson of his sword at once. And keep him under guard until justice can be served!" *Or I am out of sight,* Dunstan thought wryly.

"My lord," Peasely said, forcing a faint smile to his lips. "Now that I have resolved that unpleasantness, I would hope that you welcome me to your hall, so that we might talk."

"We can talk right here."

Peasely's smile fled. "Very well," he said with a sniff. He sat up straight and tried to look fierce, but his face was too bloated to achieve the desired effect. "I want my niece. Now. You have no right—"

"I have every right," Dunstan broke in. "You see, I have married her. Marion is my wife and no longer your concern." He waited, his hand on the hilt of his weapon, for Peasely's response.

It was immediate and extreme. Peasely's eyes seemed to pop from his head, and his skin grew red and mottled with emotion. "You lie!"

"'Tis legal," Dunstan replied. "Take your objections to the church or the king."

For a moment, Dunstan thought Marion's uncle would try to make her a widow without delay, for his lips drew back from his teeth in a fierce grimace. His bulbous eyes flicked to the battlements, however, and he paused, obviously leery of the soldiers behind the walls—and those who would step forward to avenge the Wolf's death.

Little did the coward know that his own force could easily take the poorly manned castle, and Dunstan had no intention of letting on. Quickly he seized upon Peasely's hesitation and fears.

"My father, earl of Campion, was most pleased with the match. He longs for a grandson," Dunstan remarked. In an instant, he reminded Peasely that the might of the de Burghs protected Marion and that she could well be with child. That child not only stood to inherit Campion and Wessex, but Baddersly as well, eliminating any lingering hopes that Peasely might have of retaining his hold on the castle.

Watching the message sink in, Dunstan thought Peasely would have an apoplexy, saving them the trouble of killing him, but after long gasps for breath, Marion's uncle finally seemed to gain control of himself.

"I would see her," he muttered in a more restrained manner.

"She does not wish to see you."

"Nonsense," Peasely protested. He adopted his friendly tone again. "I would see that she lives and hear her confirm that she is your wife. Surely you would not refuse me the hospitality of your hall?"

Dunstan paused. He had no intention of letting Peasely anywhere near his wife, but neither did he long for a battle that he was ill equipped to fight. If he refused Peasely's request, the man might strike, and then what? If the castle fell, what would become of Marion? Dunstan's chest constricted and his head throbbed at the thought of her at the mercy of her uncle. Alone. Defeated.

The back of his neck ached, but Dunstan resisted the urge to rub it and stared stonily at Peasely. He needed time. Simon might return at any moment. And Dunstan could send a runner to Campion, asking his father for help....

Peasely waited, a sly smile on his puffy face, and Dunstan wondered if the fool thought to take his large force inside the gates, the better to attack the Wolf. Dunstan nearly laughed, for he was not so stupid. As much as he disliked the idea, he would allow Peasely in—but no one else.

Nodding toward the far hillside, Dunstan said, "Your men may camp there. You may enter alone and see my lady for yourself."

Peasely's eyes bulged again, and Dunstan could see him struggling with anger. Obviously, his plans had been foiled, and he was uncertain of his next move. Good. As Dunstan watched Peasely, unwaveringly, he realized that it just might be better to have the man where he could keep an eye on him. Once inside, separated from his men, Peasely could hardly order a strike against the castle.

Marion's uncle licked his lips. "Surely you would not deny me a few attendants."

"You alone. And your man, the one who would kill me, may know the comforts of my dungeon, until such time as you leave."

Peasely tried to disguise his fury, but he could not hide the red stains of rage that appeared on his face. "I hardly think—" he began.

Dunstan cut him off. "Those are my terms." He knew that Peasely's only other option was to attack, and he hoped that Marion's uncle, like so many bullies, had not the courage. Obviously, Peasely would rather cloak his men as outlaws to do his killing for him than face a forthright battle.

Remaining implacable under Peasely's lethal stare, Dunstan waited until the man nodded jerkily. "Very well," Peasely snapped. He turned his mount and spoke softly to the guards behind him. Goodson was handed over to Dunstan's men, and then the rest of the soldiers began moving toward the slope, leaving Peasely by himself.

"I am at your mercy, my lord," Peasely said with a smirk, as he urged his horse onward. "I trust you will not violate my confidence."

Dunstan flicked a contemptuous glance at Marion's uncle. As much as he would like, he did not plan to murder a guest in cold blood. The king might not approve. However, let the man hurt Marion, and he would do the deed gladly. "I give you this warning," Dunstan said. "Do not lift a hand to my wife, or you will be a dead man."

Peasely sneered, apparently putting little faith in the threat. For a moment, Dunstan considered elaborating, but he had been fair—far more fair than Peasely had been to him and Marion.

"I warned you," Dunstan said, piercing those bulbous eyes with his gaze. "See that you remember it." Then he called for the gates to open.

Marion was horrified. Although logically, she knew that Dunstan could hardly refuse her uncle admittance, nonetheless she longed to run to her room and lock the door when she heard that he was here. Right here, within the nice, safe walls of Wessex. She should have stayed at Campion.

Geoffrey took her downstairs, and she was grateful for his arm, digging her fingers into it until she was surprised he did not yelp in pain. It was either that or turn tail and run. Geoffrey murmured encouragement, but she could tell he was alarmed by her reaction. And then she was in the hall, and she could think of none except her uncle.

At the sight of him, cold terror, mindless and relentless, washed over her, and she froze, staring at him with huge eyes.

"Marion," he said, more sweetly than he had ever spoken to her in her life. "How are you?"

For a moment, she could not speak, then she lowered her head submissively and murmured, "I am well, uncle." Dunstan moved to her side and was saying something, but she was still too numb to understand. Her brain told her she was being foolish, but it could not seem to convince the rest of her, which remained stiff and silent. The Wolf would protect her, she told herself, and yet the Wolf had let her uncle in....

The evening meal was a strange affair, which marked the first time Marion had ever eaten with her uncle. She had dined in her room at Baddersly, for Peasely had always said that women should keep to themselves. It all came back now, with frightful clarity, how he had let her have nothing, do nothing... *be* nothing. And despite the presence of her husband and his brothers, Marion found herself shrinking away in an effort to stay out of her uncle's sight.

Vaguely, she could hear him, his voice more cordial than she had ever heard it, as he questioned Dunstan about the marriage, stopping just short of accusing the Wolf of perpetrating some trickery. Dimly, she heard the other de Burghs, their tones harsh and angry, standing up for their brother, while Dunstan remained quiet beside her. Sometimes, she could feel her uncle's gaze, intent upon her, but she kept her own lowered, picked at her food and begged an early excuse to escape.

She was glad when Dunstan joined her, putting one of his strong arms around her as they quit the hall. He said nothing while they made their way to the great chamber, but she was thankful for his protecting presence. In their room, she was aware of Dunstan watching her, but not with his usual lusty enthusiasm. She undressed silently, while he took off his own gear and dropped it to the floor with a loud thud.

"I will send him away," the Wolf growled.

Marion slipped beneath the covers, pulling them over her despite the evening's warmth, and huddled by the edge of the bed. "Nay. Do what you must. I am fine," she said.

Dunstan whirled toward her, eyes narrowed, jaw clenched and chest bared. "The devil you are! You are not fine. You are not *you*. By faith, you are not even as lively as a wren. You are like a wraith, a ghost of yourself, and I will not have it," he added stubbornly.

"Peasely goes," he said, stripping off his hose. He climbed into bed, and although it was vast enough to more than accommodate his great bulk, he moved over to her side. She welcomed the heat that poured from him when he pulled her close, pressing her back against him.

With some surprise, Marion realized that for the first night since she had arrived at Wessex, Dunstan was not rolling her beneath him. Although she could feel his desire, a hard brand against her buttocks, he simply held her, and the tender gesture made her want to weep.

He nuzzled her hair softly and muttered, "I would have you happy, Marion." She drew in a ragged breath and tried not to cry at his gruff admission. How she loved him! It welled up in her like a great flood, washing away her fears and bathing her in comfort.

She recognized how hard the Wolf tried, in his own rough way, to make things right between them. Mercy, but he had changed from the fierce beast who had thought of her as naught but a piece of baggage to be delivered. He had come to respect her, to listen to her and to worry about her. Now, he even professed to want her happy!

Ever since his release from the dungeon, Dunstan had seemed more attentive, almost as if he . . . cherished her. During the nights, he lavished on her his passion; during the days he often sought her out for no reason other than to be near her.

Tears wet Marion's lashes as she realized just how very much this man granted her. He said he did not believe in love, but was that so very important? Perhaps she should quit wishing for something that could not be and accept what was. Even if Dunstan loved her, there was no guarantee that it would last forever, and what she had right now seemed to be awfully close.

Maybe, Marion thought, just maybe the Wolf was giving her all that he could, and she would be a fool not to be content with it.

Chapter Nineteen

Marion did not want any more battles at Wessex, so she forced a smile to her lips and insisted that Dunstan let her uncle stay, at least for a little while—long enough perhaps to discover what he was about. She kept to her room, however, joining the others only to eat.

After a peaceful afternoon spent working upon a new tapestry, Marion stood and stretched, mindful that she must go down soon for the evening meal, when there was a knock on the chamber door. Thinking it Geoffrey or Nicholas come to escort her below, she called out an invitation to enter.

But it was neither Geoffrey nor Nicholas, nor any of the de Burghs. It was her uncle who walked in and shut the door behind him, and Marion froze in horror. "So, here you are, Marion. I have missed you today. How rude of you to treat a guest with so little hospitality," he said. He stalked around the room, examining the tapestries and spare furnishings with a look of contempt before turning toward her suddenly. "But, then, you never did know how to do your duty, did you?"

Marion backed away, recognizing, all too well, the abrupt change in his tone. He had been drinking, and that meant he was capable of anything. Sitting down upon the edge of the bed, she bent her head, able to do naught but cower before the man who had tormented her so often.

"No!" he shouted. "You never could do anything right, could you? Worthless, useless spawn of my worthless, useless sister, standing between me and what is rightfully mine." Marion heard him step closer, but she remained where she was, silent and still.

"You think to take Baddersly from me, do you?" he snarled. Marion said nothing, having learned not to answer his questions even with a denial when he was in such a mood. "Well, you will not. You cannot!" His voice rose higher, his tone fierce. "I will—"

The door burst open, slamming against the wall with a loud crack, and Marion looked up to see the Wolf filling the doorway, huge and threatening and powerful.

"What are you doing in my chamber?" he growled at her uncle.

"She invited me in," Peasely said, waving a hand in Marion's direction. Hearing his easy tone, she cast him a sharp glance and was surprised to realize that he was not cowed by Dunstan. Why? Mercy, but the Wolf had been known to scare his own brothers when he was in a black humor.

"Is that true, Marion?" Dunstan asked, piercing her with his bright green gaze.

It glittered dangerously. He was tightly reined, but Marion could see that the slightest word from her would unleash his temper. Frightened as she had been, she wanted no bloodshed here in their chamber. She nodded in agreement.

Despite her response, Dunstan stood where he was, assessing her for a long moment before turning toward Peasely. "I warned you, Peasely," he growled. "See that you remember it."

"Oh, I will, my lord," her uncle said with a conciliatory smile and a mocking manner that made Marion stare at him, wide-eyed. Had he lost his senses? Perhaps he was foolhardy with drink, for why else would he bait the Wolf? Then, with one last glance that promised her retribution, he slipped by Dunstan and out of the room, leaving them alone.

"What the devil was that about?" Dunstan asked, obviously still angry and frustrated. No doubt he would have liked to slam her uncle into the wall, but had restrained himself on her account. Marion managed a tremulous smile at his patience.

"Nothing. He only sought to taunt me," she said. "You came bursting in before he did anything but bluster." It was true, she realized, and she felt a little ashamed for letting her uncle intimidate her in her very own home, in her very own room. But he had always done that....

She looked up in some surprise to see Dunstan kneeling before her. He took her hands in his roughly, but the look in his eyes was so gentle she felt the tears threaten again. Mercy, but she was a watering pot of late!

"He is nothing, Marion. *Nothing*. He cannot harm you ever again," Dunstan whispered.

"I know," she admitted. "I know it is silly, but when I see him, it is as if I am only seven again and all alone in the world—" She broke off as Dunstan's arms came around her, and she finally gave in to the urge to weep, burying her face against his neck and soaking the collar of his tunic.

Dunstan barely touched his trencher. Even if he had been starving, which he was not, his jaw was clenched too tightly to eat. He leaned back in his chair, alternately watching his wife and her uncle, and brooded. Day of God, he wanted to be rid of Peasely. How dared the bastard threaten his wife in his own chamber? Dunstan's blood boiled at the very thought.

Marion was his. *His.* And, by faith, he would protect her. It was strange and new yet, this business of having a wife, and not at all what he had envisioned. Perhaps it was his time spent in the dungeon that made him cherish every minute with Marion, but he found he no longer wanted to put her aside while he went about his business. In a way, she *was* his business.

And he wanted her back! He wanted his wife, the spirited little sprite who poked her tiny finger into his chest and argued with him, not this quiet shadow of a woman. The change in her was all Peasely's fault and Dunstan was sorely tempted to murder the man. Right now.

Dunstan's mouth tightened into a grim line at the sound of Peasely's harsh laugh. Marion's uncle and Stephen were in their cups, their tongues growing sharper with each drink, and although everyone was well used to ignoring Stephen, Peasely was a different story. Dunstan liked not his loud speech, peppered with oaths, or the look of him, full of ill-disguised loathing for his hosts.

Glancing again toward Marion, Dunstan saw the wariness in her eyes, and he wanted to smash Peasely's face in with his bare fist. Maybe he would. He imagined breaking the man's bulbous nose and what pleasure that would give him. Then he caught Geoffrey's frown of warning and remembered that Peasely's soldiers still camped outside. With a grunt, he curbed his urge to violence—just barely.

"I would retire now," Marion said, rising and whispering excuses. At her words, Dunstan nodded, moving swiftly to his feet. Although he would have liked to stay in the hall to keep an eye upon his enemy, he did not want to let Marion out of his sight, especially after Peasely had bearded her in their chamber this afternoon. When she darted across the tiles like a frightened mouse, he moved to follow.

Their attempted departure did not go unnoticed, however. "Marion!" Peasely shouted. "Surely you would not leave us yet? The night is young, and there is much to discuss."

"You can talk tomorrow, Peasely," Dunstan growled, turning toward his guest.

"But I would talk *now*," Peasely snapped. And, in response, Marion swiftly sat down upon the nearest bench, lowering her face in that submissive way that hit Dunstan like a blow to the gut. "I would talk about why a man with naught but a small and poor holding would marry the heiress to Baddersly."

Ignoring the hush that fell over the room, Peasely lurched to his feet. "He wanted a rich wife so badly that he sold himself to this sniveling creature," he said, waving his arm toward his niece.

With a contemptuous sneer, Peasely swaggered over to Marion. "I have seen the way the famous Wolf of Wessex dances around his wealthy bride, and I think it is pathetic!" he shouted. "She snaps her fingers, and he jumps. She speaks, and he follows her around like a dog, waiting for a bone!"

Dunstan heard Nicholas's outraged gasp and silenced him with a glance. This was between Peasely and himself, and he was more than ready to finish it. He stared stonily at his guest, his hand drifting to rest on the hilt of his sword, while Marion's uncle continued ranting.

Peasely's face was red and mottled as he swung toward his niece. "Methinks my little Marion has tamed the Wolf with her inheritance," he spat out. "But I am not so easily bought, my lord. Women were not created as our equals—they are to be little seen and little heard. And I would teach this one her place."

To Dunstan's shock, Peasely lifted his hand to strike Marion, who sat, still as a statue, to accept it. Too late, Dunstan realized just how far away from his wife he was, with Peasely standing between them. With a roar, he bounded forward, but just as he did Marion screamed, *"No!"* The single, defiant shout was so loud that Peasely hesitated, and she lifted her arms to block his blow easily. Then, instead of cowering, she leaped at her uncle, spewing oaths and clawing at his eyes.

Unsteady from drink, Peasely fell to the floor, with Marion atop him, kicking and gouging him with her tiny nails like some kind of wild animal. For a long moment, everyone stared in stunned surprise, then the entire hall exploded as all the de Burghs rushed to Marion's aid.

Dunstan, who was the closest, was struck with a kind of relief to see that his spirited wife was back, but then he saw the flash of silver that told him Peasely had a dagger. And in that instant, Dunstan discovered just what his wife meant to him. It came to him like a wound to his chest, sharp and clean and painful—and straight to the heart. He loved. He loved her.

And Peasely was cutting her. Dunstan saw the blade slice her arm and the blood spill, bright red upon the pale yellow of her sleeve. His vision was blurred briefly with a hot flood of dizzying anger such as he had never known. Then, with a great growl of rage, Dunstan threw himself across the rushes in a desperate reach for Peasely's wrist.

At the last minute, his quarry twisted, however, and whether by accident or intention, the dagger gored Dunstan's chest. He faltered in dazed surprise for a brief moment that could well have finished him, if Peasely had been quicker. But Marion's uncle had been slowed by drink and stunned by his niece's attack. He struggled under Dunstan's great weight, and when Marion rolled away to the safety of Geoffrey's waiting arms, he was distracted. Dunstan seized his chance, closing his fingers around Peasely's hand in a deadly grip. The two men struggled for possession of the knife as everyone in the hall looked on in hushed silence.

Emboldened by wine, Peasely thought himself invincible, but he was no match for the Wolf, who bettered him in size and strength. Dunstan was a fierce fighter, known to ignore his own injuries, and tonight he was consumed with a blood lust that blinded him to all else but the man who had threatened his wife.

"I warned you," Dunstan snarled, when he wrested the weapon away. His lips pulled back from his teeth in a feral grimace of victory, and he saw the mocking contempt in Peasely's eyes replaced by fear, raw and real, before he buried the dagger deep in the man's heart.

Heaving a great sigh, Dunstan staggered to his feet. In the stark quiet of the hall, he could hear Marion weeping, and he turned toward the sound. She was kneeling not far away, sobbing beside Geoffrey, who was trying vainly to get a look at her cut. At the sight of her blood, Dunstan wanted to howl out a protest, but instead he fell down beside her and took her in his arms.

"Ah, wren," he whispered. "What a fierce falcon you were tonight."

"'Tis but a scratch," Dunstan protested.

"A scratch that has reopened the wound Fitzhugh gave you," his wife answered. She pursed that lovely, wide mouth of hers in such a pretty way that Dunstan wanted to kiss it. Instead, he sighed and let her wrap the cut with clean linen. He had seen her own injury attended first, but then Marion had insisted on bathing his chest and rubbing on ointments and propping him up on thick pillows and . . . fussing over him.

He reveled in it.

"I swear, Dunstan, you are the worst patient I have ever had," she scolded, playing along with him as a good wife should.

"I am the *only* patient you have ever had!"

"That is not true. I was able to help a few of my people at Baddersly, when I had a chance, and some at Campion. Now I will take my place here as a healer."

Dunstan grunted and watched her hide her amusement. He had a healthy suspicion that Marion knew exactly how much he enjoyed her ministrations. She was a clever one, he was aware of that, and she seemed to know whatever he wanted, whatever he needed, without words passing between them.

That suited him to perfection, for he was not a talker. He was heartily relieved that she was not the kind of woman who begged for compliments and gifts or whined for proof of his affection. In truth, she had never mentioned love since the day of their wedding, though he found himself wishing that she would. Suddenly, knowing that he returned the emotion, he would like to hear her speak of it again, perhaps in that breathy whisper he so enjoyed, or mayhap in that high cry she released when she came in his arms...Dunstan felt himself stir beneath the sheet at the thought.

"There." She finished with the bindings, laid her hand over his heart and looked at him, her huge eyes filled with tenderness and concern. Now that Dunstan knew just how much she meant to him, this business of love seemed crystal clear. Had he not been drawn to her from the first? Well, very nearly.

And the attraction had grown until he had to have her, not only physically, but with him, body and soul. Still, he had refused to believe the inevitable, even during his stay in the dungeon when thoughts of her were what kept him alive, and afterward, when that time without her made him painfully aware of his need for her.

"Now, drink this, for it will ease the ache and make you sleep," Marion said. She reached out for a cup beside the bed, but his fingers closed around her wrist, stopping her. The last thing he wanted to do tonight was to drug himself into some senseless state. "Nay, I want no potions, wren. You may cease coddling me now."

Her head came up at that, as if she would argue, but apparently giving consideration to his condition, she spared him that aggravation. "Yes, Dunstan," she said, looking him right in the eye.

He laughed until his chest hurt with it, snorting soundly when she watched him, as wide-eyed and innocent as a babe. "Liar," he said softly.

"What?" She tried to look affronted.

"My dear Marion," he said. "I discovered not long into our acquaintance exactly when you are lying and when you are not."

That surprised her. "I do not believe you," she said, shaking her head with a teasing smile. "You only caught me now because you know I shall never cease coddling you."

Dunstan felt the low rumble of laughter gathering again, and it felt good. "Why, 'tis easy enough to see. When you lie, you look me directly in the eye in a most earnest fashion."

"Humph." She made a sound not unlike his own grunts and seemed disgusted.

"Do not be so stricken, wren. Perhaps others cannot tell as easily, for as your husband I am wont to know you well," he said. The words came out low and rough, for he hoped to soon show her just how well he knew her, every inch of her skin, every sensitive spot that made her tremble for him.

"Dunstan." She looked down at his chest, a slight frown marring her sweet face. Had he ever thought her plain? He had been mad, for she was utterly beautiful, from the widow's peak at the top of her dark head to the tips of the small toes that he liked to feel curling into his calves.

"Aye? What is it?"

She peeked up at him, her lashes so thick and inviting he wanted to touch them with his mouth until they closed and she moaned his name. "You are not angry over what my uncle said, are you? All those awful things he said about you dancing attendance upon me. 'Tis not true, of course. Everyone knows you do not want Baddersly or any wealth that I might have. I would not have you ... avoid me because of what he said."

"Avoid you?" Dunstan felt a rush of hatred for the dead man. "Peasely was a fool, and I care not what he said." He regarded her, breathlessly waiting, her great eyes full of worry, and he felt his annoyance with her kin slip away, to be replaced by the kind of peace it seemed he had spent his life seeking. "If you have tamed me, then so be it."

She smiled then, her wide mouth parting, her dimples peeking out merrily, and slowly he lifted a hand to her cheek, touching the crease brought on by her happiness. And he was awed by the depth of his feelings for her.

"Such dimples..." Dunstan whispered. Then he reached up to curl his hand behind her neck, underneath her thick hair, and pulled her toward him. He claimed her, possessing her with his mouth, and in turn, he became possessed. It was as if he had never beheld her before, never really made *love* to her....

"Your wound," Marion said, breaking the kiss. Ignoring her concern, Dunstan muttered a dismissive oath as his hands slid down to her shoulders. "You are to lie still and rest," she added more forcefully.

His answer was another grunt, and he dragged down her gown, letting her generous breasts spill into his hands. Her skin was creamy and silken, her nipples large and dark, and so enticing he was straining against the sheet. The familiar heat sparked between them, and he drew her near to suckle. She shivered. By faith, how her pleasure worked on his own!

"Tremble for me, wren," he urged hoarsely. She did, her nails digging into his shoulders as she arched toward him, gasping in abandon while his tongue tasted her, his teeth tugged gently, his hand cupping her to his eager mouth.

She smelled of wildflowers and fresh fields, and Dunstan drew in a long draft, filling his lungs and his head with her scent as he filled his hands with her ripe curves. Lifting her easily, he swept the sheet aside and moved her over him until she was straddling his naked body. He raised his knees behind her to cradle her in his lap, and she braced her hands on his chest, her fingers delving into the hair below his wrappings.

He had swelled beneath her, and she glanced at him out of doe eyes dazed with passion. "Dunstan," she murmured breathlessly. "You must not strain yourself."

He grunted in disagreement, his need for her too strong to deny, now or ever. Normally, he would roll her under him and pour himself into her, but not this night. He had no desire to set his chest to bleeding again. It might upset Marion, and besides, he was getting too old to play the invincible knight.

"Take me inside you, wren," he whispered.

If possible, her eyes grew even more huge. She needed no further encouragement but rose and fumbled with her skirts, her fingers shaking in eager anticipation. When she could not arrange them to her satisfaction, she reached up, tugged the gown and shift over her head and tossed them aside.

Dunstan's gaze swept her, and just the sight of her, naked and straddling him, was enough to set him afire. Her pale body was lush and quivering, and he felt his own shudder in response. "Now, Marion," he urged in a strangled voice, and when she did not move, he closed his hands around her hips and pulled her down upon him, impaling her in one swift gesture.

He growled low and heard her release an answering cry of pleasure. Then she threw her head back, her hair spilling over his knees, and he groaned again. She was a fever in his blood, and he had to have her, needed her, wanted her—each time more powerfully than before.

Buried full inside her, he did not stir, but grabbed a fistful of her dark mane and bade her look at him, made her see the promise implicit in his gaze, along with the yielding of his heart.

"Ride me, wren," he whispered, and she trembled in reply. His eyes were still locked with hers, his fingers dragging through her tumbling locks, when she began to rock in a gentle rhythm wholly unlike his usual fierce possession.

Although he found the difference exotic, he was soon frantic for a fiercer union, and even the wren could not keep to such a timid pace. As she began to move faster, Dunstan grunted and ground her hips to his furiously until his hoarse shout and her wild cries blended together in perfect harmony.

Marion lay across her husband's chest, thoroughly content and bemused. She should have known that despite his injury, Dunstan would find a way to join with her, for he would never be denied. As his wife, she might as well accept that truth. He might make her angry or exasperate her; he might frown and shout and argue, and sometimes he might even give in. But he would never be denied.

When she found the strength, Marion slid from his lap and fussed over him, checking his bindings and removing some of the pillows that had propped his back. She made sure he was comfortable before she blew out the candles and curled up beside him. Then she laid a hand over his heart, thankful to feel its strong beats, and closed her eyes.

Snuggling closer to his warmth, Marion listened to his breathing slow and even out. Usually Dunstan went to sleep with the promptness of a trained soldier. Sometimes he even snored, but she did not mind. Marion found the strangely intimate sound endearing, especially after what had happened in the hall tonight.

She had been so terrified by the sight of him, covered with blood and staggering.... Marion squeezed her eyes shut against the memory of those long, horrible moments when she thought she might lose him. She had known then that she could never again entertain thoughts of leaving her husband.

No matter what the future held, she would cleave to the Wolf. If he never spoke one word of affection, or learned any tender arts, she was content, for she knew, deep in her heart, that he cared for her. The Wolf might never admit as much, but the evidence was there in his eyes and his gruff behavior—if one knew him well enough to look.

And she did. Dunstan was a man of few words, a man who found it difficult to talk about his feelings, yet he showed her in a myriad tiny ways what was going on inside him. Marion had been slow to realize just how much until her uncle's hateful words had rung out in the hall. No, she did not believe that she had tamed the Wolf with her money, as Peasely had claimed, for Dunstan was not greedy. But he *had* changed.

Dunstan did seek her out, and he did attend her, and no matter how he might scoff at her romantic notions, his actions were those of a man who cared for his wife. Marion smiled sleepily. She realized that she would always have to pay attention to all the little ways in which the Wolf spoke to her for the rest of their days. And if he never mentioned words of love, she had only to look toward his deeds to find what she sought.

"Wren?" Thinking him asleep, Marion was surprised to feel Dunstan touch her gently. He entwined his large fingers with her smaller ones and brought her palm to his lips in an unusually sweet gesture.

"Hmm?" Marion murmured. She rubbed her thumb against his skin, envisioning in the darkness the hand that she had come to know so well. It was just as beautiful and powerfully stimulating today as the first time she had seen it, the back dusted with his dark hair. . . .

"I love you." His words were a harsh whisper, startling in their simplicity, and so unexpected that Marion froze for a moment, stunned to hear them spoken aloud.

She felt the foolish pressure of tears, along with a thickness in her throat that forced her to swallow hard before she could reply. "I know," she said softly. "But 'tis good to listen to you say it."

Dunstan grunted then, one of those indecipherable noises that she had come to accept so readily, and Marion closed her eyes again, warm and safe in the knowledge of her husband's love.

"Wren?" This time his voice held an edge of roughness that hinted at his displeasure.

"Hmm?" Marion answered, rousing herself again from the edge of sleep.

"I would hear you speak of this," Dunstan said gruffly.

Hiding her wide smile in the darkness, Marion leaned close to kiss his mouth. "I love you, Dunstan de Burgh," she whispered.

With a growl of satisfaction, the Wolf wrapped one heavy arm around her, anchoring her to him, and soon she heard the slow, even sound of his breathing as he sank into slumber, content.

Chapter Twenty

At dawn, Dunstan rode out to Peasely's camp with the dead man's body. He was accompanied by a small guard from Wessex, although he knew they could do little against the larger force if it came to a battle. Most of the de Burghs remained at the castle, manning its defense, but Geoffrey had insisted upon coming, claiming his superior negotiating skills might save Dunstan's life.

After much argument over the matter, Dunstan had discovered that his quiet, studious brother had a stubborn streak as fierce as the rest of the de Burghs. It soon became apparent that the only way he was going to prevent Geoffrey from coming along was by locking him up, so Dunstan gave way.

He urged his horse forward, trying to ignore the pain of his wound, aggravated by the ride. Suddenly, he longed for nothing more than to be flat on his back in bed, his wife hovering over him with that sweet concern shining in her great doe eyes. He let out a low oath and decided he was getting old.

With a grimace, Dunstan realized he would have more to worry about than a small cut, if Peasely's men proved difficult. No one had come out to greet them, and the silence of the morn made Dunstan uneasy as they approached the camp. He caught Geoffrey's eye for a brief moment, and then they topped the slope to view the enemy soldiers.

They were, to a man, dead to the world.

Dunstan was dumbfounded—until he remembered how undisciplined the guard at Baddersly had been, dicing and drinking in the hall. Without Peasely or Goodson, they obviously had done as they pleased, swilling their supplies of ale and bowing to no authority. Not one of them even stood sentry for the rest. Dunstan laughed out loud.

As they were roused and rounded up, some of the soldiers were found to be the worse for a few fights, some had slunk off, and others were too dazed with drink yet to stand. When Dunstan, as their new lord, growled out orders, however, most hastened to obey. Those who did not were either turned out or locked up, depending on how dangerous Dunstan deemed them. The rest swore their loyalty to him and waited to go back to Baddersly.

Not one drop of blood was spilled.

When Nicholas told her that Dunstan had gone out to treat with Peasely's men, Marion began sobbing, much to the dismay of the youngest de Burgh. Nicholas was plainly baffled that the same woman who had attacked her uncle so fiercely the night before could be so distraught this morning.

Although he obviously thought she was mourning Peasely's death, Marion was not. In fact, she felt precious little regret for her uncle's passing. He had tried to kill her more than once, and now she felt only relief that he would pose no threat to her or her new family.

Her tears were for Dunstan, who had left her bed without a goodbye while she still slept. Marion knew the kind of men her uncle employed, and she would not wish to lose her husband to them. After all that they had been through together—after the Wolf had finally admitted he loved her—what if he was killed out there this morning before his very gates?

A particularly loud sob made Nicholas rush out of the hall in a panic, shouting for Robin, while Marion sank down on a bench to give vent to her fears. She had saved up many a tear during all those years at Baddersly when she had stoically survived with no one to care for and none to care for her. Now she let them flow unheeded down her cheeks, for she had good reason to give in to her worries.

After consultation with an older woman from the village, Marion had discovered just what had turned her into a watering pot of late. Although she had said nothing as yet, she suspected that she was carrying the Wolf's child, and the thought that the baby might not have a father come evening made her weep more copiously.

When Robin and Nicholas returned with the news that both Dunstan and Geoffrey had been sighted approaching the gates, Marion would have cried anew, this time with relief, but the anxious looks the brothers were exchanging made her swipe at her cheeks and try to smile. She followed them outside to see for herself, and hardly gave her husband a chance to dismount before she launched herself into his arms.

Apparently Dunstan and Geoffrey were well pleased with their doings, and Marion was soon tucked under the Wolf's thick arm, while the rest of the de Burghs crowded around, pelting them with questions and congratulations. Marion resisted an urge to weep again in pure happiness.

The morning meal was a boisterous affair, for all were relieved that Peasely and his men no longer posed a threat. After the food was cleared away, the brothers lingered, to decide what next needed to be done. Although no one expected any problems with Marion's inheritance, the king would have to be informed of Peasely's death, and, of course, Baddersly would have to be taken in hand. They had just begun discussing Marion's holdings when one of the guards reported that Simon had been sighted.

Pandemonium broke out again, and the din of de Burgh voices did not fade until Simon was also seated at the table, ready to present his report to Dunstan. Marion studied him closely, with an anxious eye for his well-being, but Simon seemed none the worse for his mission. Indeed, he seemed stronger and more confident and more mature than ever, and Marion felt a sister's own pride in him.

When they had all quieted, Simon told them that he was met at Fitzhugh's primary manor by the steward, who did not allow him inside, but assured him there would be no further unpleasantness. Looking a bit disappointed by the prospect of peace, Simon continued speaking in his own terse way. He told them that Walter Avery had fled to the manor from the battle at Wessex and had promptly taken Fitzhugh's daughter to wife.

Dunstan's low grunt told Marion that he was not pleased by that news. "I am surprised Walter did not cut you down at the gates. What treachery does he plan now?" Dunstan growled.

"None," Simon answered grimly, "for he is dead."

Glancing at her husband, Marion saw that he remained skeptical, but Simon nodded in assurance. "'Tis true," Simon said. "Fitzhugh's daughter did not take well to her husband. On their wedding night she stabbed him to death . . . in their marriage bed."

Marion gasped aloud, while the de Burghs uttered several foul oaths and muttered among themselves. "'Tis one way to bloody the sheets," Stephen quipped.

Dunstan snorted. "I trust them not. How can we be sure?"

"I am sure. They sent out the body to me," Simon said. He cleared his throat. "She . . . she had ordered it left for the scavengers, but the steward gave it over to us. We buried him."

Astounded by the tale, Marion was even more astonished to see all the huge, brave de Burgh knights shudder visibly at the doings of the Fitzhugh woman. Who was she? *What* was she?

"Well," Dunstan said, heaving a sigh. "It seems she has done our work for us—"

His words were interrupted by a new shout, announcing the arrival of Campion himself. The brothers surged to their feet as one, while Marion, too, rose to greet her husband's father.

He entered the hall with his usual grace and dignity, tall and straight and drawing respect by his very demeanor. Seeming untouched by the events of the past few weeks, the earl was a steady source of intelligence and power, Marion thought. Would her Wolf ever be the same? She smiled, doubting it, for Dunstan did not have his father's even temperament.

Glancing swiftly up at her husband, Marion admired his now familiar features. He had his own strength and majesty that made men look to him, too, and that proclaimed him a fit heir to the earl. Watching the play of emotions across his face at the sight of his father, Marion felt her love for Dunstan become a wellspring, showering over them and nurturing the child she carried.

Perhaps he would never possess Campion's quiet wisdom, but Marion loved the Wolf just as he was—huge and handsome, gruff and tender, quick to rage and just as quick to burn with passion. She smiled her own secret smile to know that he returned her feelings.

Suddenly, everyone was talking at once, and Marion laughed with pleasure to see the way each son vied for

Campion's attention. They all had a tale to share, and she called for wine and ale so that the afternoon could be spent in the telling.

Like a good father, Campion listened to them all, giving each man his attention and his praise. He seemed most impressed by the way Marion had attacked her uncle, and he rubbed his chin in that thoughtful way of his until Marion had the impression he was looking right inside her.

"Now," Dunstan said, when Campion had been informed of all their doings, "I must go to Baddersly to take control of Marion's property and get an accounting—"

Marion cut him off with a gasp of protest. "No! I care not for anything from my old life."

Dunstan snorted, and his brothers scoffed loudly, giving her several choice de Burgh looks that scorned her words as female foolishness. "Well, then," Marion said more firmly, "send someone else. Simon would love to go, I am sure."

A brief, telling expression of excitement passed over Simon's face before Dunstan grunted angrily and said, "My brothers have done enough for me, Marion. 'Tis time I took control of my affairs—"

"Then stay here," Marion said.

Dunstan growled. "Do not interrupt me, wren!"

"Do not scold me, Dunstan!"

"I will not have you gainsay me, wife!"

"And I will not have you go to Baddersly!"

While all the de Burghs watched in fascination, Marion rose from her seat. Even standing, she was little higher than her seated husband, but that seemed not to matter to her. She planted her legs apart in a stance not unlike the Wolf's and poked a tiny finger into his wide chest. "You are sick of traveling, and you know it!"

Dunstan surged to his feet, his face darkened with a fury that boded ill for his wife.

"Now, Marion..." Geoffrey began, trying to forestall an argument.

She heeded him not. She simply leaned her head back to stare up at the giant of a man looming over her. "Let Simon go, Dunstan, for 'tis time for you to tend to Wessex."

"And what is *wrong* with Wessex?" Dunstan asked. "Why must I stay here?" Six pairs of de Burgh eyes met anxiously, while the brothers wondered if their little Marion was going to assault the huge knight in front of her, or if the Wolf was going to erupt in rage. Nicholas and Robin scooted back, wary of the look on the face of the eldest de Burgh, while Geoffrey and Simon moved closer, determined to protect the woman who had become a sister to them.

"You must stay here because *I* am here," Marion announced boldly. "And so is your heir." She put a dainty hand to her stomach, and stared, unflinching, up at her fierce husband.

Growling suddenly, Dunstan grabbed his wife by the shoulders, plunging the hall into anxious silence. Then Marion threw her arms around his neck, and in front of all the de Burghs, the two shared a kiss that threatened to consume them both.

The stunned brothers were shaken from their gaping by the sound of Campion's soft voice offering congratulations. Then the room erupted with the movement of the brothers, their dark heads bobbing in agreement, their deep bellows and shouts of praise ringing in the hall.

Through the press of tall, muscular bodies, Marion's eyes met Campion's, and she saw him rub his chin thoughtfully. "It seems I was wrong," he remarked.

"Wrong? About what?" she asked curiously.

"I thought that you must have tamed the Wolf, but to my mind, 'tis the other way around."

The earl had everyone's attention now, and Nicholas, casting a puzzled look at Dunstan and his wife, asked, "How so?"

"'Tis plain that Dunstan has imbued our gentle, little Marion with some of the fierce, unrestrained spirit that earned him his name," Campion answered, with a smile. "She makes a fitting wife for the Wolf."

Marion thought her heart would surely burst with happiness at the sight of the familiar tall towers rising regally into the white winter sky. Although she had come to love Wessex, Campion would always be home to her, too, for it was the first place that she had come into her own—and it was a shining example of the strength of family bonds and affection.

That notion had been a little hard to explain to her husband, who, having grown up in the luxurious castle, was unimpressed by it, and, having been surrounded by his brothers for months, was not exactly pining to see them. The Wolf, Marion had discovered, jealously guarded her love for him and for his holdings; he was not thrilled by her feelings for the rest of the de Burghs and their residence. But all of the earl's sons were returning to the fold for Christmas, and Marion wanted to be there, too.

It had taken her a week to convince her husband.

The Wolf had complained that he hated traveling, that he had seen his family more this year than during the past three combined and that he did not want to endanger the child his wife carried.

Marion had argued that Campion was only a couple of days' ride away, that she was but a few months pregnant and that it would be ill-mannered to refuse an invitation from the earl. When she sensed her husband weakening, Marion begged the journey as her gift, and, finally, after much grumbling and growling, Dunstan had acceded to her wishes.

Now, cozily settled by the fire in the solar, Marion knew a bone-deep satisfaction in his capitulation. Resting a hand upon her slightly rounded stomach, she let her eyes roam the room, lighting lovingly on the men she had come to view as brothers.

They were all here, the six of them, plus her husband. Even Simon had returned from Baddersly, where he had taken control of Marion's holdings for Dunstan. Having rid the castle of Peasely's corrupt associates, he had chosen a new steward, reorganized the defenses and had come back eager for more challenges. Although Marion knew a sister's pride in his deeds, she worried that his need to prove himself exceeded even his elder brother's and would someday put him in danger.

Of course, she fretted about them all, with the exception of Geoffrey, perhaps. Marion could not imagine the most scholarly de Burgh seeking out the pursuits of war. And yet she was concerned for Geoffrey, too, wishing that he might find himself a wife, for sometimes she caught a wistful yearning in his gaze that could not be satisfied by books or arms or anything to be found at Campion.

The youngest and most energetic de Burgh roamed the room like a smaller version of the Wolf, until he came to sit at Marion's feet. Despite her protests, he pushed a stool under them, and Robin insisted on fetching her a cushion while she tried to hide her amusement. The rough, gruff de Burghs were treating the mother of the future heir as if she were a fragile flower, and although Marion knew better, she let them.

Her pregnancy had been easy thus far, with only a voracious appetite and a tendency to become weepy to mark its passing. But then, Dunstan pampered her far more than even his brothers would dream of doing, scowling ferociously if she lifted a finger at Wessex. Smiling her own secret smile at his regard, Marion scooted closer to the fire, unaware he was watching her until he moved to her side and settled his great bulk next to her. She curled into him, warmed more by the heat of his body than by any blaze, and snuggled beneath the proprietary arm he placed around her shoulder.

Whether in deference to Marion's condition or the Christmas celebration, the brothers were not quarreling as much or as loudly as usual, and even Stephen had tempered his taunts. All in all, the solar at Campion was a perfect scene of domestic tranquillity—except for the glaring absence of the earl himself.

They were all waiting for Campion, who had called them to the solar after receiving a message from the king. Although the situation reminded her far too strongly of that day in early summer when she had been ousted from the castle, Marion told herself that not all news from the king was bad. Even the order to send her back to Baddersly had proved, in the end, to be a blessing, for how else could she have married the Wolf?

As if sensing her thoughts, Dunstan slid his great palm over her belly in a possessive gesture that acknowledged the son—or daughter—nestled inside. She smiled up at him, and his lips curved ever so slightly in response, a smile that was not one, but that had the ability to touch her heart more deeply than anyone else's giddy grin.

They could have been alone, but for the sudden hush in the room that drew their attention to Campion's entrance. He stepped to the center of the solar with regal grace, and Marion tried to judge the tenor of the news from his expression, but it was, as usual, unreadable.

Nodding to his sons, the earl spoke without preamble, as was his wont. "The king has a task for one of you," he said, and Marion saw some of the de Burghs sit up straighter, impatient for whatever battle lay ahead.

"'Tis a great sacrifice, but I know that this time one of you may be counted upon to step forward," Campion said. This time? Marion grew curious as to the king's charge and listened intently as the earl continued.

"His will is that one of you marry in order to assure the proper dispensation of his lands and protection of its people." Marion hid a smile as the brothers who had seemed so eager slumped back in their seats now, trying to disappear into the furnishings. What a hardened group of bachelors! Although she understood their reluctance, privately Marion thought she would enjoy having another woman in the family and other children to grow up kin to her own.

"I am sorry, my sons, but there is no way to escape the king's decree," Campion said, and Marion was surprised at the grim set of his features. His wise gaze held a hint of sadness that made it seem as if he were announcing a death sentence instead of a betrothal. "Since her father's death has left her not only with a sizable property, but at the mercy of landless rogues who would seek to wed her against her will..."

Suddenly, Marion became aware of tension, thick and threatening, growing in the room at Campion's words and the abrupt stiffening of her husband's arm about her shoulders.

Of whom did the earl speak? Was the heiress a child, a crone, a hag? Whoever she was, Marion felt a hot rush of compassion for the woman none wanted for a wife.

"The king wishes one of you to marry Fitzhugh's daughter."

"Fitzhugh's daughter!" Seven deep male voices rose in protest, startling Marion in their vehemence.

"She is well-known for a shrew!" muttered Robin, horrified.

"A harpy!" echoed Reynold.

"A *murderess,* for did she not kill her last husband in their marriage bed?" Simon asked, and Marion recalled the dreadful stories about the fearsome female.

Campion eyed them all with gentle sympathy. "Apparently, the king is taking a rather magnanimous view of that incident, since the groom, Walter Avery, was naught but a rebel knight who forced the wedding upon her."

"Still, 'twas a vile deed," Simon muttered, and Marion saw Geoffrey shudder.

Although she knew the situation was serious, Marion could not help but see the humor in it as she glanced around the room. Here were six strapping warriors who had not quailed before a trip to Wessex to free their brother against unknown odds, and yet every one of them had turned pale at the thought of a mere woman.

As if sensing her coming chuckle, Dunstan abruptly rose to his feet. "Let us know when congratulations are in order," he said gruffly. Then, with amazing gentleness, he helped Marion up from her seat and out of the solar.

To her surprise, Marion saw that Dunstan's face was nearly as white as those of his brothers, and as soon as the door was shut behind her, she let out a giggle at the sight.

"'Tis no laughing matter, Marion," Dunstan growled, dragging her along with him to their chamber. Faced with his most ferocious scowl, Marion was forced to quell her amusement until the last candle was extinguished and her smile was hidden by the darkness.

"Wren?" Dunstan reached for her, his tone thick with some underlying emotion.

"Hmm?"

"It appears I must thank you for saving me from the Fitzhugh wench!" he said, and then the low rumble of his laughter rang out beside her. Marion joined him, and they laughed together in bed, shushing each other so that none might hear them, until the hushing whispers turned into kisses and more serious matters pressed between them.

"'Twas nothing," Marion answered breathlessly, as she felt the familiar spark at the touch of his questing hands, rough and dear, upon her. "Methinks the Wolf was ready to be tamed."

* * * * *

Harlequin® Historical

WOMEN OF THE WEST

Exciting stories of the old West and the women whose dreams
and passions shaped a new land!

Join Harlequin Historicals every month as we bring you
these unforgettable tales.

May 1995 #270—**JUSTIN'S BRIDE**
Susan Macias w/a Susan Mallery

June 1995 #273—**SADDLE THE WIND**
Pat Tracy

July 1995 #277—**ADDIE'S LAMENT**
DeLoras Scott

August 1995 #279—**TRUSTING SARAH**
Cassandra Austin

September 1995 #286—**CECILIA AND THE STRANGER**
Liz Ireland

October 1995 #288—**SAINT OR SINNER**
Cheryl St.John

November 1995 #294—**LYDIA**
Elizabeth Lane

Don't miss any of our **Women of the West!**